No o~~ne~~
Annie Fisc~~her beautiful back then...~~

Back then—sixteen years ago—she'd worn her heavy black hair chopped off in a blunt Dutch boy that had made the natural waves stick out at odd angles, flanking her cheeks like flaps of bent leather. Between the hair and the squarish frames of her thick glasses, you could hardly see the girl's face.

Back then she was so thin, it was a wonder her legs could support her five-foot-ten frame. Mike remembered feeling sorry for her as he watched her lope toward her father's pickup.

No. No one would have called Annie Fischer beautiful back then.

But this woman standing in the doorway before him...this woman instantly made you think, "Beautiful." She had the exotic beauty of the legendary Chickasaw ballerinas from whom she'd descended. She was still slender and maybe even taller now. Almost as tall as he was, he guessed, which meant she'd grown another inch or two since high school. She was...elegant.

She looked up, smiled and extended her slim hand. "I'm Ann Fischer."

She spoke in a soft, well-modulated tone. A voice that sounded cultured, sophisticated...*and gave no indication that she recognized him at all.*

Dear Reader,

I am a daughter of Oklahoma. I was born in Tishomingo, the former capital of the Chickasaw Nation. Medicine Creek is a figment of my imagination, but many such beautiful and quaint small towns exist near the wild Arbuckle Mountains and the lush Chickasaw National Park.

In researching this story, I had several conversations with Senator Helen Cole, a prominent state leader of Chickasaw descent who has been honored in the Chickasaw Hall of Fame. Living history speaks through Helen. May her memory always burn bright.

I am also grateful to Lona Barrick and Tanya Crossley of the Chickasaw Nation Purcell Area Office for their generous assistance. As always, Linda Goodnight and Libby Banks shared valuable insights, legal details and inspiration.

As Helen and other Chickasaw women told me about their heritage, sharing family pictures, important documents, letters and heirlooms, I began to imagine a woman who was heir to this rich heritage, but totally unaware of it. What if a woman did not know her "tribe"?

Ann Fischer is such a woman. Here is the story of discovering the secrets of her hometown, what happened to her mother, what she is meant to do with her life and where she really belongs.

Her most important discoveries, of course, are finding her true love, and finding out that she is truly a daughter of Oklahoma.

My best to you,
Darlene Graham

I treasure your cards and letters. Contact me at P.O. Box 720224, Norman, OK 73070. Or visit my Web site at www.superauthors.com/Graham.

Daughter of Oklahoma
Darlene Graham

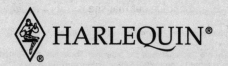

HARLEQUIN®

TORONTO • NEW YORK • LONDON
AMSTERDAM • PARIS • SYDNEY • HAMBURG
STOCKHOLM • ATHENS • TOKYO • MILAN • MADRID
PRAGUE • WARSAW • BUDAPEST • AUCKLAND

ISBN 0-373-71028-3

DAUGHTER OF OKLAHOMA

Visit us at www.eHarlequin.com

Printed in U.S.A.

This story is dedicated to Kathleen Marie Gardenhire.
Because of R.W.E.
But most of all because she is my beloved first daughter.

CHAPTER ONE

THE LAST TIME Mike Kirkpatrick laid eyes on Annie Louise Fischer she hadn't looked anything like *this*. Not at all.

Back then, she'd worn her heavy black hair chopped off in a blunt cut that made the natural waves stick out at odd angles, flanking her cheeks like flaps of bent leather. Between the hair and the squarish frames of her thick glasses, you could hardly see her face.

And back then she was so painfully thin it was a wonder her stick legs supported her five-foot-ten-inch frame. He remembered feeling sorry for her as he watched her lope across the parking lot toward her father's pickup. One of the other football players joked that it looked like she might break right in two.

No one would have called Annie Fischer beautiful back then.

No one but him.

But this woman standing in the doorway before him…this woman instantly made you think, *Beautiful.* She had the kind of beauty that was exotic, fascinating, like the legendary Chickasaw ballerinas from whom she'd descended. She was still slender, and maybe even taller now. Almost as tall as he was, he guessed, which meant she'd grown another inch or two since high school. She was elegant.

Astonishing.

"Hello," she said, and smiled in a questioning way.

"Ms. Fischer?" He held out a business card. "I'm from Home Town Realty." Actually, since Marsha had left, he *was* Home Town Realty.

She took the card and while she read it, he tallied up the years since he'd seen her. Sixteen.

She looked up, smiled again. "Of course." She extended her slender manicured hand. "I didn't expect them to send someone so quickly. I'm Ann Fischer." She spoke in a soft, well-modulated voice. A voice that sounded cultured, sophisticated, and gave no indication that she remembered him at all.

"Mike Kirkpatrick." He took her fingers lightly and felt a disconcerting thrill. Disconcerting, because the touch made him think of Gloria's hands—pudgy, always waxy with lotion—by comparison. This woman's hand was warm and smooth and her light touch reminded him of the way a dancer flitted across a stage.

As soon as they touched, a spark of recognition ignited in her dark eyes. She glanced at the card again, then her smile grew softer, more familiar. "Mickey Kirkpatrick? We went to high school together." She squeezed his hand a little tighter.

He smiled in return, wanting to say, *If you won't call me Mickey, I won't call you Annie-girl,* but she was still talking.

"Mickey Kirkpatrick. I'll be." She stepped back from the threshold. "Please. Come in. Thank you for coming here so soon. As I told your answering service, I'm anxious to sell this house and get back to my work in D.C. as quickly as possible."

As she opened the ornate paneled door wider, it creaked miserably on rusty hinges. The whole house, he guessed, was in similar disrepair. He stepped inside and saw that he was right. Yellowed peeling wallpaper. Water-stained ceilings. Warped floorboards.

He wiped his feet on a tattered rag rug inside the door.

He hated to tell her that selling her deceased stepmother's home was not likely to be quick. In a small town like Medicine Creek, real estate transactions were few and far between. He didn't want to tell her that her best bet was to plow this old relic into the ground and sell the lot to the conglomerate that was interested in the ten acres across the street.

"We can talk in there." She pointed through a set of double doors toward a massive antique dining-room table piled high with papers.

As he followed her inside, the smell of aged wood, accumulated dust and rotting papers hit his nostrils. Old people and old houses were familiar and comforting to Mike. As a Realtor, he frequently sold houses like this one after the owner had passed on. And in his role as a minister, he visited elderly church members in their old homes on a regular basis.

But this house seemed staler and more closed-in

than most. Probably because Edith Fischer had languished in the Sunset Manor nursing home for many months before her death. Edith had had no real friends who would check on her home. And unfortunately Edith had refused to go to church. She had closed off that avenue of support and comfort years ago after having angry words with Mike's predecessor. Even when the church ladies had persisted in dropping by, Edith had rebuffed them. Sad.

Even sadder, in Mike's opinion, was the fact that Edith's daughter was apparently too busy with her high-powered career in Washington, D.C. to care for her own mother—well, her stepmother, technically. But Edith was the woman who had raised Annie Fischer. And to Mike Kirkpatrick, it was the raising that counted. He figured the people who were willing to put in the daily blood, sweat and tears it took to bring up a kid deserved the title of "parent." And they deserved love and respect. People like Gloria Miller, for example. Acknowledging Gloria's good qualities somehow acquitted him of his disloyal comparison of a moment ago.

He gave Annie Fischer, who was busy clearing a space among the clutter of papers on the dining-room table, another quick assessment. As she leaned forward, her designer jeans hugged her slim graceful curves. She wore her hair long and straight now— almost to her waist, he guessed. It was pulled back from her wide brow with a thick silver clip inlaid with turquoise. The long sleeves of her creamy-white silk blouse shimmered gracefully as she moved. Her Car-

11

tier watch, diamond-solitaire ring and crimson nails flashed against tanned skin while her elegant fingers stacked the papers into neat piles.

She was beautiful, all right, but if the town gossips were to be believed, as selfish as sin.

"Sorry about the mess," she said over her shoulder. This time her smile parted her full lips and revealed perfect white teeth. No doubt she spent a fortune to keep them that way. Everything about this woman's person said, "well-maintained and expensive."

She turned back to her task. "I've only been at this for two days, and already I've found a half-a-dozen unpaid bills. Tucked into books, under couch cushions. God knows what else I'll find, so I can't simply sweep it all into the trash like I want to." She talked while she tossed papers aside in disgust. "I'm afraid there might be something valuable in this mess."

There might be something valuable here, Mike thought, *but a woman like you probably wouldn't recognize it.* Mike Kirkpatrick was a man who valued tradition. He valued old houses, old things, old stories, old people. He valued this old town. He had a vision of a future in Medicine Creek where history and progress blended together in a peaceful, dynamic small town.

Ann Fischer, on the other hand, had fled from Medicine Creek after high school, and now, according to the local gossips, she was determined to ditch everything about her past.

The funeral, a dismal graveside affair, had taken

place only two days ago. Jack Fields, the local funeral director, had called Mike the day before.

"I'm stumped, Mike. Edith Fischer's daughter is willing to pay us plenty, but other than that, she's left the poor old lady's whole disposition up to me. I need somebody to at least say a few words at the graveside. I was wondering if you could come do the honors."

As the town's only nondenominational minister, Mike often performed such services, but on the day of Edith's funeral, he was officiating at a wedding at his church. He relayed this to Jack with his apologies.

"Don't worry about it, Mike. I reckon I can say a few words myself, but even somebody as cantankerous as Edith Fischer deserves better than this. I just can't figure out this daughter. You know her?"

I kissed her once. Does that count? "Not really."

Mike studied Ann Fischer's back again.

When Gloria came over for a cookout the evening of Edith's funeral, she'd given a full report. She said that Jack Fields's wife had told her that Annie Fischer had rushed down in a rental car from Will Rogers Airport, arriving in town only a scant hour before the service.

"Sorry," Ann muttered as she continued to move the papers aside.

Mike looked around at the dismaying clutter and wondered what Annie-girl had expected to find in this abandoned old house. Lovely order? Edith Fischer had been a notorious packrat. And a sick woman for a very long time. Physically and mentally. Gloria had kept him updated about Edith, too.

Bless Gloria. She also told him how she'd donated some day-old carnations from her shop to be placed at the graveside. A little something, Gloria had said, to offset that lone ostentatious spray of spider mums Annie Fischer had ordered for the casket. Mike wondered if Ann had even noticed the extra flowers.

"Won't you please sit down?" Ann asked now, indicating the chair at the head of the table. "So have you been selling real estate since you graduated from high school?" She settled herself into a matching chair at the side.

"Uh, no. Actually I spent some time in the army." Mike took his seat and tugged at his tie.

"Oh, yeah. I think I heard that somewhere."

Mike opened the folder he'd brought with him. "When I got out of the army, I went to divinity school. After that Marsha and I moved here and started a church. I wanted to raise my kids in my hometown, give them the kind of happy childhood I had." *Right.* He had wanted a happy childhood for his kids. Except the one thing he'd neglected to do was to choose the right mother for them.

"Marsha? You mean Marsha Dodson?"

"Yeah." He laid the packet of papers he'd brought with him on the worn oilcloth and opened it. "We married right after high school. I, uh, didn't want to go off to the army and leave her behind."

"Marsha Dodson." Ann sounded nostalgic. "Wow. I haven't thought about her in ages. The most popular girl in school. And do you two have children?"

"Five."

"Five!" She laughed. A delightful musical sound that tickled his senses. "You, the senior-class bad boy, are now the father of five children?"

Mike smiled, remembering. His bad-boy days were long gone. But during those years his old man must have possessed the patience of Job. Dan Kirkpatrick, brawny as John Wayne, with a shock of steel-gray hair and a voice held low even when he could have been shouting, had inspired young and old alike as the town's championship high-school football coach for more than twenty-five years. In all those years the man had never lost his cool. Not even when a ref made a bad call. Not even when Mike and his buddies were caught drinking beer in the graveyard. Or when Mike drove all the way back from the Red River at two in the morning half-lit. The old man just held out his beefy palm for Mike's keys—and didn't return them for six months. Dan's strength and patience was the example Mike tried to follow with his own children.

And now, he, one of the worst hellions Medicine Creek High had ever produced, was the father of five beautiful children.

Sometimes he couldn't believe it himself. Though most days he was far too harried and overworked to appreciate them as much as he should. But telling this woman about Joseph, Zach, Erin, Brandon and Mary Beth—this woman who hadn't seen him at all since his hell-raising days and having her act so surprised— made him realize how far he'd come. It gave him a rush of unexpected pleasure. "I consider them my five biggest blessings."

"I'll bet you do!" There was genuine delight in her voice, and genuine admiration shining in her dark eyes as she looked him up and down.

"You don't want me to start bragging about my kids—that'd take all day." He carefully drew some papers out of the packet. "We're here to talk about your property. I hope you don't mind…Ms. Fischer—"

"Call me Ann." Something in her voice was slightly teasing, as if she was remembering their times together. Well, hadn't he thought of that the minute he'd seen her name on the memo in the office?

"All right—Ann. I hope you don't mind, but considering your mother's long-term condition, I took the liberty of coming up with some preliminary figures on this property in the event that you would contact me to conduct the sale after her death." He laid the top paper—a comparative market analysis—in front of her.

Sometimes families took offense at this tactic, as if Home Town Realty had been ghoulishly waiting for their loved one to pass on so they could make a sale. But Ann didn't look at all offended. In fact, as she picked up the paper, she looked pleased.

Good, he thought with relief, *at least this lady realizes that I'm trying to save her some time.* He knew only too well how infernally slow the real-estate market in Medicine Creek could be. While the old Victorian houses, built in territorial days, were charming, few people wanted to move to a town located in a remote valley of the Arbuckle Mountains in southern Oklahoma.

She frowned as she studied the figures. "I really appreciate this," she said softly. Then she gave him a sharp look, and he could see a flash of the tough Washington, D.C. lawyer in her expression. "Apparently my parents' property is worth more than I thought."

He nodded. If only she knew. He had been conservative in his estimate. It wasn't the house that was valuable. It was the ten acres across the street. Vacant except for the forty giant pecan trees that Annie's maternal great-grandfather Clyde Starr had planted there almost eighty years ago. Absolutely no one in Medicine Creek would've guessed what the Powers Corporation had in mind for that ten acres. Mike had been shocked when the Powers people had contacted him. But if he could get the church board to approve the funding and match the offer, he had other ideas for that pecan grove. As far as he was concerned, the Powers bunch would have to find someplace else to build their outlet mall.

And he hoped he could find them an alternative. With what Powers was willing to pay, the commission from such a sale would be the answer to his prayers. Braces for Erin, a scooter for Brandon, football camp for Zack, a computer and college for Joseph, the addition on the house so the girls could have separate bedrooms, maybe a nice minivan, instead of that junker of a pickup. His list was endless.

And, he supposed, that list might inevitably include a modest wedding for himself and Gloria. But a woman like Gloria would probably want a big wedding with all the trappings. For some reason his palms suddenly felt sweaty, his collar too tight. But he supposed a deal this important would make anybody's palms sweat.

The idea of a mall was going to stir up controversy. The corporation's plans for the land would mean uncontrolled growth for Medicine Creek. The town's genteel antique and tourism business would be overshadowed by the demand for new gas stations, restaurants, maybe even a big motel or two.

"You have a buyer?"

Mike looked at the woman seated across from him. She was unaware of all these complications, of course. Annie Fischer was Edith's only heir. Mike knew that, and he probably should have contacted her as soon as the Powers group had contacted him, giving her the option of selling her stepmother's land to Powers. But Edith Fischer had still been alive then. Alive, but slowly losing her mental faculties. He had waited, hoping the board at his church would be ready to build when the land became available.

He cleared his throat. "Yes, for the land across the street, I do have a possible buyer. But for the house, no."

"Oh? Who's interested in the land?"

"For now, the buyer doesn't want that information disclosed."

"I see. Well, it doesn't matter. Someone can install

a dump over there for all I care. This buyer interested in the land—they couldn't be persuaded to consider this old heap of a house in the deal, could they?''

He was surprised at the bitter tone of her voice. People usually spoke of their childhood homes with more affection. This house had been in the Starr family for five generations. Didn't that mean anything to her?

"The buyer has no use for the house, but might purchase it if that was the only way to secure the land. Of course, they wouldn't pay top dollar for a house in this condition. If you wanted to sell it to an individual at fair market value, you'd have to make repairs.

"If you like, I could inspect it and make a list, come up with some estimates," he offered.

"No need for any list." She held up a palm. "I want to get out of this town as quickly as possible." Again he heard the bitterness. She started looking over the other papers in the packet. "Go ahead and contact your buyer, see what they're willing to do about the house and get back to me."

"I'm certain we can come up with a satisfactory deal. I'll have to measure the place for exact square footage in order to come up with an accurate appraisal. I really don't have time to do it today. Would tomorrow work? Say, in the morning around ten?"

"Fine. Tomorrow at ten. Tell your buyers I'll be ready to sell as soon as I can go through the personal effects and get an estate sale arranged—unless they want to buy all this old junk, too." She smiled again, but this smile wasn't soft at all. This smile was grim, hard. It seemed the gossips were right—she was determined to bury her past right along with her stepmother.

"May I?" She reached over for the rest of his portfolio.

"Yes." He handed her the file. "We can sign the contract to show tomorrow."

She perused each paper with businesslike interest.

Annie Fischer's family situation broke Mike's heart. No siblings. Mother, father and stepmother all deceased. And Annie so bitter. Families should not end up like this. And what about your own family, Pastor? Right now your little family is a wild, motherless mess. His mouth twisted at the irony.

But Mike was determined that his family wouldn't stay that way. He was going to fix things if it killed him. Because, to him, family was everything.

His pager sounded—the thing seemed to bleat at him a million times a day. As he bent his head to check the harassing device, he made a wry face. Family was everything, all right. Seemed like the kids consumed every minute of every day. *What now?*

CHAPTER TWO

MIKE STOOD UP as he read the digits on his pager. "This is my son's high school, Ms. Fischer—uh, Ann. They wouldn't call if it weren't important. Would you excuse me? I need to go out to the car and use my cell phone."

"Use this one if you like." She gestured toward the phone, a greasy old black thing with a rotary dial, tucked into a small alcove next to an antique gossip bench in the dim hallway. "I kept the bill paid for Edith. She always insisted she was coming home."

"I know. I guess it was hard for you to know what to do from way up there in Washington."

Ann sighed. "None of it matters now."

He nodded sympathetically and went to make his call.

ANN PRETENDED to shuffle papers, while taking a good long look at Mike Kirkpatrick. As he seated himself on the bench and bent over the old phone, she watched in amazement.

He looked so smooth. And so clean-cut. He still had that big rugged raw-boned quality that had so attracted her and every other girl in high school, but in that white shirt, navy-blue serge suit and silk club tie he looked like a politician—or a preacher, which, evidently, he was. Mickey Kirkpatrick and Marsha Dodson had started a church? Unbelievable.

And they had five kids? And he sold real estate, to boot? How did he manage it all? The same way most successful men did, she wagered. With a lot of help from their wives. But if theirs was that kind of setup, why hadn't the school called Marsha just now? Of course, it was possible that Marsha held down a demanding job, too. Maybe even two jobs, like Mike. They had both been superachievers in high school. Voted most likely to succeed and all that.

She smiled, remembering. Mickey Kirkpatrick had probably been the only boy in the history of Medicine Creek High voted most likely to succeed who sported an earring. Back in 1983 none of the guys wore earrings, much less the chains and musical notes and crosses that Mickey Kirkpatrick kept dangling from one tortured lobe. He'd looked sort of scary. Black leather jacket. Reddish-blond hair grazing his shoulders in thick wavy tangles. Everything about him was bold, wild-looking. He'd only shaved when the coaches stepped in and forced him to, so that in Ann's memories, he seemed to have perpetual stubble shadowing his square jaw.

She stole another peek at him as he sat hunched over the phone in the dim gray light of her stepmother's narrow, high-ceilinged hallway. His ruddy complexion was clean-shaven, and his hair had deepened to the color of burnished brass, tamed close to his head in a short business cut. But his mouth, moving calmly while he pressed the phone to his ear and rubbed his brow, was exactly the same.

Those full, rebelliously expressive lips. Usually twisted in sarcasm, or smirking, or laughing. God, those lips. The rumor back in high school was that he was the world's best kisser. Started out slow and soft and just plain *killed* you before it was over. No wonder Marsha always acted so jealous, although as far as Ann could recall, he never gave her any reason to. Except for that time with her, and that was…a fluke, apparently. Because once he and Marsha had started going steady in the spring of their senior year, he had acted as if they were practically married.

Not that Ann had ever flirted with him. Oh, no, Annie Fischer couldn't even *look* at guys like Mickey Kirkpatrick. The two times they had been alone, she had hardly been able to breathe, much less look him in the eye. He was probably only being kind to a painfully shy girl, Ann realized, but dammit if something about those two episodes hadn't haunted her all these years.

That first time she had been walking home from school in a pouring November rain, the kind of sudden cold rain that always took Oklahomans by surprise after a protracted Indian summer. Annie was so concerned with keeping her latest pastel drawing safe under her cardigan that she hadn't even noticed his beat-up brown Honda Civic until he pulled into a driveway in front of her. He gunned the engine, and the exhaust fumes of the car rolled out oily and black in the damp air.

He cracked open the passenger window and hollered, ''Need a ride?''

She hesitated on the sidewalk. She was scared to death of him; she was scared to death of all the popular kids. But it was still seven long blocks to her house and her sweater was getting soaked through. Protecting the drawing was far more important than her fear.

She nodded and he threw open the passenger door.

She ran around, jumped in and slammed the door. The inside of the car felt steamy and close and smelled of his leather jacket, of *him*. A song blared from the radio: ''Pinball Wizard'' from the rock opera *Tommy*.

''Annie Fischer, right?'' he said as he jammed the stick shift into reverse.

She nodded and removed her rain-splattered glasses, then fixed her gaze out the fogged windshield as he backed the Honda into the street.

''I'm Mickey Kirkpatrick,'' he said as if she didn't know. As if his picture wasn't in the paper every week. Last week's had shown him airborne, as graceful as a young god in flight, catching the pass that had won the homecoming game against the Davis Wolves.

''Shouldn't you be at football practice?'' she asked, to show him that she wasn't completely out of it. She was trying to dry her glasses on her sweater, but the wool was so wet that her efforts only smeared the lenses.

''Coach had mercy, for once. He thinks we're gonna have a tornado.'' He grinned at this.

''A tornado!'' Her eyes went wide. ''Shouldn't we find a weather report?'' Her hand reached for the radio dial.

''Hey!'' He grabbed her fingers. ''That's The Who!''

She jerked her hand from his, and he grinned again. ''Me and my cousin almost drove to Cincinnati last year to see them.''

''Who?''

''No. It's *The Who*.'' He gave her a funny look, pointed at the radio. ''As in, this song?''

''Oh.'' She nodded self-consciously. Her parents would kill her if she even thought about going to a rock concert, much less one all the way up in Cincinnati. That was crazy. But then, Mickey Kirkpatrick was a little crazy—everybody in town knew that.

''My old man nixed that trip. I was mad at first, but in the end, I figured maybe I wasn't meant to be there.''

She gave him a questioning look and he went on, ''Eleven fans died of asphyxiation trying to get in. You didn't hear about that? Well, anyway, I figure maybe the good Lord just didn't want me to die.''

That was the other crazy thing about Mickey Kirkpatrick. He was always saying stuff like that. He was religious. No, that was the wrong word, because he didn't attend church, as far as she knew. He was more like...spiritual. Every time he made a touchdown, he dropped to one knee in the end zone. He wore a big cross—welded from two nails and tied to a string of rawhide—around his neck all the time. And he had that tiny cross on his earring, too—Annie glanced at it—but all the same, as her stepmother pointed out whenever she saw his picture in the paper, an earring was an earring was an earring. And sane boys didn't wear them.

He was definitely crazy. And now she was actually riding in his car with him.

She craned her neck and looked through the windshield up at the black clouds. "What if a tornado really is coming?"

"In November? Get real. Never happens." He rounded the corner onto Fourth Street, laughing as he created a huge arc of water from a puddle.

"Do you know where I live?"

"On Pecan Street, in that white three-story house facing the old pecan grove, right? Hey! You think that's why they call it Pecan Street?" His expression was deadpan, innocent.

When she didn't answer, he said, "Nah, probably not," and winked.

He floored the gas as he plowed through a shallow lake forming in the middle of Fourth Street and whooped, "Yee-Haa!"

Annie clutched the dash.

Mickey sang along with the next song—something about the rhythm of the falling rain. "That's a cool DJ—always has a theme. Plays great oldies."

Annie didn't know as much about music as the other kids her age. Her parents absolutely forbade her to listen to popular music. The only music allowed in her house came from the TV. But her best friend Laurie had a pretty good tape collection. Over at Laurie's house, they'd flop across the bed, listening to music and dreaming about boys, about getting kissed. Annie was a sophomore in high school and had never been kissed, which made her feel backward and homely, which she assumed she was. Her stepmom had told her so.

It started raining really hard as Mickey pulled to a stop at the curb in front of her house. He gunned the engine while he studied the dilapidated old monstrosity through the downpour. Annie knew how her home looked to outsiders; hidden behind overgrown arborvitum bushes, the windows dark, the shades always drawn, it seemed spooky and abandoned.

"Is anybody home?"

"My mother." Annie didn't elaborate.

"Oh." He shrugged. "Well, if you can wait a minute before you go in, I imagine this rain'll let up." He smiled at her.

"I guess so," she mumbled.

"Now here's a great song," he turned up the volume of the radio until it overcame the drumming of the raindrops on the car roof. "Roberta Flack."

A woman's haunting, hypnotic voice filled the confines of the little car—"The First Time Ever I Saw Your Face." The words seemed to overwhelm Annie's emotions. She couldn't just sit and listen to a beautiful song like this without feeling something, especially with the biggest hunk in the whole school looking straight at her. She didn't like him looking at her the way he was now, not while she was struggling to keep her face from showing her feelings. She turned to the window. For a second it looked as if the rain was slowing. She groped for the door handle. "Thanks for the ride," she said.

"Don't go." He grabbed her arm and her heart started to skip unevenly. "Wait'll the song's over."

He twisted his torso and draped one arm over the steering wheel and the other across the back of her seat. He started humming, then singing along with the song. What on earth was he doing?

"You should take off your glasses more often, Annie, so people can see *your* face. It's a very pretty face."

Annie's breath caught and her heart seemed to race out of control as fresh sheets of rain strafed the car. Was he teasing her? No one had ever said words like that to her. But as he leaned closer, studying her face as if truly seeing it for the first time, she saw that the look in his blue eyes was not teasing. It was...tender.

"Yes, indeed," he whispered. "A very pretty face."

Annie couldn't stand this. She wanted to leave. Now. Only, the torrential rain stopped her. She couldn't let anything happen to this drawing. It was her best one yet.

"I'm, uh, I'm sorry I've gotten your car all wet." She looked down and pulled her sweater together. The drawing was still safe in its folder, pressed against her bosom.

"Now *that* is a serious offense, young lady." He pointed a shaming finger at her. "Yes sirree, that is a very, very serious offense." He leaned closer, speaking confidentially. "Because, as everybody knows, I keep my car immaculate." He pumped his eyebrows and shifted his eyes toward the backseat.

She glanced at the litter on the floor, the smears of white shoe polish leftover from homecoming running down the back window, the petrified French fries and spills of congealed soda on the seat. She shot him a look of annoyance for making fun of her.

"What have you got there?" He nodded to where she was still clutching her sweater around the drawing.

"Just a drawing I did in art class," she admitted.

"Could I see it?"

"It's not very good." Why was her voice so shaky? Why did she feel as if she was going to cry? She wished that stupid song would end.

"C'mon. I bet you make all A's, even in art class. Let me see it."

She looked into his eyes again. Was he teasing or not? He was grinning, but sort of nicely this time. He raised his eyebrows innocently and held out a palm in invitation. Slowly she slid the folder out.

He took it and carefully opened the cover. "Wow," he said softly. "This is really good. It's amazing, in fact. These colors...wow," he ended softly.

Annie's cheeks heated up as she realized that he meant it. He was truly impressed.

"Who is it?" he asked.

"I don't know." Annie always made up her subjects. She preferred drawing imaginary people to attempting portraits of the real people around her. This one was a beautiful young woman, a common theme for Annie. The subject had long black hair and a sad expression. Her dark almond-shaped eyes were gazing tenderly at an injured bird resting on her palms.

Annie's cheeks burned as she studied her own work, and then she looked away, toward the house, where a furtive movement at one of the window shades in the living room caught her eye. Her stepmom, she knew, was peeking out at them. Edith would give her a tongue-lashing for sitting out in a car with a boy, especially the wild Mickey Kirkpatrick.

"I'd better go." She started to slip her glasses back on.

But his hand snapped out from the seat back and encircled her delicate wrist, holding it lightly in his strong fingers.

She wondered if he could feel her pounding pulse.

"Don't put those things on yet," he said softly.

Mickey Kirkpatrick really was incredibly bossy. *Stay until the end of the song. Let me see your picture. Don't put your glasses on.*

His fingers slid lightly over the sensitive skin on the inside of her wrist before he let her hand drop.

She put the black frames on and pushed them firmly up onto the bridge of her nose. "Give me my picture, please." She held out her hand. She couldn't read his expression clearly through her smeared glasses, but she was pretty sure he was grinning again.

"Not until you let me kiss you."

"What?" Her voice seemed to bounce back loudly in the interior of the car. She swept her wet hair back behind one ear nervously and licked her lips. "Are you crazy?"

He smirked and handed her the drawing. "Annie-girl, are you always this serious?"

She closed the folder and wrapped the drawing within her sweater, then pressed her eyes closed and bit her lip, determined not to appear upset. Everybody was always accusing her of being too serious, which was simply not fair. She wanted to tell him that she wasn't serious at all and that he'd know that if he'd bothered to get to know her. In fact, she could be quite hilarious when she was just goofing off with Laurie and Carrie. The Three E's they called themselves—Annie, Laurie and Carrie.

"Look at me," he said.

And she did, because now his voice sounded extremely gentle, extremely kind.

"I was only kidding about the kiss. But tell me something. I've been watching you at school for a long time now, Annie Fischer. How come you're always so serious, huh?"

She shrugged in an effort to appear cool and casual, but it didn't work because she was feeling very confused, very flustered now. He'd been watching her at school? For a long time now? "I'm...I'm not that serious..." she faltered.

"You ever been kissed?"

Good grief. Kissing again. What was he doing? Apparently boys did have one-track minds, just like Laurie's mom said.

"That is none of your business." She tried her best to sound dignified, imperious.

"Unless I'm about to be the first," he said softly as he leaned forward, forcing her back against the door.

Before she could make another move, he reached up and slipped her glasses off. "You don't need these if you're going to let me kiss you. You *are* going to let me kiss you—" his voice had dropped to a whisper and his lips were so close to hers she could feel the moist heat of his breath "—aren't you, Annie-girl?"

Her mouth dropped open and that seemed to be all the invitation Mickey Kirkpatrick needed.

CHAPTER THREE

WHEN MICKEY KIRKPATRICK wrapped his strong hand around the back of Ann's slender neck and pressed his hot mouth to hers, she thought her heart might burst.

So many sensations assailed her at once—his wonderful scent, his wonderful taste, the drumming of the rain on the roof, that haunting song, his breathing, coming harsher and faster. She couldn't think, couldn't breathe.

He was big and powerful, and his grip felt strong, yet his lips were incredibly soft and mobile. With them, he expertly teased hers farther open and then he put his tongue in her mouth! Only a little, only a teasing tip, before he withdrew it. Then he gently tugged on her lower lip with his firm ones, eased back and smiled into her eyes. But that little taste of a kiss had been enough. Enough to shoot an electric thrill straight through her. Enough to leave her wanting more.

"Man!" he whispered, and his eyes grew solemn. "What was *that?* I knew you'd taste good. You have a beautiful mouth. But, wow, what *was* that?"

As if to answer his question, he applied his lips to hers again, plunging his tongue deeper this time.

Annie had no idea what to do. Her heart thundered as she put her palms on the lapels of his jacket, but she didn't push him away. She didn't want to. Nothing had ever felt as good as this. Somewhere far in the back of her mind, a worry niggled that her stepmother was watching, but the sensation of his mouth was so powerful that for once Annie didn't care what Edith thought.

He groaned and pulled her closer, making a better fit of their bodies. And they proceeded to kiss, not, Annie realized years later, like teenaged experimenters, but like real lovers, wanting to devour each other.

When they broke apart he looked as stunned and breathless as she imagined she did, but he immediately adopted a casual macho air. ''I've been wanting to do that all semester,'' he said, and took a strand of her hair, playing it between thumb and forefinger. ''Maybe you and me should go out sometime, huh?''

Despite the kiss, this idea horrified Annie. A date? With Mickey Kirkpatrick? Number one, he was the worst of the wild guys. Number two, she'd never been on a date in her life and her parents wouldn't allow her to start with *him*. And number three, Marsha Dodson was already telling the whole school that Mickey Kirkpatrick was her guy.

''I, uh...'' She fumbled for the door handle. ''I don't date.''

''Huh?'' His voice sounded like a croak.

But she was already out in the rain and slamming the door.

She dashed up the buckled sidewalk to her front

porch, worried now that her stepmother had seen the whole thing.

Her embarrassment did not end when she got inside the house, unfortunately. A minute later Mike Kirkpatrick was banging the corroded brass knocker on the front door.

Annie peeked around the tattered plastic shade covering the bowed dining-room window and watched him hand Edith her glasses. Then she watched him run to his car, dodging puddles like the quarterback he was. Oh, God. He was beautiful. And as she watched him, a sadness settled over her. Because even then she knew. Knew that some piece of her heart, some little hope for what might have been, had disappeared down that sidewalk that rainy afternoon.

ANN SAW MIKE twist in the antique bench as he pressed the phone closer to his ear. "He what?" He raised his voice, then glanced in Ann's direction and resumed speaking calmly, but now his shoulders looked tense.

She heard him groan. Then he mumbled something like, "And where is the Jeep?" She could have sworn he added, "And the horses?" His tone was unmistakably exasperated.

She decided to go into the kitchen and make coffee, rather than appear to be eavesdropping.

She was watching the coffee drip into the carafe, absorbed in her own thoughts, when she heard him call out from the dining room. "Ann?"

"Back here. In the kitchen."

She heard his footsteps, heavy across the creaking parquet floors of the rugless living room, and then he was standing in the doorway.

"I'm making coffee. Want some?" she asked amiably.

"Uh…" He dragged a hand through his thick hair, hesitating. He clasped the back of his neck and stepped into the kitchen. "Actually I *could* use some coffee. It sure smells good."

"It's a special blend that I buy in D.C. I brought some with me."

She turned her back to him and took down two china cups—her grandmother Starr's—maybe she would ship this china back to D.C. While she poured, she asked casually, "I hope there's not a problem with your children."

Mike watched her movements, weighing his response. Right at the moment he had a crazy urge to unburden himself. Maybe she'd think the incident was humorous and give him the perspective he sorely lacked. But would telling this woman be disloyal to Zack? Would it make his son look bad? Would she even understand how things like this happened with kids?

"There is, but there's nothing much I can do about it until after school."

She handed him a cup of coffee, leaned back against the counter and smiled. She had that quality he'd seen in other Chickasaw women, a serenity that allowed them to be silent while they waited for someone to speak.

"My son Zack—he's fifteen—he and a friend decided to take a little break, instead of going to first hour this morning and, uh...there was an incident." He sipped his coffee, trying to decide how much to tell.

"Oh. I hope no one was hurt. I heard you mention a vehicle."

"A Jeep. Belongs to Zack's friend Trent. He just got his license—and the Jeep. His dad worries about him driving that thing out in the mountains. Some of those Arbuckle roads are pretty treacherous."

"I remember those roads."

"But now the Jeep is stuck in the mud out in a pasture on the Lazy J."

"Old Jerrod Cagle's place? What were they doing way out there?"

"It's a long story." Mike sighed. A story that would undoubtedly be reported with a tut-tut in Miss Ida's About Town column on Friday. Ida called her weekly newspaper *Medicine Creek Style,* posing the rag as a local shopper. Mike thought local gossiper was a better description.

"The boys—Trent is Steve Harris's boy. You remember Steve? He was in my class."

"I think so. Big guy? Curly dark hair?" She fluttered her slender fingers near her crown. "Wickedly funny?"

"Yeah. That's Steve. Anyway, the boys decided to race the Harrises' prize stallion against the car. But the horse didn't stop when he was supposed to. He threw his rider, knocked down a section of fence adjoining Cagle's land and then didn't take long to, uh, connect with Jerrod's prize mare—while the boys observed.'' His ruddy cheeks flushed a tint darker.

"I see," she said. The look on Ann's face indicated she didn't find any humor here. "Who was riding the stallion?"

"Zack." In his own mind, Mike added *of course.* It was always his Zack.

"I see," she said again. "I hope he's okay."

"Zack's big and strong. Fell on his backside. He says he's all right. Steve's wife hauled both of them back to school."

"That's good." She finally sipped her coffee, then asked, "Wasn't there some bad blood between the Harris family and Jerrod Cagle?"

"Yup. Jerrod and Steve's dad had a dispute way back when. But Jerrod has hard feelings for about half the town. Anyway, apparently he's already threatened to sue."

"Sue? For what?"

"Damages to his mare. He'll likely claim he can't breed her with superior stock now, which in old man Cagle's mind is any stock except Steve Harris's."

"Who does he plan to sue?"

"Me, I guess. And the Harrises."

"Sounds like your son is in real trouble. What do you think will happen?"

"The boys are back in class now, and I'll call Jerrod this afternoon and straighten things out. I'll probably make Zack fix the fence, maybe make him do some extra work out at Jerrod's place as compensation. Steve and Laurie will probably do the same. They're good people."

"Laurie? Laurie Whittaker?"

"Yeah. I forgot you used to hang out with her in high school. They got married after high school, not too long after Marsha and I did."

At the mention of his wife, Ann noticed how his words slowed and faltered, and his expression imperceptibly clouded. Maybe he was worrying about having to tell his wife about this incident.

She didn't blame him. She'd been a lawyer long enough to see things like this turn really ugly. She looked at him over the rim of her cup. "I don't see how you can be so calm. Trespassing? And civilly, this could be a serious tort—interference with business relationships."

Mike smiled. "Do you have kids, Ms. Fischer?"

"Ann."

"I'm sorry. Ann. Do you?"

"No. No kids. I'm not even married. It's all I can do to keep up with my career and my cat. I don't see how people like you and Marsha do it, but I admire all good parents, I really do."

He wanted to ask her about the chunk of solitaire diamond on her left ring finger, but decided to stick to his cardinal rule: MYOB.

"Frankly, some days I don't think I do the parenting thing all that well."

"Oh, you sound pretty conscientious to me."

"I try. But sometimes that's not enough. There's been more than one incident like this." He ran a hand through his rust-colored hair. "There's just not enough wholesome recreation in Medicine Creek to keep our young people occupied."

"But aren't there also advantages to raising kids in a small town? Look how quickly the school was able to notify you. And your kids also have Marsha. She was always so bright and energetic. I imagine she's a wonderfully competent mother."

He could cope with the loneliness, the fatigue, the self-doubt privately, but telling other folks about Marsha's departure was always hard for him. Not that he'd been forced to tell many people himself. The town gossips and the twittering church ladies took care of that job for him. Within twenty-four hours of the split, casseroles had started appearing at his door. Within two days, mothers in minivans were giving his kids rides everywhere. That was one reason he loved this tiny town. So what if everybody knew your business the instant it happened? Everybody cared about your pain, too.

But he wondered how long the town's goodwill and material assistance would hold out, especially with Zack regularly pulling stunts like the one this morning. He had to get his life in order, and fast.

Thus, Gloria. She had her good points and it was obvious she would make a good helpmate. "A good match," some folks at the church were already saying.

"Marsha..." He stared down into his coffee cup, then started again. "Marsha isn't living in Medicine Creek any longer."

"Not living here?" Ann blinked back her obvious shock. "Then you and Marsha are..."

"Separated, but not yet divorced. The divorce seems inevitable, though. I've finally given up on any kind of reconciliation. Marsha, it seems, has a whole new life. In fact, I went ahead and filed the initial papers. We'll have to wait on Marsha to look at the decree. I can't believe I'm even talking about the D word, much less going through it."

Ann stared at him, her beautiful brow furrowed, as if she was trying to absorb some truth too disturbing to grasp. As if she was trying to get to the heart of something beyond comprehension.

Watching her tormented face made him feel defensive as he tried for the millionth time to reassure himself that even for a preacher, a divorce was not the end of the world.

But the kernel of truth Ann finally produced was the exact same one he considered to be at the heart of his dilemma.

She turned her gaze from him and stared out the grimy cracked glass of her stepmother's kitchen window. So softly that he barely heard her, she whispered, "Those poor kids."

And with those three words, like tiny seeds gently pressed into fertile soil, Mike Kirkpatrick's affection for Ann Fischer was firmly planted.

CHAPTER FOUR

"LET'S GO SIT in the other room," Ann said as she poured him another cup of coffee. She bypassed the sagging couch in her stepmother's dust-laden living room in favor of the dining-room table where they'd been before. Experience had taught Ann that a familiar setting eased the tension in situations like this. She had apparently stumbled onto a loaded topic, and she felt the least she could do was let the man talk about it—if he wanted to. Ann had always found it easy to let people talk themselves out. It was one of the secrets of her success as an attorney. Sometimes, she found, all a person needed to solve their own problems was a sympathetic ear.

"Where is Marsha now?" she asked quietly after they'd seated themselves.

From the tense look on his face, she guessed that answering that question was going to be difficult for him.

"Is she living nearby?" Ann tried again. She certainly hoped so. *Five kids*.

A band of red inched up his neck as he gathered the papers on the table and put them back inside the accordion file. "No. Marsha is…" He let out a burst of air and hung his head. "That's the problem. I don't know where she is, exactly. San Francisco, the last time I heard from her.''

"I see," Ann said, although she didn't. How could a mother of five children not notify their father of her whereabouts?

"I have her phone number, of course."

Ann's experience as a divorce attorney made her ask automatically, ''She does send support? And she does see the children regularly?''

"Regularly? No. Her mother has taken them to meet her in Dallas a few times. I felt I had to agree to that—the kids were dying to see their mom. But no, Marsha's pretty much doing her own thing these days. She keeps promising to send more support when she gets on her feet..."

The note of defeat in his voice made Ann wince. Life was not supposed to defeat people like Mike Kirkpatrick. People like Mike Kirkpatrick conquered life. It didn't conquer them.

"How long has she been gone?" Ann asked softly.

"Almost a year." He ran a hand through his hair. "The longest year of my life, I can tell you."

"A year?" She wanted to add that without regular visits and support, a year away amounted to abandonment, but she supposed he realized that. It must have been awful for him, a small-town preacher, waking up one morning to find himself and his five children abandoned by the local beauty queen.

"You said you filed. Do you have a good attorney?" He might consider this question crass, but Ann understood the psychology of divorce cases extremely well. More than once, she'd had to convince a hurting abandoned spouse that the most pressing consideration was legal protection.

"I have a guy in Ardmore. He's done a lot of divorce settlements involving wealthy oil families. I figure he can certainly protect my puny assets. Until a month ago, I had hoped we might be able to even do this by mediation but..." He put his palms flat on the table and pushed, ready to stand up. "I shouldn't be talking to you about my problems."

"Why not?" She placed her hand over his and Mike felt an instant pull, a yearning, stronger than anything he'd ever experienced. It felt so weird, so totally surprising, that he sank back in his chair.

She took her hand away, seeming not to notice what she'd done to him. "I might be just the person you should talk to. I happen to be a divorce attorney. And I don't really know anyone in this town. I'm an outsider. I don't see you as the Reverend Kirkpatrick. To me, you're still plain old Mickey Kirkpatrick from high school."

He looked down at his hands, regaining his composure after the surprising physical reaction to her touch, then he raised an eyebrow at her. "I really don't think discussing my divorce with you would be fair."

"Fair to whom?"

As he studied her sincere intelligent eyes, Mike wondered the same thing. To whom was he being fair, being loyal? To Marsha? Or would it be Gloria now? The way things were developing, he should be telling his troubles to Gloria, not some woman he'd met only half an hour ago. Well, technically he'd met Annie Fischer sixteen years ago. But that whole adolescent encounter didn't count for anything. Did it?

As he stared into her sympathetic brown eyes, the moment he had first kissed her all those years ago— and the night that followed—came flooding back, as real as if it had just happened.

"Was it fair of your wife to leave you with five children?" she asked gently. "Whatever the reasons? Mike, I know we've just met—"

"We didn't just meet." He glanced at her. "Maybe you don't rememb—"

The clank of the brass knocker on the front door interrupted him. They stared at each other while three more knocks ricocheted like gunshots through the cavernous old house.

Great, Mike thought. Now that memory was on the table. He realized, too late, that he'd been stupid to bring it up, even tacitly. *He* was the one vulnerable to old memories, not her. Making an effort not to stare at the diamond on Ann's finger, he craned his neck toward the door while the knocker sounded again.

"Good grief," Ann said as she pushed her chair back, "I'll never get used to the sound of that ghastly old doorknocker. Why Edith never installed a regular doorbell... Excuse me." She got up and walked to the foyer.

Mike heard the creak of rusty hinges and then an equally creaky little voice chirping, "Hello, Ann dear. Remember me?" That voice was one Mike would have been happy to hear under normal circumstances, but today he resented the interruption.

"Hello," he heard Ann answer with a slight quizzical note that indicated she couldn't immediately place Ada Belle.

"I'm Ada Belle Green, dear. Don't you remember? I live in that yellow clapboard house catercorner to you."

"Ada Belle! Of course! My goodness. I haven't seen you since I was a kid. Please, come in."

Ann stepped back, and Mike saw Ada Belle tottering across the threshold. He twisted in his chair, peering through the dining-room doorway at the tiny bird of a woman. She was wearing a purple sweatsuit with pansies painted across the top and a sturdy pair of running shoes as snow-white as her hair. Mike smiled at those shoes. Ada Belle couldn't run anywhere these days—although he noticed she'd ditched her cane again. Her scrawny hands held a delicate china plate covered by a beat-up tin cake cover. Something absolutely scrumptious rested under that cover, no doubt.

"Morning, Reverend," Ada Belle called, and bobbed her white-haloed head in his direction. "I saw Reverend Mike's truck out front—" she turned her attention to Ann "—and I thought, well, if Annie's got company, anyway, maybe now's as good a time as any to pop over."

Mike smiled as he walked into the foyer. "I hope you're feeling better, Mrs. Green."

"Much better, thank you. And must I remind you

that Mrs. Green was my cranky old mother-in-law? How many times do I have to ask you to call me Ada Belle?'' She gave Ann a saucy little wink and stepped farther into the house. ''Isn't it a positively beautiful day out there?''

''Yes, ma'am,'' Mike answered. His smile got broader as he watched the old woman survey the bleak rooms.

Ada Belle had long functioned as the center of cheer and charity in Medicine Creek. And though she herself had reached the advanced stage in life where she needed a cane and home-care nurses, she still managed to deliver her famous home-baked goodies to new mothers, ailing contemporaries and the grief-stricken. That was simply Ada Belle's way.

''I brought this red devil cake for you, honey. And I wanted to tell you that I just hated to miss Edith's service. I sure did. But Mike'll vouch—I been sicker'n a stray dog.''

Mike telegraphed a smile over Ada Belle's white head, and Ann's soft answering one showed that she understood his message. Here was a dear old soul with a heart of gold and not a shred of pretense.

''Won't you join us in the dining room?'' Ann asked graciously as she took the cake from Ada Belle's gnarled hands. ''We'll make a space for this on the table and have a slice right now. I just made coffee.''

''You here to give some spiritual comfort, Reverend?'' Ada Belle asked without preamble. Her sharp eyes zipped from Mike to Ann and back.

"Uh, no. I'm here as a Realtor." Mike smiled.

"He's here to help me sell the house and the land across the street," Ann volunteered over her shoulder as she turned toward the dining room.

"Not the pecan grove?" Ada Belle said in a dismayed voice that stopped Ann in her tracks.

"Why, yes," Ann answered, but Ada Belle was looking at Mike.

Accusingly.

"She don't know, then," she said in a low voice.

Great, Mike thought. Now the cat was out of the bag—screeching down Main Street, in fact. He gave Ada Belle the same look that he gave his two youngest kids when they were squirming in the front pew.

"Don't know what?" Ann directed the question to Mike.

"I believe Ada Belle is referring to the history of the property," Mike said vaguely. "It's, ah…been in your family for a very long time."

"Oh." Ann smiled indulgently at her elderly visitor. "I know all about that, Ada Belle. But I live in Washington now and I simply can't afford to keep track of land in Medicine Creek."

"You know all about it, huh? What you don't know, sister, could flat choke a horse." Ada Belle tottered ahead of them into the dining room.

"Here, let me take that." Mike lifted the cake from Ann's hands. As he hurried into the dining room with it, he tried to think how he could put a cork in Ada Belle's gabber without actually telling her the church was the buyer interested in the land. If Ada Belle found out about that, the whole town would know his plans before lunch. And he needed time to convince the board before the naysayers and gossipers started in. The board—still unsure about committing to so costly a project—would meet again a week from Saturday.

Ann mumbled, "I'll be right back," and went off to the kitchen for utensils.

"Ada Belle," Mike said as he seated her, "I would appreciate it if you didn't tell anyone that Ann is selling her land."

"I am a poor old shut-in, Reverend. Who on earth am I gonna tell?"

Right, Mike thought. *Which is why Ida Miller over at the paper refers to you as her secret inside source.*

"Nonetheless, if you *should* happen to see anybody you know at the doctor's or the grocery store or the beauty parlor or what-have-you, please don't mention it."

"I'll wager that young woman don't know a blame thing about the history of that pecan grove. That's a shame, Reverend, and you and me both know it."

"I will see that she gets a look at the full title abstract."

"A dry old piece of paper don't tell the real story."

"It's not your place to interfere, Ada Belle. She wants to sell her property and get back to her life in Washington. A happy and successful life, I gather."

"Can't blame her for that, I suppose. Considerin' what that child must have endured at Edith's hands." Ada Belle tapped a bent finger to her thin lips. "All

I'm tryin' to do is bring some comfort to this poor girl. It's none of my affair what she does with that land. I reckon I can bite this old tongue.''

Mike relaxed. ''Thank you.'' With amity restored, he found that his mouth actually started to water as Ada Belle's shaky hand lifted the tin cover off the cake. Bits of cherry-red cake crumbs peeked through a smooth cream-cheese frosting. A homemade cake from scratch. Not often seen these days, especially by a man without a wife.

''Don't suppose you have time in your busy day for a little sliver of cake, Reverend?'' Ada Belle's keen blue eyes were teasing.

''I don't, actually. But somebody's got to eat that thing,'' Mike teased in return.

They were chuckling when Ann stepped back into the room, carrying plates, napkins and forks. Ada Belle immediately sobered, as if she shouldn't be making jokes in the home of the recently bereaved, but Ann smiled reassuringly. ''This is so nice of you,'' she said as she put a knife into the cake. ''I remember how delicious this cake tasted from my childhood days.''

''Hope I haven't lost my touch.'' Ada Belle relaxed. ''You used to come over for my red devil cake pretty regular. I remember how you and Carrie and Laurie would come over after volleyball practice. Those girls.'' Ada Belle shook her head and clutched Mike's muscular forearm with arthritic fingers. ''Those three girls used to make me laugh so hard. Smart alecks, that's what they were.''

"Only around each other," Ann responded to Mike's quizzical look. "We were shy with the kids at school."

"Well, they didn't act shy over at my house," Ada Belle continued. "They'd come bouncing in with those long legs and those big shiny black ponytails swinging down their backs. Wore gym clothes and warm-up suits all the time. Didn't care what the boys thought of them. Nossir. They were real *ath-uh-leets,* those girls were. Reminded me of my Chickasaw grandmother Jessie Maytubby. She could shoot and ride a horse better than any man. It was no surprise those girls was so strong. They all have some good old Chickasaw blood in them." Ada Belle aimed a bony finger at Ann. "And your own mama was from the proudest branch of that ancient Chickasaw tree."

"I didn't realize you played sports in high school." Mike looked at Ann with wonder.

Ann had stopped cutting the cake and had been giving Ada Belle a warm nostalgic look while the old lady reminisced. Now she turned to Mike with a more chary look. "Only volleyball. Because the season was short, my parents didn't complain too much about the practice time," she answered flatly, as if none of it mattered now. Then she turned a radiant smile on Ada Belle. "But Carrie and Laurie played every sport that girls could play. They even drove up to Pauls Valley to play on a soccer team. Funny you should mention those two. I was just thinking about them earlier, when Mike mentioned Laurie's son. I wondered what became of them."

Ada Belle frowned. "I guess you have been gone quite a while at that. Carrie moved to Oklahoma City, last I heard. Teaches high school up there—physical education, I believe. Laurie's still here in Medicine Creek, of course. In fact, she's one of the nurses that comes and visits me."

"Really?"

"Lord, yes. Goes to my church, too. Reverend Mike's church." Ada Belle poked Mike's arm, and Mike tried to grin despite a mouthful of cake.

"Really?" Ann repeated.

"Lordy, yes. You and I need to have a long visit so I can get you all caught up on the folks in your old hometown. We'll look at my pictures. I'm part Chickasaw, too, you know," Ada Belle mused. "In fact, you and me are practically kinfolk. I was best friends with your Chickasaw grandmother."

"Really?" All this was news to Ann.

"Oh, yes. Matter of fact, you ought to run over to my house of an evening, about suppertime. That's when Laurie always comes by to cook me a little something. That child is such a dear. And she and Steve have certainly stood by the reverend during his trials, that's for sure."

Mike flushed and cut an embarrassed look at Ann, who was studying him with serious brown eyes. How was it that he'd been in this woman's house less than an hour and she already knew his life story? Well, he couldn't blame it all on Ada Belle. He swallowed and dabbed his mouth with his napkin. "Uh, Steve and Laurie are the best friends a man could want. The boys play football together and, uh, run around together.''

"And get in trouble together," Ada Belle put in.

Mike turned to her.

"Oh, I done heard about that little bit of monkey business," Ada Belle said.

"From who?" Mike said. "From Laurie?"

Ann noticed that when Mike turned to Ada Belle, his face looked concerned, almost tense.

"Nope. From my other nurse, Josette Smith."

Mike muttered, "Josette Smith," as if trying to place her.

"You know, Gloria's buddy." Ada Belle's alert cornflower-blue eyes flicked sideways at Mike, and Ann sensed a new undercurrent in the conversation. "You know well and good there ain't any secrets in this town, Reverend. Especially when it comes to bad doings on the Lazy J."

"How on earth does Josette Smith know about this already?" Ann's attorney instincts picked up on the growing tension in Mike the way a mother senses a fever in her child. Tension that was riveted on the now evasive Ada Belle.

The old lady peered through her bifocals at her slice of cake. She took her time forking a tiny wedge free, then said, "I believe Gloria told her."

"Gloria?"

At the mention of that name, the undercurrent between Mike and Ada Belle suddenly got stronger.

"Yes, Gloria," Ada Belle answered tiredly, as if the very name were taxing. "She was delivering flowers to the rest home this morning. Josette dropped in there to check on poor old Gladys Pink right before she come by to see me.''

''How on earth did Gloria find out about Zack so quickly?''

Ada Belle glanced at Ann and shrugged her bony shoulders. ''Gloria Miller knows just about everything in this town. And poor old Gladys Pink. It's a shame she couldn't keep her own house the way I done.'' The old lady leaned toward Ann as if they were longtime confidants. ''Gladys is afflicted, you know.'' She tapped her temple. ''The wheel is turning, but the hamster's dead.''

Mike quirked his mouth at that one and shook his head.

''Why,'' Ada Belle went on, ''I don't know what I'd do without my nurses. I'd as soon go on ahead and die as end up vegetating over at that Sunset Manor.''

''Now, Ada Belle.'' Mike patted her arm, his voice reassuring. ''Folks look after Gladys, same as they'll always look after you.''

But he looked distracted as he shoved another bite of cake into his mouth.

Ann was trying to puzzle out the unspoken signals in this conversation, trying to figure out all these names, make the connections. All these people, still living in this town, after all this time. Changing, yet unchanging. With their lives interwoven, keeping track of one another, gossiping about one another. But at the same time, as Mike had just said, looking out for one another, counting on one another.

While her life, it seemed, was interwoven with absolutely no one's. Unless you counted Kenneth. And that was the trouble. Lately she'd discovered that she couldn't really count on Senator Kenneth Wilson for much of anything.

CHAPTER FIVE

MIKE WALKED Ada Belle to her front door, then sprinted back along the sidewalk to his pickup. As he fired up the engine, he checked his watch. He had just enough time to catch Gloria at her shop before he had to show the old McGuire farm at ten.

He didn't know how he was going to say it—Gloria got her feelings hurt very easily—but he wasn't going to let her meddling pass this time. He'd asked her not to discuss his personal business around town. The board at church was already scrutinizing his family's every move as it was. He released a pent-up sigh, once again wondering if Gloria's presence on the board was a blessing or a hindrance.

The bell on the door sounded with the familiar cheery tinkle, and Gloria promptly filled the curtained doorway that led to the stockroom.

"Mike!" She put her arms out and sailed toward him.

He gave her a hug, but kept it brotherly, distant, like the ones he'd given her for years when she'd been just another member of his congregation, greeting him after services.

Gloria noticed his stiffness immediately. "Mike?

What's wrong?'' She tightened her arms around his waist.

He kept his hands loose on her shoulders and looked down at her. Her appearance, immaculate as always, suddenly struck him as fussy, overdone. Maybe it was just that shapeless beaded denim jumper. Great for a flower-shop owner, but a little matronly for a... Suddenly he wondered, what was Gloria to him? *Girlfriend* didn't sound like the right word. Her fruity perfume wafted up at him as she wriggled free of his lukewarm embrace. ''You're upset about something.'' When he didn't respond, she slipped around the counter. With her back to him, she began to leaf through a stack of receipts. ''What is it?''

He decided to get right to the point. ''How did you find out about that trouble the boys got into this morning?''

Gloria glanced over her shoulder with her mouth pursed in a cutesy pout. ''And how did *you* find out that *I* found out?'' She raised one shoulder and batted her eyelashes.

Mike was in no mood. Gossip about his children was not cute. He kept his expression serious. ''I ran into Ada Belle Green this morning.''

Gloria dropped the feline pose. ''Oh? Where?''

''Over at Edith Fischer's house. And what difference does it make where? The point is, Ada Belle already knew about Zack's incident on the Lazy J.''

''And?''

''If she knows, the whole town'll know before

long. She said she found out from Josette Smith who found out from *you* when you were delivering flowers to Gladys Pink at the nursing home.''

''So?'' Gloria put the receipts down, facing him fully.

''So? *So?* Why is it any of Josette Smith's business that my son got into trouble on the Lazy J?''

''I didn't tell Josette. I told Gladys. Josette just happened to be in the room when I delivered the flowers for Gladys's birthday. I always make time for conversation with the older folks, you know that. And what am I supposed to talk about? The weather? Cooped-up old folks want to feel connected to the real world. I was only telling a harmless old lady about something vital and real.''

''At my son's expense.''

Gloria's jaw dropped. ''At Zack's exp— Listen to me, Mike Kirkpatrick. I think you're misdirecting your anger here. Zack is the one who misbehaved, not me. I don't think it's doing him any service to cover up his misdeeds. That's enabling, and you know it. He has to suffer the consequences of his behavior, and if that includes being embarrassed in front of the whole town, so be it.''

Mike raked tense fingers across his scalp. Why did conversations with Gloria always get twisted up like this? Somehow she always made him feel wrong, lacking. But he had to admit this time she was right.

''I don't want to protect Zack from the consequences of his actions. I just don't like the whole town knowing what my children are up to before I do.'' He bit his tongue, refraining from adding, *And I don't like you running around town talking about my kids as if they were your own.*

Gloria sighed. ''There's no help for it, Mike. People will talk. I found out about Zack over at the school this morning. Mary Elder—Erin's English teacher?— she's well aware of how much I care about your kids, and she knows you and I are…getting close. *She* brought it up. I was just delivering the corsages for the teacher-appreciation banquet tonight—''

''Dang!'' Mike whacked his forehead. ''The banquet! Erin is getting an academic achievement award for her writing, but I told the building committee at church we would meet at seven.'' He groaned in frustration. ''I really should get their input before the board meeting next Saturday.''

Gloria sighed again. ''Poor Mike. You can't be everywhere at once. The plain truth is, those children need a mother.''

''They have a mother.''

''Well, yes. And we both know what kind.''

Mike blinked at that. Gloria was right again. But even if there was no defending Marsha, even if he was no longer sure he wanted to, he didn't want Gloria attacking her. ''I've got to get going. I have to show the McGuire farm in less than—'' he checked his watch ''—twenty minutes.''

Gloria swung her hips around the counter and bustled across the small space that separated them. She tilted her body close to his and placed a placating palm on his lapel. ''Don't be angry at me, Mike.

Please. We can't let Zack's problems come between us. I want to help you with the kids, you know that.'' She rubbed her fingers up and down his lapel. ''I love those kids.''

''I know,'' he conceded. He enclosed her fingers and lowered her hand from his chest. He gave it an extra little squeeze before letting go. He didn't want to hurt her feelings.

She favored him with a tentative smile. ''Listen, how about if I go to the banquet and watch Erin get her award? I have to pick up the centerpieces afterward, anyway. They're on loan.''

Mike returned her smile, hoping it didn't look as careworn as he felt. ''Thanks.'' It seemed as if he was always thanking Gloria these days. ''But I think I can ask her grandma to go with her. I'd better get going.'' He darted out the door.

GLORIA WATCHED Mike climb into his pickup and throw one long arm over the seat as he backed onto Main Street. He was such a good-looking man. And he was definitely all man. And a preacher to boot! Ever since Marsha had left town, Gloria couldn't help thinking that at last God had answered her prayers.

Much to her confusion and dismay, Gloria Miller had suffered in silent spinsterhood since high school. She'd had a few dates, but those relationships had always quickly disintegrated. Why?

She was very careful with her grooming. She was hardworking, responsible, charitable. Was it her blasted weight? But no. Women far heavier, far homelier than Gloria, had husbands, children, homes. Why not her?

When Preacher Kirkpatrick, a man she had adored from afar for years, had miraculously become a single father last year, she'd seen her chance for happiness at last. He'd known her as a friend first, had become aware of her fine qualities of character at the church. In Gloria's mind that was a definite plus. Because for a man like Preacher Kirkpatrick, character counted.

But she worried. What had made him so testy and impatient this morning? So withdrawn? He'd practically pushed her away just now. Lately she'd felt things were reaching a critical impasse between them. And their relationship wasn't progressing the way she'd hoped. A healthy man like Mike should be needing the physical comfort of a woman. But he actually seemed to be avoiding that aspect of their relationship. Every time they were alone, she felt as if she was pressing too hard. Like just now.

But she was only pressing because timing was critical. Now, when he was still smarting from the shabby treatment by his flashy wife. Only now, when he was lonely and vulnerable, would a man like Mike Kirkpatrick be able to fully appreciate a solid woman like herself.

Gloria knew she was no beauty, knew she could try harder to control her weight, but she reasoned that if she could get Mike Kirkpatrick to see her as a helpmate, a mother for his children, he might eventually accept the tradeoff.

Yes, now was the time. He was vulnerable, having

finally given up on his flighty wife and filed for divorce. But if much more time passed, Gloria feared he might adapt to the demands of single fatherhood, and then she would lose her trump card—her ability to help him manage those children. And what would happen once he got involved building this new church? And there was always the terrifying possibility that he might meet someone else.

She frowned, tapping a red nail on the phone next to the cash register. So, Ada Belle Green had been at Edith Fischer's house this morning?

When she'd delivered the casket spray to the funeral home the day before yesterday, Jack Fields had told her that Edith's daughter still hadn't arrived in town. The poor man was getting nervous, thinking he might be doing the graveside service on his own. Goodness. Gloria shuddered at the thought of dying such a lonely death.

So she had volunteered to attend, although Edith had never ordered so much as a carnation from Gloria's Secret Garden. But if you were aiming to be the preacher's wife, it didn't hurt to stay on good terms with the town mortician.

Thank goodness Jack Fields had called an hour later to say that the daughter had arrived. Now Gloria wished she'd gone to the service, anyway, or at least pumped Jack for information about the woman.

Gloria couldn't dredge up much of an image of Annie Fischer in high school. The girl had been one of those brainy kids who had hovered in the background. Shy. Skinny. Gloria's jealous instincts hummed as she wondered if Mike's withdrawn attitude had something to do with this new woman in town. Well, there was more than one way to find out things around here.

She flipped her Rolodex and punched the number with a long sturdy acrylic nail. "Ada Belle? This is Gloria Miller... Fine, honey, just fine. And how are you doing these days?"

ANN ROLLED UP her sleeves and put her mind on the dirty work ahead of her. She'd just as soon dump all this stuff into the trash, but she hoped against hope that some item from her real mother could be found among all this junk. Her desperate, sporadic search over the past two days hadn't uncovered anything, not even a photograph. She was simply going to have to conduct a more methodical and thorough search.

She looked around at the furnishings and boxes and litter that filled Edith's bedroom to overflowing. After her father's death, her stepmother must have become even more driven in her peculiar cycle of hoarding and purging. There were duplicates and triplicates of everything, much of it obviously other people's garage-sale cast-offs. Throw pillows, plastic flowers, books, clocks and lamps.

She found some plastic garbage bags under the kitchen sink and dumped all the old magazines and newspapers into one. Then she made two piles—trash and Goodwill—of Edith's clothing on top of the bed, being careful to search every pocket. After she'd worked in the bedroom for a while, she decided to muck out the decaying condiments left in the refrigerator so she could lay in some fresh supplies. She was sick of eating fast food. She sponged the inside of the fridge with bleach solution, scrubbed the sink with what was left of her stepmother's cleanser and mopped the curled-linoleum floor.

But though she worked like a Trojan, the morning seemed to drag by. The minute she'd closed the door on her visitors, an eerie sadness had settled on her, which she couldn't shake off.

She'd watched from the bow window in the dining room as Mike guided Ada Belle down the sidewalk to her house. Though he was older now, he seemed somehow the same. Would she always have these feelings around him?

She imagined that even if the two of them were in a room with a thousand other people, she would still be keenly aware that he was there. It had been like that in high school. If she had a class with Mickey Kirkpatrick, his presence was a distraction for the whole semester. If he was slumped in a desk in the back of the classroom, her concentration was blown. Instead of her usual easy A, she would barely squeak by with a decent B.

And now here he was again, just as attractive as he'd been in high school. No. Now he was *more* attractive. Maturity had made him downright charismatic. His jaw was fuller, his build more solid, more powerful. The faint lines at the corners of his eyes seemed to accentuate his easygoing teasing personality. Those few strands of gray at his temples…she'd

wanted to rake her fingers through that short-cropped
hair. And his mouth! How was it that she had found
herself immediately wanting to kiss that mouth again?
For a woman who was supposed to be engaged to be
married, that was most disturbing.

What Ada Belle had said about her Chickasaw heritage had also been disturbing. Of course, Ann knew
that she was some part Chickasaw. Half the town of
Medicine Creek was part Chickasaw.

But Ann had never bothered with the paperwork,
if, in fact, any existed. Back when she was first considering law school, a school counselor had told her
about a program that paid for one's education if one
agreed to come back to Purcell and do legal work for
the Chickasaw government. Ann had passed on that.

But now she found she wanted answers. What exactly had Ada Belle meant when she said her people
were "the proudest branch of that ancient Chickasaw
tree"? Why hadn't Edith or her father ever said anything like that about her mother's people?

While she'd covered the cake and cleaned up the
plates, Ann had tried to remember her mother. But as
always, the images were frustratingly blurry.

If she closed her eyes and really concentrated, she
could hear her mother singing as she gently stroked
her little girl's long silky hair with a big brush. But
what was the song? What were the words? And what
had her mother looked like as she sang it? Suddenly
Ann burned to know everything about June Starr. But
it seemed that everything about her real mother had
been obliterated by Edith Sloan Fischer. A cold con-

trolling woman whose attitude about life was tighter than a straitjacket.

The suffocating memory of Edith kept intruding while she sorted through the woman's decaying possessions. When she finished in the kitchen, she turned her attention to the living room and made groupings of useful items that might be appropriate for an estate sale. Upstairs in a spare bedroom, many small electronics were still in their original boxes, dusty and faded now, apparently never used. Ann recognized several Christmas gifts she had sent Edith over the years. Her father must have insisted on keeping these.

Yet there was no functional order about the place, no evidence of the flow of life. And there were no signs of lasting relationships, either. While Edith kept meaningless material things clutched tightly to her, she'd had a habit of discarding the things that mattered most. Mementos. She hadn't even kept many photographs of herself and Nolan. This was what worried Ann. Edith hadn't had a sentimental bone in her body. Why would she preserve any of June's things for Ann? With a fresh pain, Ann remembered how her mother had drawn wondrous graceful drawings for her from the time she was a baby. She could remember those drawings clearly. But Edith had always been quick to toss out anything personal, anything artistic…anything connected to June. Ann closed her eyes, hoping that she would find something.

She thought again of that day when Mike Kirkpatrick had first kissed her.

"Young lady!" Edith had screeched as Ann had

tried to bolt past her up the stairs. "What were you doing out in that car with that wild Kirkpatrick boy?"

"Nothing." Ann froze on the bottom step, but she didn't turn around.

"Don't lie to me! I saw you kissing him. Are you out of your mind? The whole town knows he's practically married to that silly Dodson girl. Don't you care what people think of us?"

"I…" As always, Ann had no idea how to respond when her stepmother started in like this.

"What have you got there?" Edith demanded.

"Nothing."

"Let me see it!"

Slowly Ann withdrew the folder containing the drawing of the young girl holding the bird.

Edith snatched it.

"When are you going to stop wasting your time like this? Honestly, Ann Louise, you need to concentrate on your trigonometry, instead of doodling this sort of dreamy junk. You won't get the kind of scholarships you need from a drawing. And this thing is so morbid-looking! I swear. Now go to your room and do your homework. And don't you ever let me catch you with that Kirkpatrick boy again. Here."

Edith thrust the drawing toward Ann as if it was worthless trash.

Relieved that the drawing had survived Edith's tirade, Ann had grabbed it and dashed up the stairs.

Ann opened her eyes, hating the sight of all this meaningless junk as much as she hated the memory of Edith.

She stomped across the scarred wood flooring and threw up the sash on a window overlooking the street. But the fresh air didn't help, because below she saw her eighteen-year-old self, hurrying down the sidewalk with a suitcase toward the faded green Ford Maverick she'd bought with her earnings from the beauty parlor...

"Young lady!" Edith screeched from the front door. "You get back in this house!"

"No!" Ann whirled on the woman. "I'm never going back into that house again."

"Stop acting like a fool! You cannot make it on your own and you know it...." Edith's tone, though threatening, bordered on hysteria, and as she ranted on, shredding Ann's plans for freedom with every word, Ann realized something important for the first time. Even if her stepmother didn't love her, having Ann in the house had somehow given shape, legitimacy, to this bitter woman's days. Without Ann, Edith would have no one to control. No one to blame for all the money she spent. No one's hair to chop off when it should have been allowed to grow. No one's drawings to tear into shreds.

Edith charged down the sidewalk. "Answer me!" she demanded. But Ann hadn't heard the question, and besides, as far as she was concerned, there was only one answer here—to get herself as far from this woman as humanly possible. She closed the trunk of the Maverick and gave Edith the benefit of one long cold stare with her dark eyes before walking around to the driver's-side door.

"You're acting just like your mother's moody people." Edith's voice dripped with contempt. "All this fuss over a little drawing."

Ann turned on her. This wasn't the first time Edith had insulted the Chickasaws, but it would be the last time Ann would have to hear it. "I won an award for that drawing. It was important to me." She got in the car and slammed the door.

Edith clutched the handle, bending down to look in the open window. Ann saw the beginnings of panic in her face. "If I had remembered that, do you think I would have torn the thing up?"

"Don't give me that. You were having one of your fits because I wouldn't arrange my room to your liking. Now just get away from the car."

But Edith clutched the handle more tightly. "I had to show you who was in charge! A woman can't let a child talk to her that way." Edith, still clinging, raised her voice as Ann started backing the car out. "And I will not have you poking holes in the wallpaper! What will I tell your father?" She wailed as she trotted alongside the car.

Ann jammed on the brakes. "Tell him," she said through gritted teeth as she peeled Edith's fingers off the door handle, "the truth. Tell him I love him, but I refuse to live in the same house with you—the woman who tears up my drawings."

Edith's face grew white. "Leave, then." She shouted as Ann backed away. "But don't ever come back. I don't want to see your face in this house again!"

Of course, Ann had come back, but only twice. Once for her father's funeral...and now for Edith's.

Her jaw hurt and she became aware that she was gritting her teeth now just as she had on the day she left. Suddenly she could no longer bear to be in the musty old house surrounded by the remnants of Edith Fischer's stagnant life.

She looked out over the rooftops and the quiet tree-lined street. It was truly a gorgeous day, and she decided to leave the rental car in the carport and walk the few short blocks to downtown.

MAIN STREET STILL LOOKED much as it had when Ann was a child. Buildings that dated back to the 1890s when the famous ranch—Starr of the Arbuckles—and the train depot and town built to serve it—had first been established.

The old railroad depot had been converted into a quaint museum now, surrounded by a charming park with a half-dozen picnic tables, large trees and a seasonal tableau that stood between antique lampposts. Right now there was a scarecrow surrounded by pumpkins and decorated hay bales in anticipation of Halloween. A calligraphy sign propped on one of the hay bales read: Design Courtesy of Gloria's Secret Garden.

Along the main drag there appeared to be more antique dealers and gift shops now, fewer dry goods and shoe stores. The drugstore was in the same place. It had a new name, but it was the same old Rexall.

She stopped at the Murray County National Bank,

still charmingly housed in its original sandstone
building with the corner clocktower. In the hushed
dim interior the smell of old wood competed with the
tang of new carpet and fresh paint. "I'd like to close
my deceased stepmother's accounts," she explained,
and was directed to an old-fashioned teller's window.

Closing the accounts would be a simple matter. At
least her father's will had made it clear that all remaining monies and property reverted to Ann upon
Edith's death. She didn't have a certificate of death
yet, but in a town of less than five thousand, official
documentation hardly seemed necessary.

When she made her request, the teller peeked over
her bifocals and said, "And I suppose you'll want to
empty the safe-deposit box, as well."

"My parents had a safe-deposit box?"

"No, *they* didn't. It was Edith's. She maintained it
for years."

"But I don't know where Edith's key is."

"You don't have the spare? Customers are always
issued two. It's customary for people to leave one
with someone in case of an emergency." The woman
frowned. "This isn't mentioned in the will?"

"No." Ann was puzzled. "The will was my father's." What on earth would her stepmother have to
put in a safe-deposit box? "You can't open it without
her key?"

"No. The bank has one key and the customer has
another. Both are needed to open the box."

Ann knew that. As an attorney she knew that. It
was just that this news was so stunning she wasn't

thinking clearly. There had never been any mention of a safe-deposit box. That key could be anywhere in that old house.

"There's no other way?"

"The bank can drill the box open at the customer's request."

"Okay. That's what I want to do." Anything to speed up her exit from this town.

"All right. We'll need proof that you're the executor—no need for a death certificate, everybody knows Edith has passed—and the fee will be two hundred dollars. I can deduct that from Edith's savings."

"Two hundred dollars?"

The woman nodded sympathetically.

Ann could afford to pay that much, but it seemed an unnecessary expense when she hadn't even searched for the key.

"Let me try to find the key first. I haven't really looked for it, and the house is...my stepmother had a lot of things."

"I understand. The whole town's aware that Edith was...a collector. Just bring the key in whenever you find it. The stuff in that safe-deposit box isn't going anywhere. I guess you'll need to do some sorting, anyway, to preserve family mementos and other important things before you hold an estate sale or anything. Is that what you're planning to do? Have an estate sale?"

Important things. Ann seriously doubted that the things that were important to Edith were important to her. But she smiled at the woman and said, "I really haven't thought it all through yet. Even though I was aware that Edith wasn't well, her death still came as a shock. My stepmother and I were not…close.''

The woman stopped writing and looked at Ann. ''Yes. So I hear.'' She readopted a sympathetic face. ''We are so sorry for your loss,'' she added, clearly an afterthought.

Ann wondered exactly what Edith had told the townsfolk about her strained relationship with her stepdaughter. A self-pitier of the first order, Edith was good at playing the martyr, the victim. And small towns, Ann knew, had some kind of honor code about taking care of their own no matter how difficult the relative might be. Which would probably place a woman who ran off to Washington and avoided the stepmother who'd raised her about one rung above an ax murderer.

She accepted the meager cash left in Edith's accounts and was relieved when she was out in the sunshine on the sidewalk again. She glanced up and down Main Street. Across the way she spotted the flower shop—Gloria's Secret Garden—that had supplied Edith's funeral spray. She decided to go ahead and pay the bill in person.

Like every other building on Main Street, Medicine Creek, the place had been charmingly restored. A pink-and-white-striped awning stretched cozily over a wide window and a paned-glass door. Colorful seasonal banners fluttered sideways in the top half of the door, which was flung open, admitting the fresh air and fall sunshine. An old-fashioned shop bell tinkled as Ann pushed the bottom half open. The place was thoroughly pleasant, bursting with the usual plants and flowers artfully displayed among substantial antiques, homey gifts and elaborate craft items.

"Hello!" Ann called out.

"Be right there!" a cheerful female voice trilled from an open door at the back.

But when the woman emerged, she gave Ann a somber appraisal. She spread her palms on the small glass counter. "May I help you?" She was stocky. Short. With dyed-red hair carefully arranged in a chic cropped style. Her loose-fitting denim jumper twinkled with beadwork and sequins atop a full bust. She exuded the aura of an efficient and prosperous shop owner, but didn't seem pleased to see Ann.

"I'm Ann Fischer, Edith Fischer's stepdaughter." Ann gave the woman an encouraging smile. "I thought I'd drop by to pay for her funeral flowers."

"Yes. I know who you are. I have the ticket right here." The woman's rings flashed as she withdrew the bill of sale from a stack. "That will be $221."

Ann didn't comment on the price and proceeded to write the check.

"So, you're selling Edith's house?" The shopkeeper stated it as if she knew it for a fact.

Ann glanced up. "Yes. I'm sorry…you are?" She didn't want to be rude, but she wasn't going to discuss her business with a stranger, either.

"Gloria Miller." The woman produced a simpering smile. "I own this shop. And I know Mike Kirkpatrick—that's how I know about Edith's house. So, did he make it over there today?''

"Yes, he did.''

"I see. What have you decided to do about the contents? I imagine Edith had quite a few antiques tucked away in that old place. I could name you a decent price if you want me to come over and have a look.'' Gloria's rings flashed as she efficiently wound a sash of ribbon.

Ann continued to write the check as she searched her memory. Ada Belle and Mike had mentioned someone named Gloria. This woman? What was it they had said? That she knew everything in this town? Hadn't Mike seemed miffed that Gloria already knew about his son's misbehavior?

"I really haven't decided what I want to do yet.''

"Well, estate sales are so cumbersome. And people usually don't make a dime. I could take the whole mess off your hands in one fell swoop.'' Gloria returned the bolt of red ribbon to its allocated spot beside the other shades of red on the rack behind her. "If you let me take care of it, you could get back to...Washington? without any more worries about all that old stuff.''

"We'll see. How do you know Mike Kirkpatrick?''

Ann meant only to deflect Gloria from probing about Edith's possessions, but at the mention of Mike the woman seemed suddenly wary.

"Why do you ask?''

"Just wondering. Is he your minister?''

"Well, as a matter of fact, he is. But—'' Gloria

drew out the word as she tapped an already tidy display of gift cards "—our friendship actually goes a little deeper than that." Her demeanor became demure. "Actually Mike and I...we're becoming very close. Some people act like we're all but engaged. But you know how folks in a small town are."

Ann tore the check from its binding.

Gloria plucked it between thumb and forefinger, then glanced at it before sliding it into a drawer. "Thank you. I don't normally accept out-of-town checks. But we all know who you are and we all know where to find you." She smiled. "Will you have to return to Washington immediately, or will you be staying for a few days?"

Again Ann searched her memory. This woman seemed vaguely familiar—from high school, perhaps. Ann would guess they were about the same age. "I...I don't know. I'm hoping to close on the sale of the property as soon as possible."

"Well, Mike'll do a good job for you. He's very...energetic. And as honest as the day is long."

"Of course."

"Thank you for your business, Miss Fischer. It is still *Miss* Fischer, isn't it?"

"Yes. It was nice to meet you, Gloria. The casket arrangement was lovely. Thank you for doing it on such short notice."

"No problem." Another smile. This one faintly catty.

Ann left the florist shop thoroughly confused. Mike Kirkpatrick was "all but engaged" to that woman?

She didn't seem like his type. And the way he'd
sounded when he'd talked about Marsha today—still
so sad and weighed down by the whole separation
and divorce—he didn't seem like a man entertaining
thoughts of an engagement.

CHAPTER SIX

OUT IN THE FRESH AIR again with the strained exchange in the flower shop behind her, Ann realized she was hungry. She looked at her watch. Well, no wonder. Noon.

She had planned to go by the grocery store for sandwich supplies, but when she peered down the block, she spotted a small café. A green awning proclaiming Pie in the Sky rippled in the fall breeze above a pale yellow brick facade. The place looked a lot more inviting than the fast-food joints out near the interstate. Ann didn't remember this restaurant being here when she was a kid.

But next door the cluttered, dusty-looking display window of Hobbs Hardware was arranged exactly as it had been when she'd made all those boring trips there with her father.

After lunch she'd go to Hobbs and get a new doorknob for Edith's back door. The old one wouldn't stay locked in a stiff breeze. It was amazing that Edith's home had sat unoccupied and yet nothing inside had been disturbed. Only in a small town…

After Hobbs, she'd walk down the block to the Sooner Super and get some fruit and sandwich fixings. She felt an involuntary wave of freedom and

contentment at being able to do all her errands efficiently—on foot, no less—within a few short blocks,
instead of struggling to coordinate subway stops and
change trains as she did in D.C.

PIE IN THE SKY was filled with luscious aromas. Coffee. Burgers on the grill. And, of course, freshly
baked pies. Ann's stomach actually growled as she
waited while the woman behind the counter rang up
a ticket. The long narrow room was crammed full of
booths and tables covered in red-checked oilcloths,
and bustling with customers.

Farmers in plaid flannel shirts, retired couples from
the RV village out at Arbuckle Lake, teenagers in
letter jackets with "Titans" monogrammed across the
back, were served by waitresses in athletic shoes,
jeans and Pie in the Sky sweatshirts hustling to and
fro.

Because of all the activity, Ann didn't spot Mike
Kirkpatrick in a back booth until the woman behind
the cash register led her to a booth against the wall.
He was laughing, engaged in an animated conversation with a man in a red ball cap.

A waitress brought a plastic menu, water and sil-
verware rolled in a paper napkin. She poised her pen
over a pad and said, "Know what you want?"

"Uh, no. I don't," Ann admitted as she studied the
list of amazingly varied fare.

"The special today is Ma's meat loaf," a pleasant
baritone voice announced from behind her.

"Hi, Reverend Mike!" the little waitress chirped.

"Hi, Jessica. Go ask your mom to fix Miss Fischer a lunch special. You won't regret it," he assured Ann as she smiled up at him.

"Red devil cake and Ma's meat loaf. A few more days in this town and I'll have to switch to elastic waistbands."

"You? Fat? Never! Why don't you come and join me and Steve Harris? You know, Laurie's husband? Back there." He pointed to the rear booth, and the man in the cap gave her a smile and a little two-fingered salute.

Ann remembered Steve the minute she took a closer look at him. She suddenly recalled the time he'd dressed up like a sheriff—complete with a fake paunch and a toy gunbelt—on Halloween. He'd banged on Laurie's door and "arrested" her for being "way too pretty." How wonderful that those two finally got together.

"I'd like that," she said.

"Ann." Steve stood as she approached. He took off his cap and enclosed her hand in his work-roughened one. "You look great! How long's it been since we saw each other last?"

"Quite a while." She smiled. She slid into the booth, and Mike slid in right beside her. Natural enough, she supposed. Steve was a very large man.

Ann enjoyed getting reacquainted with Steve, and before long Jessica appeared bearing platters loaded with savory meat loaf, mashed potatoes and gravy, and buttery lima beans. After she refilled the men's coffee, brought an iced tea for Ann and added a plastic basket of the softest, lightest yeast rolls Ann had ever seen, Mike said, "Let's bow our heads."

He quietly said a simple prayer of thanks to which Steve intoned, "Amen," and Mike added, "Dig in!"

They did. Even though she'd had a slice of Ada Belle's cake at ten that morning, Ann had never been so hungry and the down-home cooking at Pie in the Sky tasted wonderful.

Before she finished, the men had cleaned their plates, ordered up pie and signaled for coffee refills.

"You gotta take one little bite of this," Mike insisted when his slice of coconut-cream pie arrived. He was aiming a forkful toward Ann's lips when an angry-looking old man appeared inside the door of the café. As the red-faced man removed his cap and glared around the room, the buzz of conversation in the little restaurant grew subdued. When he spotted Mike and Steve, he stomped around tables and chairs to the back. All eyes followed him.

"Here comes trouble," Steve muttered, and pulled on his own cap, tugging the bill down tight.

"I figured I'd find you two in here stuffin' pie in your faces," the man shouted when he got close. "What're you gonna do about those hellion kids of yours? What're you gonna do about my mare?" He glared at Steve.

"I know you're upset, Jerrod," Steve said calmly, "but I've taken the boy's Jeep away from him and—"

"And Trent and Zack will work on your ranch to pay back every penny of the damages," Mike chimed in. "We were planning to bring them out to your place after school. We've already given the boys a good talking-to."

"A talking-to? If them devils was my kids, I'd beat 'em with a horsewhip!"

Ann gave an involuntary gasp.

Cagle fixed a hard glare in her direction, and under his gaze something in her tightened. She recognized those cold eyes. She was aware that this was the owner of the Lazy J ranch, but she could have sworn she'd seen him somewhere else before. The memory refused to come clear, but the feelings accompanying it were strong—and negative.

"I'll be. This here's gotta be June Starr's kid." Every word the man said spewed hostility, but the sound of her mother's name coming from his mouth gave Ann a real chill. She shivered, visibly, and Mike turned to her with a concerned frown.

"This is Ann Fischer," Steve said mildly. "Ann, Jerrod Cagle. Owns the Lazy J."

Ann nodded stiffly, deliberately resisting giving this man her hand—or even a cordial smile.

"I know what you two are up to," Cagle said, resuming his earlier tirade in a voice loud enough for the whole restaurant to hear. "Schmoozin' this woman to get your hands on that pecan grove. Sendin' your kids out with their vandalism to distract me when I'm trying to sell my land to the Powers people."

"Now wait just a minute—" Mike started to rise.

"No, you wait just a minute, mister!" Cagle

pointed a finger in Mike's face before he got out of the booth. "You may be the holier-than-thou preacher to all these folks, but I know you're just tryin' to cut me outta that land deal. And this big-city lawyer—" he jabbed the finger at Ann "—is too stupid to know what she's sellin'."

"It's rude—" Mike's hand flashed up faster than a striking snake and knocked Cagle's finger aside "—to point. And don't talk like that to the lady." He stood.

Ann stared up at Mike openmouthed. He had positioned himself between Cagle and the table, between Cagle and *her,* to be precise. And in less time than it took to blink, his color had risen, his chest had expanded, his breathing had grown rapid, his eyes were flashing, and in general, he looked ready to beat Cagle to a pulp.

This was the town preacher? No, Ann realized, this was the aggressive high-school jock who had never been completely tamed.

"You always was a goddamn piece of work!" Cagle seethed and leaned in, practically nose to nose with Mike.

Everyone in the restaurant—waitresses, farmers, teenagers—stared, waiting to see who would land the first punch.

"Now calm down, Jerrod." Steve slid out of the booth. "You too, Mike."

"I'm calm," Mike said. But his tone was low, threatening. When Cagle backed up, Mike jerked his head at the door. "I suggest we finish this at my office."

"Fine by me." Cagle jabbed his stubby finger at Mike again. "Let's go." He turned and stomped to the door.

"Ann, I'm really sorry our lunch got disturbed this way." Mike was pulling a couple of twenties out of his billfold. His mouth was still tight, but he did look calmer. "Please. Enjoy your pie."

"I'm sorry, too," Ann said quietly. "But you don't have to buy my lunch." She reached for the bills as he laid them on the table.

"I want to." He covered her hand briefly, capturing her gaze with his. "I'll see you tomorrow."

"At ten." She nodded.

"Bye, Ann," Steve said.

"It was nice to see you again, Steve."

"I'll tell Laurie we visited. She'll want to see you while you're in town."

"Yes. Please have her call me. I've kept Edith's phone connected."

"I sure will." Steve winked jauntily as they turned to go, but as he and Mike made their way through the restaurant, returning two-fingered salutes from farmers along the way, they moved with a weariness that said they weren't looking forward to the coming confrontation.

OUT ON THE SIDEWALK Mike said, "Can you believe that guy?"

"Lookin' to get his ass kicked. But still, we gotta fix this screwup."

Mike smirked at Steve's pun and checked his watch. "Man! I'm supposed to pick up Mary Beth." He whipped out his cell phone and punched a number. "Come on, Mom, answer."

After waiting impatiently, he said, "Shoot," and snapped the phone shut. "Here." He pulled his keys from his pocket and handed them to Steve. "Would you mind going over and opening my office? Let Cagle have a good rant until I get there. I have a feeling you're going to have better luck reasoning with him than I would, anyway."

"No problem." Steve took the one key Mike held apart from the set. "Where're you going?"

"Over to Gloria's." He stepped into the brick-paved street. "I'll have ask her to fetch Mary Beth from kindergarten again—" he broke into a trot "—so I can deal with you-know-who," he yelled over his shoulder.

Steve waved his understanding.

When Mike ducked into the flower shop, Gloria crooned, "Well, hello!" as she looked up from a stack of papers at the counter. "You're back!" She stuck out her lower lip. "But I'm afraid I don't have time for lunch." She acted as if the earlier tension between them had never happened. She sailed around the counter and pursed her lips in a little mew as she leaned up to his face.

Something about her strained cheerfulness set Mike's teeth on edge, but he gave her a dutiful peck on the cheek, anyway. "I'm not here for lunch. I've already grabbed a bite at the Pie with Steve."

"Oh? Did you see your new client? I thought I saw her going into the Pie. You know, Edith Fischer's daughter?"

How in the devil did Gloria know every time anybody in this town so much as took a poot? No doubt she'd soon hear that he'd nearly lost it in the Pie, and so would the church board before the day was over. "Yeah, I saw her. In fact, she ate with us."

"Did she?" Gloria's voice raised an octave.

"Listen, I really don't have time to chat. Jerrod Cagle is coming to my office."

"I kind of remember her from high school. Remember how thin that poor girl was?"

"Who?"

"Edith's daughter. Annie. Isn't that her name?"

"She goes by Ann now. Gloria, listen." Mike did not have time to indulge Gloria's insatiable curiosity. Right now he desperately needed her help. "I'm in a bind here. Could you do me a favor?"

Gloria rolled her eyes toward the big service clock above the arrangement cooler and sighed. "Mary Beth again?"

Mike raked a hand through his hair and nodded. He hated imposing on Gloria, but what choice did he have? And hadn't she insisted that she wanted to help him with the children any way she could?

"I've got to go deal with Cagle immediately and—"

"Don't you worry. I'll bring Mary Beth back here

and she can help me make bows. But really, Mike, you must find a sitter for your little girl, much as I love having her in the shop with me.'' She drew something out of a drawer below the counter. ''I have a business to run here. I can't always be hanging this sign out.'' She set the hands of a Be Right Back paper clock, walked around the counter and leaned forward to prop the sign at the front of the display window.

Her denim jumper stretched over her ample backside, and Mike glanced at it critically, instantly chastising himself for doing so. He reminded himself that a beautiful body wasn't everything a woman could offer a family and that Gloria had many other qualities he admired. She was organized, industrious, punctual, generous....

She finished adjusting the sign and turned from the window.

''You're right.'' He ran a hand through his hair again. ''I should find someone, but I keep hoping I can get by until Mary Beth's in first grade. She feels more secure if she can come to the office with me in the afternoons. I do my phone calls and work at the computer, and she usually curls up on the couch with her blankie for a nap. It works out okay—usually.''

''Except for today,'' Gloria said, ''and last Wednesday. And that Friday when you had to go out and show that farm.'' She smiled up at him, despite her lecture.

''I know.'' He glanced out the display window and saw Jerrod Cagle's pickup lurching to a halt in front of the Home Town Realty office. ''But this is different. Cagle got hostile in the restaurant about that deal with the boys, and I just don't want Mary Beth around the man when he might fly into a rage.''

Gloria shuddered. ''What a nasty old man. I certainly understand.''

''I promise I'll try to find someone from the church to pick up Mary Beth from now on.'' He was already backing toward the door. ''I really, really appreciate this. I just don't know where else to turn on such short notice.'' He stopped at the door and sighed heavily. ''I could wring Zack's neck for causing this kind of trouble.''

''Oh, Mike.'' Gloria rushed forward and laid a hand on his lapel. She tilted her head and tsked. ''What in the world are we going to do with that boy?''

We. Lately, Gloria had been using the *we* pronoun more and more often. But as far as Mike was concerned, he and Gloria were a long way from being *we.* He'd hardly touched the woman. And yet they'd become inexorably entangled in the past few months. Gloria had been so accommodating. Always there. Always prepared. It had started with those casseroles she'd dropped by the house. The kids had scarfed them up. Then one Sunday morning he had found himself standing next to her, serving up sausage at the church's pancake breakfast. While they dished up the food in their matching red-striped aprons, people had started joking with them as if they were a couple. It was all good friendly fun. But with their twinkling eyes and jovial laughter, folks had let their fondness for Gloria show. Many in his congregation had never warmed to Marsha. Looking back, he realized he shouldn't have let that cozy little scene happen.

After that, their relationship, always friendly enough, had become more…interdependent. Well, not really interdependent, he thought with mortification. *He* was the one who depended on Gloria. Little by little Gloria had helped him survive this first year without Marsha. And he hadn't known how to refuse that help when his children were hurting.

He shouldn't have let things get this far, but here he was turning to Gloria for help again.

And lately it seemed as if she wanted something from him, expected it. He flinched at the possibilities as she reached up and touched the tip of his nose as if he were a naughty little boy. "Well, we'll worry about Mr. Zack later. You'd better get going."

"I'll come and get Mary Beth as soon as I get rid of Cagle." He darted out the door.

Seemed like he darted everywhere these days, he thought ruefully as he sprinted toward the realty office. Here was yet another fire to put out. And he had not liked the look on Ann's face when Cagle accused him of schmoozing her. No, he had not liked that look one little bit.

Tomorrow he'd have to face her and explain this pecan-grove deal.

CHAPTER SEVEN

JERROD CAGLE'S ACCUSATIONS about Mike Kirkpatrick's plans for the pecan grove had taken Ann by surprise. She'd been telling herself that she didn't care what the buyers did with the land. And she didn't. But Cagle had implied that Mike was manipulating her because of some shady deal. That had surprised her. And inside the Hobbs Hardware store, she was in for more surprises.

The interior of the store was no surprise, of course. Everything about it had remained basically the same for years. The same tarnished cow bell tinkled over the door when she pushed it open. The same oily, painty, metallicky smells greeted her nose. The same aisles were crowded with the same faded displays of wallpaper and paint, hinges and hammers. The same old guys loitered around in billed caps and overalls. Three of that sort gave her alert looks from the bins of nails near the door. Good grief. It was the twenty-first century, but in Medicine Creek, she supposed a woman in a hardware store still drew attention. She walked past and waited at the counter with her back to them.

The men resumed their conversation.

Loudly.

The first man said, "Yep. Jerrod Cagle has just been itchin' for an excuse to drag Mike down, and now that kid has gone and give it to him."

The second man chimed in. "Kirkpatrick's in way over his head on this whole land deal, anyway, if you ask me."

"What deal are y'all talkin' about?" man number three asked, as if he was out of the loop. Ann's gut tightened when she realized he was playing the straight man, and this conversation was being staged for her benefit.

Man number two: "Ain't you heard? Cagle told me Mike's got some big developer on the string. Plans to bring a big mall in here."

"A mall? Here in Medicine Creek?"

"Yeah. That's how they do. Put it between the metro areas like Dallas and OKC." *Oklahoma City*. "That way, people from all over the place drive to it. Tryin' to get a bargain, you know, 'cause it'd be one uv'em…whatchamacallits."

"Outlet malls," man number one supplied.

"Hope the preacher knows what he's doin' this time. You get one of them things in a town, it'll destroy the place faster'n a number-five tornada. All kinds of riffraff come in because of places like that. They bring in the shoppers by the busload, you know."

"Don't know what Preacher Kirkpatrick is thinkin'."

"Cold cash. That's what he's thinkin'."

"If you had a pack of kids headed for college, you'd be worried about money, too."

"But if Kirkpatrick gets his way, the town's gonna lose the pecan grove."

"Some folks don't know the value of that pecan grove, if you ask me, or much of anything else."

Ann's cheeks blazed. Had she stepped into the midst of some kind of local controversy? The idea of a mall that would bring shoppers and tourists by the busload, a mall that would change the face of this sleepy historic town—that idea hadn't even occurred to her. Suddenly she remembered that Mike had the papers prepared for the sale of the pecan grove before Edith had even died. He'd been forthcoming—or was it disarming?—about that fact. Had he been waiting for Edith to die so he could close this deal?

"May I help you?" A short, pleasant-looking woman in a muslin carpenter's apron materialized out of a side aisle.

"Susie?" Ann said. She was certain this was Susie Hobbs, granddaughter of the kindly man who had run this store when Ann was a child. Susie, two grades behind Ann in school, had always looked younger than her years. She used to come to the upper-level art classes to ooh and ahh over the older kids' work. Especially Ann's. Still cherub-cheeked and blond, Susie looked very mature now, but she hadn't lost the old openness that Ann had liked.

"Yes?" Susie said, still smiling. "Do I know you?"

"It's Ann." Ann spread a palm on her chest. "Annie Fischer."

"Oh, my!" Susie put out her hand, grabbing Ann's forearm. "Of course. I heard you were back in town because of...because of Edith. I was sorry to hear she'd passed on."

"Thank you." Ann smiled.

"You look great!" Susie enthused. "Life in Washington must agree with you."

"I enjoy it."

The old men by the nail bins were completely silent, no doubt eavesdropping. Ann almost expected them to whip out carpenter's pencils and take notes.

"How long are you going to be in town?"

"I don't know." Ann sighed. "I plan to sell the house, but I haven't decided whether to fix it up first or just get rid of it." She dropped her voice. "I may have a buyer who doesn't care if it's in good repair."

"Myself, I've always longed to see that old beauty restored." Susie got a faraway look in her eyes. "It could be grand." She lifted her hands and spread her fingers like a painter framing a landscape. "Maybe in shades of vermilion and cognac with a soft Basque beige."

Susie made it sound so easy.

"But there's so much to do," Ann confided. "I hardly know where to start."

Susie nodded sympathetically. "That bad, huh? We can help. We can give you a price break on materials if you decide to do major work. And I know the names of lots of contractors and subs. Sometimes it's hard to get workmen in a small town.''

Ann felt better. No wonder Hobbs Hardware had stayed in business for fifty years with this kind of helpful attitude.

''I assume Mike's your real-estate agent?''

The silence over by the nail bins grew positively Stygian.

Susie flapped a hand. ''Mike's great. He helps people get old houses in shape all the time.''

''Yes, he seems very professional. Right now I just need a few basic things to get the place secure and clean. A door lock. Some big heavy-duty garbage bags. A wide broom. Window cleaner. Stuff like that.''

''You bet. Follow me.'' As they passed the men huddled around the nail bins, Susie smiled. ''You boys need anything special or you just counting nails?''

That brought tobacco-stained grins from the trio.

As she edged by, the second man looked at Ann knowingly and touched the brim of his cap. ''Ma'am.'' Then he glanced at his buddies.

Their shifty crinkled eyes told Ann that the earlier artificially loud conversation had definitely been for her benefit.

Good grief. A land-development flap. Weren't small towns supposed to be dull places where nothing ever happened? She hadn't experienced this kind of intrigue even in the legal trenches of Washington, D.C.

BACK AT EDITH'S HOUSE, Ann dragged a thirty-gallon trash can from the old storage shed to the middle of the living room. She lined it with one of the bags she'd bought at Hobbs Hardware, tied on a tattered apron of Edith's, rolled up her sleeves and started sorting and pitching.

While she worked, she replayed that overheard conversation. Much as she hated Medicine Creek, hated the sad memories of her childhood that being here evoked, hated this house, these things, even that land across the street, the town represented the only past she had. As she considered starting a new life as Mrs. Senator Kenneth Wilson, she needed to know as much as she could about her old one. And that meant finding something of her mother's to ground her, give her a history.

So for emotional and practical reasons, she had to keep looking.

She pitched and sorted with a new sense of purpose, and by late afternoon, her fevered search had taken her to the third floor.

In a dusty bent grocery box, one of many that she had wrestled down the ladder from the attic door in the third floor hallway, she was finally rewarded.

The box had ''Annie'' scrawled across two sides in ballpoint pen. Ann pried the pieces of twine off the ends and then unpeeled the strips of drying tape that bound the lid.

She knew what she had found the instant she peeked under the lid and saw folds of an old prairie-style dress. The garment looked strangely familiar. It was a circle skirt and peasant blouse in multiple shades of red, blue and yellow calico with rows and rows of navy rickrack. As Ann touched the fabric, she knew that the dress was the link to the past she had been seeking. Her breathing grew rapid.

Within the folds lay a small yellowed note. She recognized her father's strained writing immediately.

Dear Daughter,
You are too young to understand why, but someday your mama would have wanted you to have this. It is her Chickasaw ceremony dress.

Dad

That was all he'd written, but it was enough. Ann folded the note, the only thing her father had ever written to her. She closed her eyes, remembering a time—she must have been ten or eleven—when she had asked her father to tell her about June. Nolan Fischer was rail-thin by then, worn down by years of Edith's carping and years of working under the hot Oklahoma sun in the stone quarry. His hands had felt as dry as limestone dust when he touched Ann's cheek.

"Baby doll, Mama Edith doesn't like us to talk about the past." His voice had sounded dry, too, as exhausted and threadbare as his worn overalls.

Mama Edith.

For a while the couple had encouraged that unlikely moniker for Ann's stepmother. It hadn't worked. Even as a five-year-old, Ann had seen the hypocrisy

in using a term of endearment for a woman as un-
pleasant and repressive as Edith was. By the time she
was eight, Ann stuck to the more formal "Mother"
or simply "Edith" when she spoke of the woman.

How had Nolan managed to save these things for
her? Edith would have gotten rid of anything remi-
niscent of June the minute she came upon it.

But for once, Nolan had somehow gone against
Edith's wishes and in doing so, left Ann a small piece
of her mother.

"Mama," Ann whispered as she reached out to
touch the rickrack along the ruffles of the long skirt.
She lifted the dress from the box and buried her face
in the remotely familiar fragrance of the fabric. When
she looked up, her gaze caught on what lay below the
dress, and her breathing ceased altogether.

For a suspended moment in time, her heart in her
throat, Ann stared down into a strong likeness of her
own face.

The young woman in the eight-by-ten black-and-
white photo smiled up—youthful, fresh, beautiful—
wearing the white-feathered off-the-shoulder boa
commonly used in old high-school graduation portraits in the sixties. She gazed steadily from beneath
a broad smooth brow framed by long, coal-black hair.
Her face looked innocent and kind. With shaking
hands, Ann raised the picture and felt as if she was
studying her own cheeks, her own smile, looking into
her own eyes.

She sat back on her haunches and lost track of time.
She had never seen a picture of her mother this large,

this clear, this detailed. As she stared down at the face that so resembled her own, a long sad silence stretched back through the many years of her mother's absence. Years that could never be regained. Years when her mother had been hidden from her. A shadow person. In a box. In the attic.

As she let her gaze travel over the picture, it landed on a chain sparkling down her mother's throat. At the end shone a large jewel, almost hidden in the fluff of boa. Ann remembered that piece—a star sapphire at least as large as a nickel—because her mother had once let her wear it, briefly, when she was very small.

Where was that necklace now? Ann hadn't seen it since…since she was five years old, she knew that much. Edith and Nolan had certainly never mentioned it. Had it gone back to her grandmother Lydia? She stared off into space, remembering the vivid blue of the thing. Maybe that was what Edith had kept locked away in the safe-deposit box at the bank.

She turned her attention back to the contents of the box, eager for more memories of her mother. There were other, more mundane articles of clothing. There was a small tattered quilt. A carved wooden horse.

And there were snapshots. Some of Ann as a baby. One, a madonna-and-child pose where one-year-old Ann was being tenderly held in her mother's arms, brought tears to her eyes.

Mama.

Anger welled up in Ann. "Why didn't you show these to me?" She whispered the accusation to the empty room. "Why?" But the dead couldn't answer.

Kneeling there, surrounded by the evidence of her stepmother's irrational jealousy and her father's passivity, Ann was overcome by a desperate need for comfort. She clutched the framed photo to her breast and stumbled down the stairs. In the dining room she pulled her cell phone out of her bag and dialed.

At his town house, she got Kenneth's voice mail. "Hi," she said brightly. "It's me. Would you call me on my cell as soon as you get in? I just...I just need to hear your voice."

It was almost seven o'clock Washington time. He was probably at a reception or dinner, but she dialed his office, anyway. "Is Senator Wilson still there?...Ann...Ann Fischer."

Several seconds ticked by before Kenneth answered. "Ann?"

"Kenneth? Thank God you're there!"

"Why are you calling me at the office? I mean, is something wrong?"

"No, nothing's wrong, exactly. I mean, I'm all right. It's just...oh, Kenneth. It's so awful here. My stepmother's house is a wreck, and digging through all this old junk is depressing. I miss you. I need someone to be with me now. Coming back to this town has been...so damned hard. I found an old picture of my mother and—"

"I know it's hard. And I wish I could be with you. You have no idea how I wish I could be there, instead of here facing Bruebaum's filibuster on the environmental bill. It's a crucial time, a critical time...." Ann got up to pace the darkening living room while Senator Kenneth Wilson listed all the reasons he couldn't fly "all the way out to Oklahoma" right now.

"I know," she agreed quietly while he talked on. "I understand." One of the reasons Kenneth loved her, he reminded her often, was her independence. It took a special kind of woman to be married to a U.S. senator. An independent woman. But standing in that gloomy living room with the boxes of Edith's junk closing in around her, Ann had never felt so bereft, so needy, so *dependent.* She wanted to rage at Kenneth that even a strong woman needed support sometimes. Was this marriage going to be a one-way street? she wanted to scream.

Instead, she sank to the dusty couch with the picture of June on her lap and listened to him complain about his overbooked schedule, his migraine, his regrets and his guilt for not being with her.

In the end she let him go to his important meeting, and though he promised to call her early the next day, she hung up the phone feeling worse, not better.

She turned on a couple of lamps and propped the portrait on the table and finally ended up standing at the bow window in the dining room, staring out. The sun was setting low over the steep-pitched roofs of the aging houses across the street, and she thought of Ada Belle in her cozy house across the way. Her childhood haven. Perhaps it could be so again.

She checked her watch, remembering Ada Belle's invitation to "run over of an evening, any evening." Five o'clock. She walked to the front-parlor window, where she could see in that direction, and pushed aside the rotting lace sheers.

A red Honda CR-V was parked in Ada Belle's driveway. Lights glowed, soft and golden, through the sheers of the downstairs windows.

Ann went to the bathroom and washed the dust from her hands. She refused to mope around in this horrid mausoleum when her best friend from high school and the sweetest old lady on the face of the earth were sitting nearby in a warmly lit house.

CHAPTER EIGHT

LAURIE HARRIS answered Ada Belle's door, looking fresh and professional in pink nurse's scrubs that had "TLC" and a silhouette of praying hands stamped on the breast pocket.

The unruly brunette ponytail of Laurie's high-school days was gone. Now her hair lay in a short, well-behaved pageboy. She was a bit heavier around the hips and her formerly flawless skin was camouflaged under carefully applied makeup. But her eyes were the same. Dark brown. Soft. Kind.

"Hi, Laurie. Remember me?"

"Annie?" Laurie cried, and broke into a huge grin and grabbed Ann in a hug before she had a chance to answer. "I can't believe you're really here. Ada Belle!" She hollered toward the back of the house. "Look who's here!"

Ada Belle appeared at the dining-room door, leaning on a cane, wearing a paper dinner napkin tucked into the neck of the pansy sweatshirt.

"Sorry I just popped over," Ann explained. "I couldn't remember your phone number."

"It's all right, child. That's what I wanted you to do. Come on in. Come on in." Ada Belle beckoned with her hand.

Ann stepped inside. Laurie had turned away and bent over a little table next to a gold velvet recliner. "Here," she said, and handed Ann a card. "Before we forget, that's Ada Belle's phone number and—" she turned it over "—that's mine."

The card was pink and read Tender Loving Care Home Health.

"Thank you." Ann slipped it into the pocket of her jeans. "Next time I'll call." She eyed the napkin at Ada Belle's throat. "Am I disturbing your dinner?"

"Not at all. Laurie just set out a coupla bowls of stew on the table."

"I can add one for you." Laurie smiled in invitation.

Despite the huge lunch at Pie in the Sky, Ann realized she was famished again. What was it about small towns that encouraged one to eat?

"Thank you, but only a small bowl."

After they settled down around the mahogany dining table and Ada Belle mumbled a quick grace, they ate. And talked. And talked.

In no time Ann felt as comfortable as she always had in this dining room. It looked very much as it had more than sixteen years ago, though there were even more photos of friends and family sprinkled about. Gently faded floral wallpaper. Worn Persian rug. Beveled-glass hutch, groaning with antique silver and crystal. Ada Belle's environment was as cozy and warm as Edith's was drab and cold.

"I had lunch with Steve today," Ann informed Laurie.

"He told me. We talk on the cell phone about ten times a day. Keeps him from getting lonely out in the field with only horses for company and keeps me from going insane while I run around on the back roads with only horses' asses for company."

"That Steve's a keeper," Ada Belle said. "He cooks dinner for their young'uns so Laurie can stop by of an evening and fix dinner for this old lady."

"Actually our kids are off at football and cheer-leader practice about half the time, anyway, and it takes an RN to check Ada Belle's evening meds, then test her blood sugar and inject her insulin. So I usually stay and eat with her while I'm here."

Ada Belle patted Laurie's hand. "This girl's my lifeline."

"And for me, coming to Ada Belle's is my treat at the end of a long hard day."

Ann smiled. "I can imagine."

"Now, tell me about your life," Laurie insisted. "We were all so proud when you landed that big job in Washington."

Ann felt guilty for not staying in touch with her old friend. Why on earth had she rejected the whole town right along with Edith?

"I love my job. We handle some very high-profile cases. Very challenging."

"Where do you live? An apartment?"

"Actually I managed to get into a very nice condo last year over in Rosslyn. I ride the subway to work."

"Riding a subway to work. I can't even imagine that, can you, Ada Belle?"

Ada Belle, nibbling a cracker, shook her head.

"What do you do on weekends?"

"I take in the culture—art museums, plays, opera…" Ann's voice trailed off. Suddenly it all sounded so sterile.

"Sounds exciting. And I imagine your work keeps you pretty busy," Laurie encouraged.

"Yes. And I also have a wonderful cat—"

"No man?" Ada Belle, always candid, blurted. "Pretty thing like you ought to have a man."

Laurie rolled her eyes. "Welcome back to Medicine Creek, Ann."

"Well, yes. In fact, I've been involved in a relationship for a while now, but his work is even more consuming than mine. His name is Kenneth Wilson. He's a senator."

"A senator?" Laurie had been efficiently stacking dishes while they talked, but now she stopped. "So is it serious?"

"Well, lately, the whole thing's evolved into talk of marriage."

"Evolved into talk of marriage?" Ada Belle scoffed. "I swear. The way you young people talk. Has this fella proposed or not?"

"He gave me this ring, but we haven't set a date. His schedule is grueling. He's…well, we haven't set a date."

"He gave you a ring!" Laurie gaped and grabbed Ann's hand to inspect the large diamond. "How exciting!"

"Yes. At the moment he's trying to decide whether

to run for senate again or hold out for a presidential appointment. He's highly respected in his home state."

"Which is?" Ada Belle again.

"Kansas."

"Kansas, huh?" Ada Belle peered at the ring, too, then nodded grudging approval. "I imagine this senator's crazy about you, honey."

Ann had recently developed secret doubts in that regard, but she wasn't about to share her worries during this happy reunion dinner. The fact was, this emergency trip to Medicine Creek had come at a time when the tensions between Kenneth and her were at an all-time high. She had always ascribed Kenneth's moodiness to stress and fatigue from the demands of his job.

But last month, when he'd proposed in a way that made marriage sound more like a wise career move than a sacred commitment, she had begun to question the relationship. How could you date someone for two years and not really know him? In the hectic social whirl of Washington, it was completely possible. Now, from the distance of a thousand miles, surrounded by the peace and quiet of her old hometown, Ann was seeing Kenneth in a different light.

She decided to change the subject. "And speaking of men, Laurie, I can't believe you ended up with Steve Harris!"

Laurie, a thirty-four-year-old mother of two, actually blushed. "Mike played matchmaker."

"He did?"

"Yeah. Before he went off to the army, he fixed Steve and me up on a double date with him and Marsha."

"And now your teenage sons are friends, imagine that."

"Trent is actually a year older than Zack, but I held Trent over for a year after kindergarten. He has always struggled in school. Those two are great friends. Marsha never did like Zack running around with an older kid, though."

"Marsha," Ada Belle muttered, and swiped her lips with her napkin as if to wipe away a foul taste.

Laurie turned compassionate brown eyes on Ann. "Do you know about Mike and Marsha's situation?"

"Only a little."

"It's sad."

"It's disgusting," Ada Belle interjected.

"Now, Ada Belle," Laurie's voice was steady and kind.

"Don't 'Now, Ada Belle' me," Ada Belle snapped. "I cain't figure out why this whole town ain't ready to string that woman up by the thumbs. She had the finest man God ever gave a woman, not to mention those five cute kids, and she just run off!" She flicked her bony fingers sideways in disgust. "Just run the heck off!"

"Maybe we shouldn't be repeating stories about Mike's personal business in front of Ann like this," Laurie said.

"You listen here, sister." Ada Belle aimed a

gnarled finger at Laurie. "I never repeat anything. At least not to the same person."

Ann and Laurie smiled at each other.

"Besides," Ada Belle continued, "this girl's bound to find out about that family if she sticks around this town more'n a week. She already heard about the trouble out on the Lazy J."

Ada Belle leaned her frail torso confidentially in Ann's direction. "No disrespect to the reverend, honey, but ever since that witch Marsha run off, that Kirkpatrick household has been jumpin' like a box o' bugs. It's a regular asylum over there. Yes, it is. And it's startin' to tarnish the reverend's reputation."

"Mike's kids are bright, adorable—"

"And growin' up wild as weeds!" Ada Belle declared. "They run around this town like a pack of stray pups."

Laurie sighed. "Poor Mike. I think he's overwhelmed. His congregation has become divided over this. Some are even calling for a replacement minister until Mike can get his personal life in order."

"And there's some that think getting his personal life in order means getting hitched up with that Gloria creature," Ada Belle huffed.

For some reason Ann's heart sped up, as if an unseen threat had crept into the room. "Gloria? You mean the woman who owns the flower shop?"

Laurie nodded. "She's very popular over at the church. There are certain members of the congregation who've made no secret of the fact that they think Mike and Gloria would make a good match."

"But I ain't one of 'em," Ada Belle said. "Just 'cause old Gloria can whip up a mean meat loaf, and just 'cause she's president of the Ladies' Guild, and just 'cause she makes it her daily business to suck up to the Kirkpatrick kids' teachers don't mean she's the right woman for our reverend. She's a busybody, is what I say. Runs in the Miller blood. Her aunt Ida's cut from the same cloth. Don't tell Ida you broke a fingernail unless you want to read about it on the front page of that town tattler of hers."

"Miss Ida Miller writes the local weekly shopper," Laurie clarified. "She calls it *Medicine Creek Style*."

Ann smiled at that.

"Gloria's a real piece of work, if you ask me. Matter of fact, that woman phoned me today. Wanted to know what you look like." She touched a bony finger to Ann's arm.

"Me? Why would Gloria want to know about me?"

"'Cause Mike has had dealings with you. She's a jealous thing. But she can get as jealous as she wants, that don't mean they're getting married. No, sirree."

"But Mike told me he's not even divorced yet." It was an effort to put the brakes on this outlandish discussion.

"No, but he has every right to be," Ada Belle pronounced.

Laurie gave Ada Belle a censoring look.

"Well, by Gingo, he does!"

A moment of strained silence passed before Laurie explained, "What Ada Belle means is, Marsha's al-

ready living with another man.'' Then she added
sadly, ''And it seems pretty clear she'd met him before she left town.''

''Livin' in sin,'' Ada Belle put in contemptuously.
''Plain old adultery, don't you see.''

But Ann, an experienced divorce attorney, knew
there was seldom anything ''plain'' about adultery.
Again she wondered how Mike Kirkpatrick's marriage could have unraveled like this, and again she
told herself it was none of her business. ''I wanted to
ask you both about something else,'' she said.

''What's that, honey?'' Ada Belle took a shaky sip
of iced tea.

''I was in Hobbs Hardware today and…well…''
She didn't really know how to say this without seeming paranoid. ''There were some men in there talking
loudly, and I got the distinct feeling they were talking
so that I would hear what they had to say.''

''Unkempt old guys?'' Laurie inquired. ''In grimy
overalls and billed caps?''

''You know them?''

''No. But this town's crawling with them.''

''Same old butts on the same old Coke machines.''
Ada Belle laughed.

''Pardon?'' Ann didn't understand the joke.

''The same old men sit around on top of that old
freezer-style Coke cooler over at the Texaco,'' Laurie
explained.

''And the teenage boys are just as bad,'' Ada Belle
said. ''Hangin' out in front of the drugstore like a
bunch of stray mongrels.''

"I see. Anyway—" Ann steered back to subject "—these guys were talking about the pecan grove and how Mike is planning to sell it to a company that intends to build an outlet mall on that land. Have either of you heard about that?"

Laurie and Ada Belle exchanged glances.

"Yeah, well, Steve told me about Jerrod Cagle's scene at the Pie," Laurie said.

"Jerrod Cagle—that boy's always got a kink in his slinky." Only someone of Ada Belle's advanced years could call a man of sixty a boy.

"Ada Belle, you said something this morning, something about what I didn't know could choke a horse. I believe that was the way you put it. I've been wondering about that."

Ada Belle looked down and smoothed the napkin on her chest. "I oughtta keep this old trap shut."

"Please," Ann urged. "Is there something about the pecan grove that I should know?"

Ada Belle bit her lip like a child that wouldn't tell, then looked at Laurie for reassurance.

Laurie nodded.

"You promise this won't affect your dealings with Mike?"

"I can't honestly promise anything."

Ada Belle sighed. "I suppose somebody's got to tell the child," she murmured to her lap.

Ann leaned forward, all ears.

"To think the old council grounds could end up being a tacky shopping mall," Ada Belle mused.

"The council grounds?" Ann asked.

"I better start at the beginning. This whole thing started so long ago I expect none of it matters much anymore, but still… I remember how Lydia suffered, how she worried, after June died."

"Lydia? You mean my mother's mother?"

"Yes, indeed. Lydia Bennett Starr. Born in 1915, the same year I was. Me and Lydia shared a little shotgun-style house in Dougherty after our parents sent us to town to attend the high school. That's how it was in those days. Couldn't travel those steep rocky Arbuckle roads every single day, so we stayed in town as boarders."

Ann felt like she was hearing this for the first time, although surely someone must have told her these things when she was a child. She had been in Lydia Starr's little frame house a time or two. Nolan and Edith had taken the little girl by after church as a matter of duty. Ann remembered sitting on Lydia's itchy couch, her feet pinched in shiny patent-leather Mary Janes and her hair clipped back in painfully tight curls. The old woman always stared at Ann with forlorn black eyes, hardly speaking, never even touching her. Ann now realized, after seeing June's picture, that she must have reminded her grandmother of June. So much so that her very existence probably brought the old woman pain.

Once, the adults had come to words in front of Ann. Angry words about the old house on Pecan Street. "You deeded it to June," Edith had argued, "so now the place belongs to Nolan…and this child."

Ann remembered Lydia Starr's black eyes snapping

to life, flashing from Nolan to Edith and back. "But not the pecan grove, I didn't! Neither of you are Indian! And you can't touch that land!"

"Tell me about my grandmother," Ann encouraged Ada Belle.

Ada Belle's piercing blue eyes studied Ann's face. "That would surely be my pleasure. I have wanted to tell you what I know ever since you was a little girl. But Edith stood in the way. She came over here once, early on, right after Nolan married her. She said that she and Nolan had come to an understanding, and they did not want me to upset you with stories about the past."

"The past?"

"Meaning your mother, I expect."

"But why?"

"That is sure a mystery, ain't it? I always figured if I told you, and Edith found out, it would only make your life under Edith's thumb harder. But Edith and Nolan are gone now, and I think you have the right to know some things. But I need to move to my recliner first. My legs are achin'."

Laurie helped Ada Belle hobble to the living room, and Ann finished clearing the table. After they tucked Ada Belle's favorite afghan around her bony legs, Laurie lit the gas-log fireplace, then got comfortable on the couch while Ann took the nearby rocker.

Ada Belle started in on the story again, her reedy voice spinning out into the room like an unbroken thread.

"Lydia gave birth to June—your mother—out on

the Lazy J ranch while the War was still on, early in 1945, I reckon. I believe June was the last Starr child born out on that ranch. Albert Starr, Lydia's father-in-law, had barely been able to hold on to the ranch during the depression. But the Starr family felt like that ground was practically sacred. It had been in their family ever since the Chickasaws were moved to Oklahoma.''

''You're talking about Cagle's Lazy J?'' Ann was incredulous. ''My family owned the Lazy J?''

''Lordy. I forget that you don't know a thing about the Chickasaws or even your own family. Yes, hon. Your clan owned all one thousand acres of the Lazy J from way back in the Indian Territory days. Called the place the Starr of the Arbuckles—spelled star with two r's like the family's name. They owned a lot of land in this here town, too. But that pecan grove is the last of it now. Bet you didn't know that place was an old Chickasaw meeting ground. The capital of the Chickasaw nation was Tishomingo, of course, but they met in that pecan grove quite often. There were lots of secret meetings in the old days. The word Chickasaw means rebellion, you know.'' Ada Belle gave Ann a sharp look. ''Bet you didn't know your very own great-grandfather planted those trees.''

Ann didn't. ''Tell me more.''

A great wave of emptiness passed over Ann as Ada Belle talked on about the artistic, prosperous, kindly, upright Starr family, the people Ann had never known. Ada Belle kept mentioning that she, Ann, was the last of them. Ann felt as if a very real part of her was missing, like pages torn from a book. But gradually the emptiness filled with the sound of Ada Belle's voice as she reminded Ann that the house down the street had been a Starr house long before Edith had infected it.

"You think about those trees, honey. Those are your family trees." Ada Belle chuckled at her pun. But to Ann it was not a joke. Right then, she began to think about the pecan trees in a new way. Her mother was dead, but the trees—trees that June's grandfather, Ann's great-grandfather, had planted with his own hands—didn't deserve to die right along with June.

"Ada Belle, you said Lydia worried after June died. Why?"

"Why? Well, I don't hardly know how to say it, child." Ada Belle's creaky voice grew hushed. "Lydia worried that your mother had been, you know…murdered."

Ann sank back in the rocker as if she'd been struck. *"Murdered?"* Ann had been expecting to hear that Lydia had worried about what would become of the ranch or about Ann's welfare, for heaven's sake. But murder? "But my mother fell," she protested. "Off a horse…out in the mountains…near the ranch."

"I know that's what they told you. And that's what old Doc Fields called it—an accident. A fall. And all of us believed it. The Starr ranch was abandoned in those days, Lydia and June being the only Starrs left and livin' in that house you've got now—the Starr house. I don't know what Lydia thought she was gonna do with that land. Anyway, June was the only one who ever went out there in those days. She'd go there to ride. Kept her horse on another place nearby. Well, come to think of it, she kept that horse on Jerrod Cagle's daddy's place. That's how them two met. June would go out to ride that horse. I expect Jerrod saddled it up for her a time or two, and then he got to romancin' her.''

Ada Belle took a sip of water. Ann and Laurie waited, spellbound.

"Anyway, June was a pretty good horsewoman, but she took lots of risks. Rode that horse like a wild woman, even rode it into town sometimes, prancing right down Main Street. No one doubted it when they said she took a tumble on the rocks. But many a time when I visited Lydia after June's death, she brought that accident up. It worried her mind, it did. You see, she never got to see June's body. They said it looked too bad.''

Upset, Ada Belle pressed her hankie to her lips.

"After they found June's horse wanderin' around, all banged up like he was, well, several days passed before they found June's body. So many ravines and rocky cliffs out in those old Arbuckles.'' Ada Belle finally stopped to catch her breath.

Ann could hardly believe this story. No one had even so much as hinted that her mother's death was anything other than an accident.

"Ada Belle, are you sure you're remembering correctly?'' Laurie asked gently.

"'Course I'm sure. A person don't forget about serious business like this."

"Who did Lydia suspect?" Ann asked. It was the obvious question.

Ada Belle stated the answer as if that were obvious, too. "Why, Jerrod Cagle, of course."

CHAPTER NINE

"CAGLE?"

"Yes, hon," Ada Belle confirmed quietly.

The cozy living room became as quiet as a church while Ann stared into the soundless uniform flames of the gas fire.

Ada Belle leaned back against the headrest of the recliner. "I could use a sip of water."

Laurie jumped up to get it.

"We are tiring you out, Ada Belle. Maybe I should go. You can tell me about this another time."

"Hon, at my age, you never know if there's going to *be* another time."

"Now, Ada Belle," Laurie handed her a small glass to drink from.

"Now, Ada Belle. Now, Ada Belle," the old lady mimicked before she took a sip of water. "Tarnation! I get so sick of having my hand patted and folks saying 'Now, Ada Belle.' If a body is ninety-three years old, the big clock in the sky is ticking pretty fast, and there ain't no reason to pretend otherwise."

"But there's no point in dwelling on it, either." Laurie's voice was firm.

"Easy for you to say," Ada Belle countered. "You ain't the one facing her Maker."

Ann interceded in their spat. "Tell me more about this Cagle theory," she suggested.

"It weren't no theory." Ada Belle's attention returned to Ann. "It's just what Lydia claimed. And no one listened to her but me. You have to understand, Lydia had been a recluse for many years, poor thing was so depressed and all. And..." Ada Belle hesitated, then tightened her lips.

"What is it, Ada Belle?" Laurie prompted.

"It's not very nice, and I doubt Ann will like to hear it."

"I want to hear everything," Ann said calmly. "Hearing about this doesn't hurt me, Ada Belle. Except for my mother, I hardly remember these people. This is all ancient history to me."

Ada Belle nodded. "Well, Lydia was drinking pretty heavily by then." After an apologetic shrug at Ann, the old woman continued. "So nobody in town listened to her, and she just died that way, shut up in that house, brooding about June to the end. But I always wondered if Edith had some kind of suspicions about the whole thing, too. The way she made such a point of hushing me up...."

"Did Cagle have an alibi?" Laurie was obviously as caught up in the story as Ann was.

"As I recall, his daddy said he'd been working on their place from dawn to dusk on the day June's riderless horse wandered up. Said he could account for every minute of the boy's day. *Boy.* Jerrod weren't no boy. He was in his twenties when June died, but he still lived out there with his daddy. Jerrod was a loner, even in those days."

"Why did Lydia suspect him?" Ann asked, leaning forward.

Ada Belle laced her fingers over her middle. "Jerrod had been sweet on June back when they were younger. Like I said, he probably met her one of those times when she went out for a horseback ride. But Lydia always thought he actually had his eye on the Starr of the Arbuckles. And sure enough, he bought it from Nolan the minute June's estate was settled."

"How did my father and mother end up together, by the way?" Ann had never seen so much as a wedding picture of her parents.

"Oh, I don't rightly know about that one. June, she could've had her pick of all the young men from here to Sulphur. But she took up with Nolan. Seemed like it was right after Jerrod Cagle made that scene in town that night."

Laurie frowned and started to say something, but Ann raised a palm, signaling to let Ada go on while she could remember.

"They kept company for only a short while before the wedding was done, and then, next thing you know, they was movin' into the big house down the street. June wanted Lydia to live with her there, but Lydia wouldn't hear of it. Nolan was quiet, kept to himself, a putterer. But I do remember how handsome he was. Maybe June felt safe with him." Ada Belle tapped a finger to her lips, thinking.

"Ada Belle—" Laurie glanced at Ann "—you said Jerrod made a scene in town?"

"Oh, yes! That's the part I left out. I reckon Jerrod and June was gettin' a little more friendly during her horseback rides than Lydia knew. One night Jerrod brought his daddy's car, a 1951 Ford, pale green—now why would an old woman like me remember something like that? Anyway, he rammed that car right up in front of the T.G. and Y. store on Main Street where June had herself a little job. Went in there hollerin', demandin' to see her. Made a real big scene. The manager threatened to call the sheriff. Lydia was very upset about it."

"June married someone else, and that's why Lydia thought Jerrod Cagle killed her?" Laurie sounded skeptical.

"And I was five years old by the time my mother died," Ann said sensibly.

"Well, it don't exactly make sense. But I do remember that the thing that haunted Lydia—haunted me, too, if you want to know the truth—was them marks."

"Marks?"

"Like cuts almost. On June's neck." Ada Belle touched shaky fingers to the crepey skin at her own throat. "Doc Fields never did explain them deep marks. Lydia said it was from her necklace gettin' tore off when she fell. She had a bunch of men out searching for that thing for days and days after they found June's body. Searched all the rocks and ravines, even looked up in the trees. But they never did find it." Ada Belle's voice was growing raspy, and Ann wondered if it wasn't time to let her rest, but Laurie popped out with one more question.

"What necklace?"

Ann sat as still as a stunned bird. She already knew.

"A blue star sapphire as big as the end of my thumb." Ada Belle held her thumb up to demonstrate. "The Starr of the Arbuckles."

WALKING HOME IN THE MOONLIGHT, Ann found herself drawn across the street to the pecan grove. It was a magical place, rimmed by giant cedar brakes in the north, rolling meadows in the east, and the ancient Arbuckle Mountains, ascending like guardians, to the south and west.

The moon, as full as a pumpkin, must have shone like this, she imagined, during those long-ago Chickasaw gatherings in this grove. Some clouds scuttled past, and the wind picked up, making the treetops whisper like voices from the past.

Sadness overcame her as she laid a hand against the rough bark of a giant tree, and Ada Belle's words echoed in her mind: "Your very own great-grandfather planted those trees." A great-grandfather Ann knew nothing about. And what about her mother? What if someone really had murdered June? Ann could hardly bear the thought. She pressed her forehead against the tree, and the tactile sensation of the bark triggered a memory...

"Hi." His voice seemed to come from nowhere. The mist among the trees was so still, the air so quiet

on that long-ago November night that she could hear
the leather of his jacket squeaking before her eyes
adjusted and she saw his silhouette, standing like a
dark statue between two of the trees. Her heart started
to pound, but she didn't move.

His hands were firmly jammed into the pockets of
his jeans, a gesture of nervousness...or harmlessness?
He was a guy, after all. And he was large. And it was
dark out here. Edith would screech her head off for
sure if she found out Ann had been alone in the grove
with a guy like this. She should turn and run—right
now. But she didn't. Instead, she waited as he walked
toward her, keeping her hand on the tree trunk, with
the rough bark cutting into her skin.

"I hope I didn't scare you." He took a step forward
and she edged closer to the tree, as if it might protect
her from wild-boy Mickey Kirkpatrick.

"I...I've seen you walk over here at night before.
And ever since, well, you know—" he glanced over
his shoulder at her dark house "—I've...I've been
wanting to talk to you. Alone. Actually, I called you
a couple of times. Did your mom tell you?"

Ann shook her head.

"Well, that sure sucks." He turned his head toward
her spooky old house again, and the moon outlined
his handsome features, setting her pulse into higher
gear. "Do they know you're out here?"

She finally got a word past her lips: "No."

"Good. I mean, I don't want anybody to bother us
or... I don't want to get you in trouble or anything."

"What do you want?" It came out in a whisper

that embarrassed Ann. Why couldn't she ever act cool? Say something funny? Or at least something halfway normal.

"I...I can't stop thinking about you," he said. The admission was as hushed as the mist swirling at their feet and hung there just as eerily.

Ann's heart raced. He was crazy, but he wasn't that crazy. Something about the way he dropped his head told her he was speaking the truth.

He sighed and stepped closer. "So there it is. I can't stop thinking about you." He released another huge sigh, and she felt the warmth of his breath; that was how close he was now. He placed his palm on the tree trunk right above her head. The raised arm emphasized his size, opened his jacket and let his intoxicating scent drift over her. "And I keep wondering...how did you feel about what happened? You know, that kiss? I can't stop thinking about *that,* either. Am I crazy?"

"You have a girlfriend." Again it came out in that stupid choked whisper, and now she was also looking down at the ground, for heaven's sake. *Look him in the eye!* she commanded herself. And she did. Big mistake.

His blue eyes shone with glimmers of tortured sincerity, catching the distant moonlight. "I know I do. That's why I feel so bad. Marsha's been my steady since school started. So how come I keep thinking about you all the time?"

"How should..." Annie gulped and her rapid breathing formed crystalline puffs in the cold moonlit air. "How should I know?" She fixed her eyes on his throat. Another big mistake. Even in the dark, she could see his pulse pounding wildly above the neck-band of his white T-shirt.

"What I've gotta know is, are you thinking about me the same way?" Her heart thudded three times before he added unsurely, "Or not?" When she still didn't answer, he said, "Look, I don't do stuff like that all the time. I'm not a player. Okay?"

She nodded, and despite her resolve stared down at the ground again.

"It's just that ever since I kissed you, I've been wondering if Marsha's...or maybe it was just that kiss. It would help if you'd just tell me how you feel."

How did she *feel?* When the moonlight was filtering through the towering trees and lit the side of his handsome face like some beautiful ancient painting? When his soft mouth breathed only inches from hers? When his sad eyes seemed to be holding his soul out for her to take if that was what she wanted?

When it looked like he might actually kiss her again?

"I mean, did you like it at all? Do you want to do it again? Or am I crazy? Please—" his voice was croaky and he leaned even closer "—tell me."

Ann's eyelids fluttered up, and just as she saw the moon duck behind a veil of cloud, he pressed his mouth to hers. Her lips had formed a small "O" of surprise at the moment of contact, and he groaned softly against that open oval. She answered with her own involuntary deep-throated sound that seemed to unleash something fierce in him.

And then they were kissing again, just as they had in his old Honda Civic, only this time they were standing, so that when he snaked his arms under her open coat and pulled her hard against the full length of his muscular body, there was no question about what *this* kiss meant. In fact, in Ann's mind the press of their bodies answered all his questions—and hers. Except one. Was it always like this?

He released her abruptly and drove his hands through his wild hair. "God!" he cried. "This is making me crazy! I've never kissed anybody like that! Where the hell did you learn to kiss like that!" He whirled from her and slammed his palms against the tree trunk, then pressed his forehead against his fists.

This guy was a little scary, Ann thought, except she herself felt the urge to do something like that. Instead, she stood there, clutching her middle, shivering and biting her lip like a scared rabbit.

But Mike Kirkpatrick turned on her again, and he grabbed her again, and again, she allowed him to assail her mouth.

This time they slid down the length of the tree trunk onto the leaves at its base, still locked in a hot kiss. When they broke apart long enough to look into each other's eyes, he whispered, "God," then stretched out his long legs and angled her into his lap. He pulled her knees up and curved around her with her bottom tight against him, then he tenderly arranged her skirt over her knees, ending up with her head on his shoulder tucked under his chin.

"You've never kissed like this before, have you," he stated.

No, she hadn't. And she had never been held like this. Ever. She closed her eyes against the seduction of it, but she could not resist. It felt too safe, too right, being held this way. Breathing in time with him. Feeling the solidity and curve of his chest and the way his arms seemed to reach everywhere around her at once.

"All I want to do is hold you," he said. "Is that okay?"

But he ended up doing more than holding her, and it became a lost night, a long night. A night when his warm, insistent mouth, his soft talk and wild kisses, put a spell on her, a mark on her. A night fraught with anxiety as Ann wondered if her parents—or anyone else, for that matter—would discover them as they tasted each other over and over. A night when he put his strong hands on her. Everywhere. His sure firm touch communicating that he ached to do much more than he allowed himself.

"I'm grounded, but I sneaked out of my bedroom window and walked over here," he told her at one point. "I know you come here on Thursdays while your folks are at bingo, right?"

Ann nodded. "I get restless. I can't stay in that house alone on Thursday nights."

He pressed his lips to her forehead as if he understood. "Can we meet here again?"

"No."

He answered her refusal with a kiss so fierce it might have bruised her lips.

"Are we falling in love or something?" he said at the end of it all when she broke away from him for the final time. They were facing each other, out in the open, in the unclouded moonlight. Anyone might see them. Ann looked around furtively. He didn't seem to care.

She wanted to say, "I might be," but she wasn't about to admit that when ten-to-one he'd be back in Marsha's arms the very next night. Marsha's parents, Laurie had told her, were hosting a big party for the football players and the cheerleaders after the final game of the season.

"You need to decide what to do about your girl-friend." She took a backward step.

He hung his head. "I deserve that. I'm sorry, Annie," he said as she continued to back up. "I should never have touched you this way. But sometimes I see you at school and I just get crazy. I won't bother you again until I've made a clean break with Marsha."

But the clean break never happened. Marsha got suspicious and tightened her hold on her boyfriend. Ann could guess what weapons the perky blonde had used when she heard a rumor later in the school year that Marsha Dodson was pregnant and that come graduation, Mike Kirkpatrick was joining the army— right after their wedding.

Ann's stepmother got suspicious, too.

She accused Ann of having "wild blood" when she caught her coming back from the pecan grove the following Thursday. Ann had stayed waiting too late, long after her parents' headlights had swung into the driveway, hoping against hope that Mike would show up. But Edith appeared out of the mist, instead, clutching her faded wrapper over her flat bosom.

"What in the world are you doing out here?" she snapped.

Shortly after that, Edith put Ann to work in a friend's home-based beauty parlor, unrolling odorous perms. "You need to keep yourself busy earning money for college, instead of slinking around in that pecan grove at night looking for trouble," she'd said.

Ann sighed, touching the tree bark in memory and with fresh understanding. Wild blood? Edith, she suspected now, had been jealous of June, and by extension, Ann, all her life. But why? She supposed Edith had even disliked these trees.

It didn't matter. What mattered was that she and Mike had stayed locked in their separate prisons. Those kisses, it turned out, had been potent enough to haunt them, but not potent enough to free them.

And now? Ann had no idea how Mike felt about her now. One thing was for sure, he had bigger worries than a pregnant girlfriend. And Edith was dead.

And the house was Ann's, with all its history, with all its secrets.

Secrets about her mother's death. Even if Jerrod Cagle were responsible for her mother's death, how could Ann prove such a thing twenty-eight years later? How could she prove anything?

She was shamed to realize that she, a competent attorney, had never insisted on seeing a single document pertaining to her own mother's death. When Nolan had died so many years ago, Edith had insisted on complete control of everything and had rejected Ann's help.

Ann had told herself then that she'd washed her hands of the past and Medicine Creek. But here she was, back in Medicine Creek, and as embroiled in the past as ever.

She wished for the millionth time that she'd enjoyed a normal childhood. Siblings. Sports. Fun. But as her therapist friend had reminded her many times, you can't have a better past, no matter how much you might wish for it.

She rubbed her palm on the tree lightly. What would become of these beautiful giants when the land passed to its new owners?

The voices of the old men in the hardware store talking about "that outlet-mall deal" echoed in her mind. Didn't she have the right to know what would become of her family's land? Didn't she have a *duty* to find out? Ada Belle had made her little joke about "family trees," but for Ann, these trees were beginning to feel like the only family she had. She had a few more questions for Ada Belle.

And she would also have a few pertinent questions for Mr. Mike Kirkpatrick, the Realtor, when he arrived the next morning.

CHAPTER TEN

THE CREAKY DOORKNOCKER banged twice at ten o'clock on the dot. Mike—this time casually clad in jeans, a white golf shirt and a black leather jacket that Ann would never have expected a preacher to wear— seemed massive as he stepped into Edith's dark little foyer. It was as if his raw maleness overcame the dead energy in the house. Even the scent of his fresh aftershave created a sharp counterpoint to the musty interior.

His handsome smile didn't hurt, either. "Morning, Annie—uh, I mean, hi, Ann." He instantly blushed.

Before Ann could tease Mike about his slip, a tiny child in overalls and a faded striped T-shirt peeked around his leg. Her two corkscrew pigtails were of the same variegated strawberry shade that Mike had sported as a youngster. She clutched a Little Golden Book to her chest while she regarded Ann with Mike Kirkpatrick's blue eyes, set in Marsha Dodson's pixie face.

"Hi." Ann smiled at her, then looked up to see Mike's apologetic smile. "And who is this young lady?"

"This is my favorite sidekick, Mary Beth—"

"Mary 'Lizzabeth, Daddy," the little girl corrected, then gave Ann a shy glance.

"My daughter," Mike explained.

"Well, hello, Mary...Elizabeth," Ann said, feeling unsure of herself. This was a surprise—somehow she'd never expected to actually meet any of Mike's children, let alone today. "Are you out helping your daddy?"

The little girl nodded solemnly as she studied first Ann, then the dark interior of the house.

Mike dropped to one knee and bracketed Mary Beth's tiny torso with his big hands. "Like I told you, this will only take a little while, sweetheart. You've got your book with you. So you just sit over there—" he pointed to the couch "—and practice your reading, okay?"

The child nodded as she continued to take in the gloomy living room with intelligent blue eyes that didn't look at all sure about this place.

"Mary Beth," Ann said quietly, "I found some crayons and paper in the dining room yesterday. Do you like to color?"

"And draw," Mary Beth offered shyly.

Ann pulled back the heavy living-room drapes, took crayons and paper from the dusty old breakfront in the dining room and placed a sofa pillow on the floor next to the coffee table. "Want to sit here?" She patted the cushion and Mary Beth settled herself obediently.

Ann squatted down nearby and took a black crayon and started to draw.

"It's a bird!" Mary Beth exclaimed, and looked up at her father in delighted surprise.

"Miss Fischer is a very talented artist," Mike explained.

Ann blinked and smiled up at him.

"Well, you used to be anyway, in high school."

"Yes, I suppose I was. It's like riding a bicycle, I guess." Ann took another sheet of paper. "Once you get the hang of it, Mary Beth, you never forget how." This time she sketched a swift graceful rendering of a horse.

Mary Beth looked directly at Ann. "I love horses," the child said sincerely.

"Then I'll draw several for you."

Mary Beth's eyes shone and Ann finally got the smile she'd been angling for.

After she'd made a few more simple sketches for the child to color, Ann stood. "Okay." She smiled at Mike. "That should keep her happy. Where do you want to start?"

"Let's go ahead and get the initial papers signed."

They left Mary Beth busily coloring and went to the dining room.

"I'm sorry," Mike said when they were out of earshot. "I forgot to mention that I would be bringing my daughter. Mary Beth has been sort of...needy lately. On Saturdays I try to take her with me."

"I understand. She's a precious child." Again Ann wondered how he managed. It must be an untenable situation. Abandonment gave children such deep insecurities. Ann knew all about that.

The photograph of June Starr sat propped on the table where Ann had left it the night before. "Wow," Mike breathed. "I don't have to ask you who this is."

Ann looked down at her mother's beautiful face. "She was lovely, wasn't she?" She ran her fingers over the scrolled frame. "I found an old box of my mother's things in the attic. I was looking for Edith's safe-deposit-box key."

"She was very pretty. The resemblance is amazing. Do you remember her at all?"

"Unfortunately no. In fact, I've never even seen this picture before."

"You're kidding. No one ever showed you this?"

"It turns out they didn't show me a lot of things. Edith, I suspect, didn't much care for my mother. I'm beginning to wonder what else she disposed of. I have a feeling she simply overlooked this box. My dad had sealed it up tight and put it away in the back of the attic."

Mike regarded the picture and thought of his own children. If he got involved with Gloria, would she wipe out all memories of Marsha? Sometimes she acted like that was exactly what she wanted to do. As angry as he was at Marsha, he didn't want that to happen. She had been a good mother for many years. And the children love her. A prayer flitted through his mind: *Lord, help me find my way through this mess.*

He looked at Ann's profile as she studied the picture, glimpsing the sad lonely child she must have been.

"We'd better get busy." She laid the picture aside, and they seated themselves at the table. "I'm sorry, but before I sign anything, I need the full story on this property." The sad little girl had vanished, and the tough businesswoman had taken over.

"A large development firm is considering some Lazy J land between town and the interstate as a possible location for an outlet mall." Mike was glad for the opportunity to explain Jerrod Cagle's tirade in the café. "The Powers Corporation contacted me months ago, wanting to find a site. Cagle has the idea that I'm steering them toward your pecan grove."

"You're not showing them Cagle's land?" Laurie had told Ann that Mike was the only active Realtor in Medicine Creek since Marsha had left.

"No. He wants an exorbitant price for that rocky strip of land and, besides, I don't do business with Jerrod Cagle. We've crossed swords a time or two."

"Really? About Zack?"

"About the future of this community."

She raised a quizzical eyebrow.

"Jerrod Cagle is all about greed. Always has been. Way back when, he tried to sell some of his land for development as a granite quarry that would have been visible from town. Later, he wanted to sell that same strip for a bingo hall. We stopped him both times, but it wasn't easy. Ever since then, he's tried to paint me with a broad brush: the meddling goody-goody preacher, stuff like that. That's not where I'm coming from at all. I just happen to love Medicine Creek and I want to see it grow the right way. I actually have a vision for the town's future.''

"Tell me about it.''

"I want some growth, reasons for our young people to stay, of course. But at the same time, I want the town to retain its historic charm, to evolve at a comfortable pace.''

"You don't want it to change too much,'' Ann supplied. "I agree.''

"Right.'' He gave her a small frown. "But I didn't think you saw it that way.''

"It's funny, I really enjoyed my walk downtown yesterday. It gave me a feeling of…peace. A few years of battling big-city life changes your perspective, I guess.''

Mike smiled. "Makes you appreciate a place where you can still see white-flowering plum along the creek beds,'' he enthused. "Where you can stand on a ridge and see fork lightning five miles away, where you can look up and see red-tailed hawks circling…''

"Where the corn is as high as an elephant's eye.'' Ann grinned.

Mike blushed and cleared his throat. "Okay, call me a dreamer. But if you've ever seen a herd of white Charolais cattle dotting a bright green field of winter wheat like—''

"Statues?'' Ann's smile grew wider.

Mike had to laugh at himself. "Like *marble* statues, to be exact.'' He smiled into her eyes. "You know what I mean.''

"I do." Ann nodded. This town was fortunate to have a man like Mike Kirkpatrick to care so passionately about it. Anyone, she thought, would be lucky to have Mike Kirkpatrick in their corner. Again she wondered what had gone wrong between him and Marsha.

"The buyer I have in mind for your land will respect that vision and this community."

"Your prospective buyer, will they want to remove my trees?"

Her trees? When had the pecan giants become *her* trees? she wondered.

"I thought you didn't care if that land became a toxic dump."

"Something has changed my mind."

To his puzzled look, she responded, "My great-grandfather planted those trees."

"Oh, that."

"Ada Belle told me."

"I see."

"And you didn't want her to."

He looked at her sharply. Okay. He hadn't wanted Ada Belle to tell her that. But when he met Ann Fischer that first day, she had acted as if the Starr property was something she wanted to dump. "I thought you just wanted to get out of this town."

"I do, but I don't want to be the person who breaks the link in generations of Chickasaw tradition."

"What else did Ada Belle tell you?"

Ann cast a cautionary glance in Mary Beth's direction.

"Mary Beth." Mike walked into the living room and squatted on his haunches next to the coffee table where the little girl was coloring furiously. "Sweetheart, would you mind waiting in Daddy's truck while I talk to Miss Fischer?" He flipped one of the tiny pigtails affectionately with his finger.

"Da-dee!" Mary Beth did not look up from her busy work. "I'm not done coloring."

Ann walked to the double doors and caught his eye. "Mike, maybe you'd like some—" she tilted her head toward the kitchen "—coffee?"

When the kitchen door swung closed behind them, Ann said, "Ada Belle told me that my mother's death might not have happened exactly in the way I've been told."

Mike seemed confused. "You mean Edith?"

"No. I mean my real mother, June. Ada Belle isn't convinced that June's death was an accident. When I was a child, they always told me she took a bad fall off her horse out in the Arbuckles. But Ada Belle said June's mother always thought there was something strange about that story. Ada Belle claims June might have even been murdered."

Mike looked dumbstruck. "Murdered?"

"Ada Belle said—this is so weird, Mike—that June's mother, my grandmother Lydia, always wondered if Jerrod Cagle killed her."

"Cagle?" Mike folded his arms over his chest, frowning. "Jerrod's no saint, but *murder?* Sounds a little farfetched. I mean, why didn't your grandmother go the authorities? Why didn't your father, for that matter?''

"How should I know? I was only five. I'm going to try to talk to Ada Belle some more about it. She got very tired telling me as much as she did.''

Mike nodded. "You have to be careful not to tax her.''

"I'll be careful.'' Ann became pensive. "Anyway, as you can see, the pecan trees are not the biggest of my worries. But I'd like to preserve them...for a lot of reasons.''

They stood assessing each other for a moment. The mention of the pecan grove stirred a mutual memory that seemed to swirl in the silence around them. The memory of a moonlit night, in the mist, under a canopy of giant trees.

"Listen.'' Ann broke the spell. "I think I want to separate the house from this whole pecan-grove deal. I've got to go through all this junk, anyway, and I've decided I might as well fix up the house, sell it separately and make a profit. In the meantime—'' Ann drew a fortifying breath ''—I've decided I want a little more time to think about what I want to do with that grove.''

A little more time? Mike felt his chest tighten and his breathing speed up. With a little more time, the board might actually find that replacement for him. Then any plans for building his dream church on the beautiful grounds of the pecan grove would die.

In other words, with a little more time, his whole world could fall apart.

WHEN KENNETH HAD NOT called her back by lunch-time, Ann made up her mind. If she wanted to find out more about the Starr family from Ada Belle and if she wanted to get some answers about her mother's death, she would need to extend her stay. She also needed time to decide what to do about the house and the pecan grove. Perhaps, most of all, she needed time to decide what to do about her relationship with Kenneth.

She called the senior partner at her law firm and obtained an indefinite leave of absence. It wasn't difficult, since she hardly ever took vacations and hadn't had a single sick day in her entire tenure. Her comp time alone amounted to three weeks. "I appreciate this, Sal. I'm not sure how long I'll need to stay in Medicine Creek. I've run into a couple of...surprises out here."

Yeah. Surprises. And the biggest one was Mike Kirkpatrick.

For lunch she took sandwiches over to Ada Belle's—an aide was there checking Ada's vital signs. They talked about June again, but Ann kept the meal short and cordial. Then she went back to Edith's house for another round of sorting and packing.

When the doorknocker sounded late in the afternoon, Ann's first thought, with a flutter of her pulse, was that it was Mike, back to finish measuring the house for the appraisal.

But she opened the door to face Jerrod Cagle.

"Mr. Cagle?" Instinct kept her from opening the door fully.

"Miss Fischer." He doffed his cap. "May I speak to you for a moment?" His mien, very polite, was the exact opposite of his behavior in the restaurant the day before.

"I suppose." The hinges gave a spooky creak as Ann opened the door a bit wider.

"May I come in?"

Ann hesitated, then nodded.

Looking wary, Cagle stepped inside. His gaze traveled up to the water-stained ceiling, then up the dark staircase. "I ain't been inside this old place for years."

Ann's gut tightened when she thought about why Jerrod Cagle might have been inside her childhood home. His admission only added fuel to Ada Belle's story.

Her suspicions were raised further when his gaze traveled to the fireplace mantel where Ann had lovingly propped the picture of June Starr. His mouth drew down at the corners as he stared at the smiling young woman. The flash of bitterness Ann caught before he looked down at his cap gave Ann a chill. He glanced guiltily around the room. She kept her distance from him.

"So why are you here?" Ann asked. Again some instinct prevented her from offering the man a seat.

"I understand you're getting ready to sell this old house and—" he jerked his head toward the street "—that vacant lot over there with it."

It's not vacant, Ann thought. *According to Ada*

Belle it is full of memories of council fires and drums and chanting dancers. "I'm considering it."

"Then I'd like to make you an offer. A real good offer, if you know what I mean."

"Then you should contact Mike Kirkpatrick. He's my real-estate agent."

"No need. I'm prepared to offer you cash. Right now. More than fair. I'll buy this place and everything in it. That way you can get back to your business in Washington."

Ann frowned. She glanced at the picture of her mother, then at Cagle's craggy face. What did he want with this house?

"What do you plan to do with it if you don't mind my asking?"

"I expect I don't have to tell you that this old heap is in terrible shape. I'd have to tear it down—that can be costly, you know—then I have a buyer for the land."

"For *all* the land?"

"Yes, ma'am. Think about it. My offer would get you out of here, free and clear, cash in hand."

Ann wondered if Cagle was simply trying to beat Mike to the punch. Mike had indicated to her that his buyer wasn't planning a mall, but Cagle didn't know that. Ada Belle's story about Lydia's suspicions weighed heavily on her mind, and suddenly Ann didn't feel safe with this man in her house. She looked at the picture of her mother, and a memory began to surface, like an image floating into focus on Polaroid film.

"Mr. Cagle, I'm expecting someone soon, so I'm afraid you'll have to go now." She tried not to act nervous as she walked toward the door.

The knocker sounded as if on cue, and despite herself she jumped and put a palm to her chest.

She let out a pent-up breath and stepped around Cagle. When she threw open the creaky door, there stood Mike Kirkpatrick. "Cagle," he said flatly, "I recognized your truck."

Jerrod Cagle didn't reply. He glared at Mike as he squared his hunched shoulders and twisted the cap in his hands.

"Hi, Ann." Mike smiled at her.

"Hi. Come in." She moved aside for him.

"I'll be going now." Cagle stepped stiffly forward. "You just remember something, ma'am." He stopped and aimed the wadded-up cap at Ann. "There's certain folks in this town who'll tell you any kind of lies to get what they want. You think about my offer. Neat and clean, and *no strings attached.*" He turned his back on them and stomped out onto the porch and down the steps.

Ann and Mike stood in the doorway together and watched him slam the door of his truck and roar off down the street.

"Busy guy."

Ann looked up. "Oh?"

"He just came from my office. He's suing us over the horse."

"Oh, Mike, I'm sorry."

"But in the same breath, he offered to drop the

lawsuit if I'd get the Powers Corporation to buy his land. You know, that piece that's near the interstate exit.''

"Are you going to do it?"

He gave her a sharp look. "I don't plan to deal with Cagle. I'll find somewhere else for Powers to put its mall.'' He followed her into the living room.

When they were seated on the couch Ann said, "I called my office a while ago and requested a leave of absence.''

"Oh?"

"I've decided to stay here for a while. I've got some things to sort out.''

"I see," Mike said, but he didn't exactly. Did she mean "things" as in Edith's estate or "things" as in this relationship with the senator that he'd heard about from Gloria, who'd heard about it from Josette, who'd heard about it from Laurie. He wanted to ask Ann about the man behind that ring on her finger. Were they deeply in love? Serious? *No, dumb ass, they're engaged in a sort of casual, not-too-serious way.*

Or did she mean "things" as in the truth about her mother's death?

Ann was staring at the picture on the mantel. "You know, if Jerrod Cagle dated my mother, I imagine other people in town would know about it.''

Mike frowned. "Ida Miller might. She's about Jerrod's age.''

"That makes sense. He was older than June, so someone his own age might remember him better than her contemporaries. I'd just like to know if he had a mean streak back then—and a long-standing interest in the Starr of the Arbuckles.''

"Why?"

"Ada Belle said folks could never decide if he loved June or just wanted to get his hands on that ranch.''

"Interesting.''

"He also just offered to buy my property.''

"Interesting.''

"Is that all you can say? *Interesting?*''

"It is interesting, don't you think?''

"Well, yeah. But don't you think it's also kind of creepy?''

"Hey, everything about Jerrod Cagle is creepy. He must have changed a lot from the days when your mother dated him. After all, she ended up with your dad, who was a pretty quiet guy, as I recall. Did Ada Belle tell you how your parents got together?''

Ann smiled. "Yes, she did. He may have been quiet, but I gather my father was really good-looking.''

"No surprise there. He certainly fathered a beautiful daughter.'' Mike felt himself flush. He hadn't meant to blurt that out. It seemed every time he got around this woman, he threw off his clerical collar, his reserve, and all his common sense.

"Apparently Nolan won June over with his gentle ways. According to Ada Belle, that infuriated Jerrod, who continued to carry a torch for her.''

"I hate to say 'interesting' again, but, man, it really is.''

"I know." Ann stood and crossed to the mantel. She picked up June's picture and contemplated it. "There's more. Just before you arrived, I remembered something disturbing."

Mike frowned. "Tell me about it."

"Cagle came to see my mother here when I was about five."

"Really?"

"Yes. I remember she drew some pictures for me to color—to keep me busy."

"Like you did for Mary Beth."

"Yeah. I was repeating a pattern, I guess. Anyway, I was in the dining room, but I could hear them arguing. June said that her mother had told her she couldn't sell the land to a white man. Cagle sounded furious. My sense of that conversation is that June had promised the land to him at some point. Probably when they were dating."

"This is strange. How he ended up with the ranch and all."

"It gets stranger. I vividly remember Edith peeking around the swinging door of the kitchen. I looked up from my coloring, and when she saw me, she let the door fall shut, soundlessly."

"Edith? What was she doing here?"

"She had worked as hired help for the Starrs since high school. She did my mother's laundry. But I don't remember much about her from back then. Edith was just a grumpy laundress until she became my stepmother."

Mike looked stunned. "I never knew that."

"There's a lot we don't know, Mike. When my mother died, she was the last Starr—"

"Except for you."

Ann looked up at him, her expression startled. "Except for me," she repeated slowly.

"Anyway, my dad didn't want anything to do with the ranch, probably because June died there. He retreated into a passive shell and never even went back out to the place. Within three months he'd sold it to the highest bidder..."

"Cagle."

Ann nodded. "And within another three months, my father married Edith. The rest, as they say, is history. Or my sad childhood, if you're looking at it from my point of view."

"Which is the only point of view I care about."

"It is?" She turned to him, eyes wide.

Mike hesitated, then admitted, "You bet it is." He'd said it and he meant it. He was starting to care about this woman more every time he saw her. "Tell me about your childhood. Why was it so sad?"

"It's hard to explain. I know everything looked normal on the outside."

"Not exactly," Mike said kindly.

Ann locked eyes with him. "It was Edith. She was so...hostile all the time. I never could do anything right. She dominated my father and me. And my father let her. He also let her spend the proceeds from June's estate as she saw fit."

"Why didn't your Starr relatives do something about that?"

"My mother—"

"—was the last Starr."

"Except for my grandmother Lydia. She had always suffered from depression and had withdrawn from my grandfather and the Starr family years before. According to Ada Belle, she also had a drinking problem."

Ann's voice was flat, but Mike could tell this admission bothered her. He nodded sympathetically.

"Ada Belle says that after June died," she went on, "Lydia became worse. She wasn't interested in anything except sitting in that little house on Dewey Street and grieving."

"What about Nolan's people?"

"Come on, Mike. You know what the Fischers were like. Sweet, but lazy. And just a tad bigoted. If they'd spent their time improving their own situation, instead of running down others', they wouldn't have been nearly so poor. I imagine they were not too happy when Nolan impulsively married an Indian girl, whether she had money or not, and were not too sad when the Indian granddaughter finally left town for college."

Mike let a respectful silence settle before he spoke. "It seems to me all those adults were too busy feeling sorry for themselves to take care of a little girl."

"I was cheated, Mike." He could tell it took a lot for her to admit that out loud. He wanted to take her in his arms right then and there, but he didn't want to do anything to diminish her strength at this critical moment.

"You sure were."

"Nolan and Edith, they…they squandered my heritage."

"No. No one can do that. Maybe they sold the ranch, maybe they spent the money, but you still have your family history. All you have to do is dig for it. It's like treasure. Hidden. In this town. In this house…"

"In those trees."

Mike caught a breath, eased it out gently. "I figured this was coming."

"Did you?"

"Sure. You're having second thoughts about selling the pecan grove, because you've found out what it meant to your family. I can understand that."

"It feels like the last link to my real family. I don't know. I might…I might want to preserve those trees. But I keep thinking, where does that leave you?"

"With a seller who has cold feet. It's happened before."

"Mike, work with me. All I want to know is what your buyer will do with those trees. Isn't there some way to make a deal where they have to save them?"

"Maybe. I need a few more days."

"A few more days?"

"Yes. My…buyer is having an important board meeting a week from today. I wish I could tell you more, but right now this board is a little skittish. Until I talk to them, I don't want to let the cat out of the bag."

BUT THE CAT, in fact, was plastered all over the front page of *Medicine Creek Style* the following Friday. Ida Miller's cutesy headline shouted, Where-Oh-Where Will The New Mall Be?

Gloria slapped the paper on the counter in the Secret Garden. Her stupid aunt! She'd been afraid Ida had overheard her that day when she'd phoned Jerrod Cagle to tell him the pecan grove was up for sale. Gloria hadn't really lied to the man. She'd simply let him jump to his own conclusions—that Mike's buyer for the grove was Powers. She'd hoped to get Cagle to stop that deal by buying the grove himself, thus getting that woman out of town. Because if Mike got the board to approve the purchase of the land, he'd throw himself into building the church and then he might never get around to marrying her.

Ever since the Fischer woman had come to town, Gloria could almost *feel* Mike being distracted by her. *Ohhh!* Gloria fumed as she turned and started snipping the stems off this morning's delivery of carnations. That woman! If the pecan grove was out of the way, maybe that woman would leave town. If, if, if. *Snip. Snip. Snip.*

According to Josette, who had heard it from Laurie, Mike had been over at Ann Fischer's house every day this past week. Herding this contractor and that subcontractor over there. Why couldn't Skeeter Morgan just take his Bobcat over and do whatever lot grading that needed doing and leave the bill in the screen door as he did for everybody else in this town? But no, Mike had to accompany old Skeeter, had to make sure the job was done right—and Mike always managed to see Miss Perfect in the bargain.

That was what Gloria had taken to calling Ann Fischer in her mind. Miss Perfect. All Mike had talked about for the past week was that old house and how fast it was shaping up and what a great job Miss Perfect was doing cleaning it up. Ever since that woman had come to town, Mike had acted as though he'd had a spell cast over him. *Snip.*

In the meantime, this business about the mall had come up. And now dear Aunt Ida was making a ruckus about it on the front page of her diddly little paper. Snip-snip-snip-snip-SNIP.

Leave it to her aunt to start a front-page fight over the whole thing. Ida, who fancied herself some kind of journalist, had to pick this of all times to present both sides of a story and whip up a controversy.

The opposing factions would side up, as they always did in this town. Even now, somebody was probably reading the article aloud over sausage and eggs at the Pie. People would waste no time before voicing their bullheaded opinions. Folks who wanted the mall in the town versus folks who wanted to keep the smelly diesel buses loaded with tourists out by the interstate.

And if Gloria knew Medicine Creek, the folks who were against bringing the mall into town, would end up being the most vocal. Which meant the pecan grove would be available for Mike's church.

The bell on the shop door clanged and Gloria turned. Erin Kirkpatrick slipped inside. Twelve years old, the spitting image of her father and frisky as a filly, Erin Kirkpatrick needed a mother in the worst way. Even if she couldn't be a real mother to the girl, Gloria had made up her mind to civilize this child. Or at least fatten her up. She was as thin as a willow reed.

Erin slid onto the stool beside the counter and propped her freckled chin on her palm. "Hi." The word came out dejectedly.

"Hi, sweetie. Why aren't you in school?"

"The band left for the San Antonio contest this morning. I didn't have the money for the trip. What's one more triangle dinging in the back, anyway? They've got ten."

Gloria's heart sank. If only she'd known! She would have paid Erin's way. "Oh, honey." Gloria swept around the counter and grabbed Erin's shoulders. "I'm so sorry." She folded the child in a hug. "There's always next year." She swept back Erin's thick wavy hair. "Surely every seventh grader didn't go, did they?"

The Medicine Creek band was the town pride, along with the state-champion football team. Kids started out marching and playing in fifth grade. By seventh grade they were permitted to go on the field trips with the high school.

"Everybody went but me and Clayton Stuart. His mother wouldn't let him because of his asthma. I didn't want to be stuck in a study hall all day with just me and Clayton and old Ms. Brewer. Her breath makes me wanna puke!"

"Are you skipping school, then?"

"I told them I was sick and coming over here. Please don't tell my dad."

Gloria considered. She should pick up the phone this instant and tell Mike that Erin had shown up at her shop. But she didn't want to. She wanted to use this opportunity to…influence the child. "Okay. I won't tell him. But this can't happen again. Skipping school is serious."

Gloria picked up the phone and dialed the school. She slid a crystal candy dish full of M&Ms toward Erin. Erin grabbed a handful.

"Shirley?" Gloria said into the phone. "It's Gloria. I have Erin Kirkpatrick here…. No, she's fine. Just a touch of nausea…. Well, of *course* you tried to call Mike…. Oh, don't I know, dear. That poor man. Well, it's okay. He knows I'll look after Erin."

Gloria hung up and gave Erin a bright smile. "All taken care of. How would you like to work at the computer with me this morning? I'll show you how to enter the invoices. Then at lunchtime we'll track down your dad and all have a nice big lunch over at the Pie."

"He won't come. He's at that lady's house, tearing wallpaper down."

"Tearing down wallpaper?"

"Yeah. In the dining room. They couldn't find anybody to do it soon enough to suit her. Seems to me she's awful picky. Have you met her?"

"Well, yes. I have. And she's very…sophisticated, very…nicely groomed."

FREE FREE
BOOKS! GIFT!

PLAY
BANGO!

AND CLAIM 2 FREE BOOKS
AND A FREE GIFT!

BANGO

5	19	32	54	73
6	17	41	50	6
13	22	FREE	52	
5	24	44	46	
8	21	35	47	75

BANGO

9	19	44	52	71
4	20	32	50	68
11	18	FREE	53	63
7	27	36	60	72
3	28	41	47	64

BANGO

38	9	44	10	38
92	7	5	27	14
2	51	FREE	91	67
75	3	12	20	13
6	15	26	50	31

★ **No Cost!**
★ **No Obligation to Buy!**
★ **No Purchase Necessary!**

TURN THE PAGE TO PLAY

PLAY BANGO!

AND GET THREE FREE GIFTS!

It looks like **BINGO**, it plays like **BINGO** but it's **FREE**

HOW TO PLAY:

1. With a coin, scratch the Caller Card to reveal your 5 lucky numbers and see that they match your Bango Card. Then check the claim chart to discover what we have for you — 2 FREE BOOKS and a FREE GIFT — ALL YOURS, ALL FREE!

2. Send back the Bango card and you'll receive two brand-new Harlequin Superromance® novels. These books have a cover price of $4.99 each in the U.S. and $5.99 each in Canada, but they are yours to keep absolutely free.

3. There's no catch. You're under no obligation to buy anything. We charge nothing — ZERO — for your first shipment. And you don't have to make any minimum number of purchases — not even one!

4. The fact is, thousands of readers enjoy receiving our books by mail from the Harlequin Reader Service®. They enjoy the convenience of home delivery…they like getting the best new novels at discount prices, BEFORE they're available in stores…and they love their *Heart to Heart* subscriber newsletter featuring author news, horoscopes, recipes, book reviews and much more!

5. We hope that after receiving your free books you'll want to remain a subscriber. But the choice is yours — to continue or cancel, any time at all! So why not take us up on our invitation, with no risk of any kind. You'll be glad you did!

YOURS FREE!

This exciting mystery gift is yours free when you play BANGO!

Visit us online at
www.eHarlequin.com

It's fun, and we're giving away
FREE GIFTS
to all players!

PLAY BANGO!

CALLER CARD

SCRATCH HERE! →

YES! Please send me the 2 free books and the gift for which I qualify! I understand that I am under no obligation to purchase any books as explained on the back of this card.

YOUR CARD ↘

BANGO
38	9	44	10	38
92	7	5	27	14
2	51	FREE	91	67
75	3	12	20	13
6	15	26	50	31

CLAIM CHART!	
Match 5 numbers	2 FREE BOOKS & A MYSTERY GIFT
Match 4 numbers	2 FREE BOOKS
Match 3 numbers	1 FREE BOOK

(H-SR-OS-12/01)

336 HDL DFUL   **135 HDL DFUK**

NAME   (PLEASE PRINT CLEARLY)

ADDRESS

APT.#   CITY

STATE/PROV.   ZIP/POSTAL CODE

The Harlequin Reader Service® — Here's how it works:

Accepting your 2 free books and gift places you under no obligation to buy anything. You may keep the books and gift and return the shipping statement marked "cancel." If you do not cancel, about a month later we'll send you 6 additional novels and bill you just $4.05 each in the U.S., or $4.46 each in Canada, plus 25¢ shipping & handling per book and applicable taxes if any.* That's the complete price and — compared to cover prices of $4.99 each in the U.S. and $5.99 each in Canada — it's quite a bargain! You may cancel at any time, but if you choose to continue, every month we'll send you 6 more books, which you may either purchase at the discount price or return to us and cancel your subscription.

*Terms and prices subject to change without notice. Sales tax applicable in N.Y. Canadian residents will be charged applicable provincial taxes and GST.

If offer card is missing write to: Harlequin Reader Service, 3010 Walden Ave., P.O. Box 1867, Buffalo, NY 14240-1867

BUSINESS REPLY MAIL

FIRST-CLASS MAIL   PERMIT NO. 717-003   BUFFALO, NY

POSTAGE WILL BE PAID BY ADDRESSEE

HARLEQUIN READER SERVICE
3010 WALDEN AVE
PO BOX 1867
BUFFALO NY 14240-9952

NO POSTAGE
NECESSARY
IF MAILED
IN THE
UNITED STATES

"Well, so are you!"

Gloria cringed at the fact that Erin had already intuitively picked up on the fact that Gloria felt threatened by the other woman. To hide her chagrin, she plucked yellowing leaves off a nearby geranium. "You know, a woman who makes all kinds of money as an attorney would naturally be picky. I'm sure she's used to the best of everything, used to having everything her own way."

"I guess." Erin popped more candy in her mouth.

Gloria couldn't tell if Erin had gotten the point. She didn't want to make the child feel insecure, but she had to find a way to hint that Ann Fischer was the kind of woman who might take their family away from this small town, whether it was true or not. Gloria had to make Erin an ally against this woman.

"I don't know why Dad thinks *he* has to tear that wallpaper down for her. If you ask me, he just wants to do it."

"Why do you say that?" Gloria wheedled. Did Erin know something she didn't? "After all, real estate is your dad's job."

"Realtors don't go around doing handyman work for people."

"Well, no..."

"And what about you, Gloria? He was supposed to take you to hear that speaker up in Pauls Valley last week and he forgot all about it! If you ask me, that's not fair!"

Gloria turned away and raked the pruned leaves into the trash. No use letting the child see how upset

she was about that. Mike had called and apologized.
Said he was working late. It sounded like a bad cliché.
Later she'd found out that he'd been at Ann Fischer's
house, helping her measure the pitch in the attic for
central heat and air.

"Anyway," Erin continued, oblivious to Gloria's
growing unhappiness, "I'd like to tell that woman a
thing or two. She should quit taking up my dad's time
when he's got five kids to take care of."

With sudden insight, Gloria snapped out of her
glum mood. "Goodness, Erin," she pretended to
chastise the girl, "we would never want any of
Preacher Kirkpatrick's children to say anything unkind to a stranger. We must be cordial to Ms. Fischer
while she's visiting in Medicine Creek."

"I get so sick of being the preacher's kid."

"Now, Erin."

"Well, *somebody* oughtta send her a message."

A message? "Let's get started on the computer,"
Gloria steered the child toward the desk in the back.
"You know," she snapped her fingers as if an idea
had just hit her. "Invoices are dull. I've got a program
that makes flyers and greeting cards and such. You
can type in *any* message you want." She gave the girl
a meaningful look, then added, "Maybe you could
make up a pretty flyer about my Halloween specials?"

"Neat!" Erin enthused as she seated herself at the
desk.

Gloria felt a niggle of guilt as she looked down at
the child hoping Erin would take the hint and create

a "flyer" for Ann Fischer as soon as Gloria left her
alone. But if she was going to have to resort to covert
measures to stop Mike from pulling away from her,
so be it. She sure wasn't looking forward to that board
meeting on Saturday. It would be tricky, pretending
to support Mike's goal on the one hand while under-
mining it on the other.

CHAPTER ELEVEN

"I HOPE TO GOODNESS you can explain this." Julius Harn tossed a copy of Ida's front-page article onto the long folding table as the Windrock Nondenominational Church board settled into their seats. Harn, an elderly farmer who was tough as a cob and deaf as a post, considered himself the chief steward of the church's financial resources and had a habit of dousing the lights and flicking off the air-conditioning.

Karen Pierce, another board member, craned her neck to see the headline. "Yes, I was shocked to read about that, Pastor. Surely you aren't going to sell the Fischer property to a bunch of folks that'll come in here and ruin our town."

Mike had been afraid of this. Emotions were already running high. Thanks to Jerrod and Ida, the whole town thought they had a stake in the mall issue, and about half of them thought *he* had some kind of hidden agenda about that land. Well, maybe he did, and it was time to get it on the table. "Not exactly. Let's get started."

When the five-member board, including Gloria Miller and Mac and Mercy Reardon, was comfortably seated, he said, "Let's open with a short prayer."

They held hands and Mike asked for the standard

blessings—patience, generosity, self-control—then he slipped in, "And give us the wisdom to separate idle gossip from the truth and make a decision here today that will be for the good of all in this community."

Everybody said, "Amen," but Julius Harn frowned at Mike as soon as he raised his head.

"All right." Mike spread his palms on the table. "We have a whole lot of ground to cover today, but first things first. Despite rumors you may have heard, I have not been negotiating with the Powers Corporation about that pecan grove. Like all of you, I don't think a giant mall only a few blocks from our quaint shops on Main Street is a good idea. That's why I'm hoping you'll consider my idea, instead." Mike took a deep breath. "I'd like us to buy that land and build our new church on it."

There was a stunned, bug-eyed silence, and then Karen Pierce said, "Oh, my."

"A new church?" Julius Harn was practically shouting. "You are talking about a new church when the damage is barely repaired on this one."

Mike suppressed a groan. Last summer, Zack and his friends, shooting off illegal fireworks out back, had accidentally set the Boy Scouts' paper-drive trailer afire. Drifting embers had ignited the church roof.

"Julius, that's all in the past," Gloria intoned smoothly.

"The hell it is—pardon my French, Pastor—but that little bit o' business cost a bundle and it raised our insurance rates."

Mike put up his palms. "I know. And that's why Zack and the boys weed-whacked the parking lot all summer."

"We *need* a new building, anyway," Gloria insisted.

"I'm thinkin' what we need is a new preacher."

"Julius!" Mercy Reardon exclaimed. "Not with the pastor present!"

"You agree with me and you all know it." Harn slapped the table. "Somebody's got to be the daddy around here. We cannot go out and commit this congregation to some horrendous debt when Mike doesn't even know what his own future holds. We shouldn't even be talking about buying land. We should be talking about getting ourselves a pastor that don't have so many irons in the fire all the time." He turned his grizzled head toward Mike. "I'm sorry to be so plain-spoken. But facts is facts. This sure ain't the time for a new church."

Mike bowed his head and closed his eyes.

"Julius, you are being unkind," Mercy mumbled.

"Kill the messenger if you want to." Harn flapped a hand at her. "These things have got to be said."

"Maybe this isn't the best time to build a new church," Gloria interjected, "but I gather Ms. Fischer is ready to sell the land as soon as possible and go home to Washington. It's a beautiful site, and we should grab it while we can. Am I right, Mike?"

He nodded and opened his eyes. Bless Gloria for steering this discussion back to the matter at hand.

"We could buy the land now—it's going to take

time to clear those big trees, anyway—and while we pay off the land, Mike could get his bearings, get his family life in order.'' She smiled at him meaningfully. ''I think we all agree that Mike has been a good pastor. And a personal crisis can befall anyone.''

The Reardons raised their eyebrows in agreement.

''I'll give you that.'' Julius looked sheepishly at Mike. ''Never saw a better preacher.''

''But, Pastor.'' Mac Reardon, a mild-mannered reasonable man, had finally decided to speak. All heads turned to him. ''I don't know how to say this but, well, you've been under a lot of strain lately and...''

''Go on, Mac,'' Mike encouraged.

''Well, there was that incident between you and Jerrod Cagle last week at the Pie.''

''Flashed your famous temper again, didn't you?'' This was Julius. Mike squinted at the man. He hadn't lost his temper since high school, but to some folks in this town, that was only yesterday.

''Julius, do you have the church's financial figures that I asked you to bring with you?'' Mike asked quietly.

''Course.''

''Then with this—'' he drew a real estate document and some photographs of the pecan grove from a file ''—the board has the data you need to decide on the purchase of the land. Please bear in mind that as Ms. Fischer's Realtor, I am obligated to continue to market that property for her at fair market value. And we may have to agree to save the trees in order to get her to sell. Now, to avoid any conflict of interest, I'd like to excuse myself from this meeting.''

"Mike.'' Gloria followed him as he headed out the door. When they were out in the hall, she said, "Don't worry," in a low voice. "I can get them to see the light.''

MIKE HAD BROUGHT a few prospective buyers by the house even before Ann had begun the renovations, but after that article about the pecan grove in Friday's *Style,* the old Starr house needed a revolving door.

People, people, people, roamed in and out from morning 'til night. Unfortunately most of them were nosey townsfolk who simply wanted a peek at the old place. They ventured inside almost cautiously, wide-eyed, poking around with avid curiosity, having absolutely no intention of bidding on the property.

But even when they weren't serious buyers, Ann was amazed at Mike's grace and patience, at how easily he could get people to envision what the changes would look like, at how he could charm even the triflers into sharing his enthusiasm—*her* enthusiasm now—for the hard work ahead.

With so much to do, it became impossible for Ann to jump up and leave every time someone wanted to drop by, and Mike told her it wasn't necessary. They had, in fact, begun to function like a team. He'd bring the folks in, introduce Ann, and she'd offer some of her specially blended coffee, brewed to perfection in the antique silver samovar on the breakfront and served in her grandmother's china cups. Then Ann would discreetly disappear while Mike showed people around. Sometimes he'd give her a wink when they passed through on their way to another room.

In that next week there were a lot of lookers, but no takers. Mike encouraged Ann to hold out for top dollar. He reinforced their strategy as they walked the grounds of the house the following Thursday.

"If my buyer for the grove falls through, and this place really does end up across from an outlet mall, someone could eventually resell it as a commercial property, as a restaurant, an antique emporium or maybe even a museum," he encouraged her. "You don't want to give it away."

"I won't, but this whole process is nerve-racking."

"I know. But now we've created quite a buzz about this old house. The architecture of the place is incredible." He leaned his head back and raised an arm toward the roof pediments. "Just look at that lacy millwork up there. Even in its crumbling state, this place attracts people. After Edith moved to the home, kids would poke around out back. That's when I started watching the house for her. There have even been silly rumors that this old house is—" He stopped himself.

"Haunted?" Ann guessed. After an awkward pause she added, "Don't tell me these are rumors about my *mother*."

"No." Mike said firmly. "It's just the kind of dumb talk that swirls around an old house in a state of disrepair. And we are fixing that as fast as we can, aren't we?"

But Ann's brow had already creased into a sad little frown.

"Ann, look." He faced her and took her lightly by the shoulders. "There's always a lot of speculation and history and rumor attached to an old house like this. And after Ida's article, people are especially curious." He released her and ran a hand through his hair as he looked up. "You know, we should just throw open the doors and let the whole town have a good look…" He snapped his fingers. "That's it!"

"What?" His sudden excitement made Ann forget her sorrow.

"An open house! We could weed out all of the busybodies that way. Everybody could get a look at the house—and at you—and then maybe the speculation and rumors would finally settle down. We might even snag a real buyer in the process."

Ann liked the idea immediately. "But how can I possibly get this place ready soon enough?"

"That's just it! You don't. You make it clear you're throwing the doors open and selling the place as is. All we have to do is show the potential in one key area." He took a step and swept one long arm toward the bow window. "Like that dining room, for instance. You could even serve your special coffee in those antique china cups. Add some old-fashioned cookies. All you'll have to do is clean up the clutter everywhere else so buyers can see the potential."

Ann sighed. "Three stories of junk? It's taken me a week just to clear a path."

Mike nodded. "I see your point. Even if we keep

it simple, we've got a lot to do to get this old girl presentable. But we've got a little time. I couldn't do an open house this coming weekend, anyway. It's Oktoberfest at the church. When did you say the painters were coming?''

"Monday, but—"

"Could you at least get the dining room in shape by, say, the following Saturday? November fourth?''

"I'll try." Ann raised her shoulders and spread her fingers as she looked around. He was making it all sound so easy! "I don't know if I can be ready by then, but my schedule is certainly wide open. Maybe Laurie would help me if I ask her.''

"I'll help."

How readily he said that. Ann looked up into the face of the good man standing on the buckled sidewalk beside her. "Mike, you've got so much to do with your kids and your church and all..." Ann's voice trailed off because his eyes...oh, his eyes. She realized she should never look into this man's eyes, because there was too much to see there. Too much kindness. Too much intelligence and humor. Too much...of the old fun-loving Mickey Kirkpatrick, someone so full of life and passion that his eyes were a dangerous thing.

"But I want to," he said softly, simply.

She reasoned that he had as much to gain from closing the sale on this old mausoleum as she did. "All right. As long as you really want to."

"Then we're all set!" He clapped his hands and rubbed them together, staring up at the front of the house again. "That means we'll have to get the announcement over to Ida by next Wednesday if we want it to appear in Friday's *Style*. A week from Sunday will be a perfect time for an open house. Say from two to five? I'll be through with church services, people will be out visiting and taking Sunday drives." Mike's enthusiasm built. "Let's go inside and write up the announcement right now."

When they stepped inside the foyer, he eyed the neatly packed boxes of serviceable goods Ann had stacked near the front door. "Hey! What're you going to do with all this stuff?"

"I planned to get rid of it before the painters started on Monday."

"Why don't you bring it to the Oktoberfest rummage sale on Saturday? You could meet my kids, some of my congregation. It might even be fun."

Ann hesitated.

"Laurie and Steve will be there," he coaxed.

Ann smiled. "I've never been to a rummage sale."

Mike looked scandalized. "Never been to a rummage sale? Woman! Think of all the great junk you've been missing out on!"

"I've got plenty right here, thank you." Ann swept an arm over the still-cluttered living room.

"But this is your chance to turn junk into an electronic keyboard for the youth group." He pumped his eyebrows. "And there'll be great food and singing and games and... Come on, you've just gotta come to Oktoberfest." He grinned. "The preacher insists."

Ann smiled. He was the most persuasive, charming

man she'd ever met. No wonder his congregation had grown by leaps and bounds in only a few short years.

So on Saturday afternoon Ann showed up at the church with her rental car packed to the gills.

The congregation was buzzing like a crowd at a carnival around dozens of tables and booths set up in the sunny gravel parking lot. The church buildings— two large cinder-block structures—were very ugly and the location was worse. The whole compound sat on a treeless lot not far from the railroad tracks.

The teenagers had a baked-goods sale table under the walkway between the two buildings. A hand-lettered poster board sign read Help with the Ski Trip. There were craft booths, a silent auction inside the church building and steam tables waiting to be loaded with catered German-style food from a restaurant in nearby Sulphur. Ann was impressed.

She carried some boxes to the sale area, where two smiling middle-aged ladies in identical starched aprons put out their arms to help her. She spotted Mike, standing under an oak tree, looking handsome in his black leather jacket, sipping coffee from a foam cup and talking to some men. When he saw Ann, he waved, said something quickly to the guys, then strode toward her.

"Can I help?"

"Reverend," one of the ladies gushed, "look at all the lovely stuff this young woman brought for our sale." She held up a box that had never been opened. It contained a blender.

"Yes. Isn't she generous? Ann, meet Kathy and

Cindy Parker. They're sisters-in-law. Ladies, this is Ann Fischer.''

The women froze, then quickly formed polite smiles that looked as stiff as their aprons. ''Edith Fischer's daughter?'' one said.

''Yes.'' Ann smiled.

Silence.

''Well, you ladies enjoy the bounty. I'd like to introduce Ann around.'' Mike took Ann's elbow in a protective gesture. ''Come on, I want you to meet my son.''

''Can it wait until I finish unpacking these boxes?'' Ann smiled at the ladies again. This time their answering smiles reflected a trace of approval.

''Sure. I guess he'll be here for a while. He's helping the guys set up the moonwalk.''

An hour passed while Ann and the ladies got the work done, and in the process Ann was friendly and helpful, letting Kathy and Cindy see that she wasn't some mother-hating ogre who had abandoned Edith Fischer in her old age. She tried not to think about why the opinions of Mike's church members mattered to her. Two weeks ago she hadn't cared one whit what anybody in this town thought of her. Now that was changing. And Ann was afraid to examine why.

Mike eventually brought his son over to the tables. Funny, Ann thought when she spotted them walking toward her, this kid didn't have the look of a troublemaker. His blond hair was clean-cut, and his clothes were neat and casual. He was tall and thin and, except for that glint of Kirkpatrick humor in his blue eyes, he exuded a quiet, almost shy demeanor.

"Ann, this is Joseph," Mike said as he clapped a proud hand on the boy's shoulder.

Joseph. Now Ann understood. She had been thinking she'd be meeting the rebellious Zack. But this was the oldest son, the baby born to Mike and Marsha sixteen years ago, shortly after they'd graduated from high school.

"Hello, Ms. Fischer.' The boy extended his hand.

Ann shook it and noted how Joseph had a hint of his father's Scottish good looks, but without the raw edges. Something about his face was more…refined …sweeter than Mike's had been as a teenager.

"Call me Ann." She smiled.

"Okay, Ann." His posture was relaxed, confident. "Are you staying for our little shindig?"

Ann glanced at Mike. He raised a questioning eyebrow: Was she?

"Oh, you've got to stay and have some knackwurst and sauerkraut," Kathy enthused. "It's delicious. The reverend serves it up himself."

"He wears lederhosen and a fancy German-style apron. Very cute." Joseph tossed his dad a teasing grin. "You don't want to miss it."

"I guess I could stay and eat." Ann smiled at Mike.

She stayed for the entire day and the entire evening, and thoroughly enjoyed every minute.

She found Laurie at the children's face-painting

booth, working rapidly, applying a hasty heart to a toddler's chubby cheek.

"Hi." Ann eyed the long line. "You look busy."

"Terribly. I think I got duped," Laurie explained without looking up. "Zack is supposed to be helping me, but when Melissa Banks showed up towing her little sister, Zack suddenly had to go to the john. He hasn't come back."

"I'd offer to go find him, but I don't know what he looks like."

"Don't bother. He hasn't been that cooperative." Laurie shook her head and sighed. "Painting snakes and skulls on the little boys, ants and spiders on the little girls."

"Oh." The more Ann heard about Zack, the more she wanted to meet this character. "Maybe I can help." Ann was glad she'd worn old jeans and a simple oversize chambray shirt. She started to roll up the sleeves.

Laurie nodded toward the empty chair on the other side of the card table laden with paints and brushes. "Bless you."

Before long the line of little kids and parents forming in front of Ann stretched out into the parking lot. It seemed every child at the Oktoberfest wanted one of Ann's delicate designs. Bright fall leaves and butterflies and rainbows.

Brandon Kirkpatrick stepped up, making no secret of who he was and why he was back to get his brother's handiwork—a bull's eye—wiped off his cheek. "Kids keep tossing popcorn at it." He was a snaggle-toothed cutie of about seven, running a hand through his spiky, copper-colored hair in the same way his father did.

"Can you do Pokémon characters?" the child asked in all seriousness.

"Sorry." Ann gave him a regretful look. "How about an eagle?"

"Neat!"

Even the preteens started wandering over to watch Ann work. Something about a lanky redhead at the center of the cluster of giggling girls caught Ann's attention. With her tawny hair, square jaw and fiery blue eyes, that child had to be a Kirkpatrick.

She wasn't giggling. She was watching Ann with her head tilted and those blue eyes squinting. Ann, more sensitive than most to hostile vibes, cast a smile at the child and kept painting.

"Yoo-hoo! Erin, honey!" It was Gloria Miller, dressed in a red vest of crocheted rosettes and a matching broomstick skirt, waving and rushing toward the group.

"I need you girls to come and help." Gloria placed one hand on her heaving bosom as if out of breath.

"Oh, hello." She twisted her head and gave Ann a cool smile. Her full lips were delineated in the exact same shade of red as her outfit. "I see you're helping us out today."

Laurie swished a paintbrush in water and said, "Ann, this is Gloria Miller."

"Oh, we've met!" Gloria chirped. "And how are you, Laurie?"

"Fine, thank you." Laurie dipped the brush in yellow paint and proceeded to craft the daisy on her little customer's cheek.

"Hello, Gloria," Ann said, tilting her face up into the sun. Under the vest, the woman wore a white blouse embroidered with tiny edelweiss. Was she trying to match Mike's lederhosen?

"Oh, there you are, honey." Gloria turned to the child who had come up beside her. "Ann, this is Erin Kirkpatrick. Mike's daughter." Gloria linked her arm with Erin's.

This woman, Ann thought, was certainly putting her mark on Mike's family.

"Erin, this is Ann Fischer. You know—the lady *from Washington* who's selling the old house on Pecan Street."

"Hi." The child's greeting was clipped, devoid of any warmth.

"Nice to meet you, Erin." Ann smiled at her. "Are you having a good time?"

"Yeah." Again the word was bitten off on its way out.

Fortunately Gloria hustled the girls away, and Ann was able to forget about the frosty encounter by concentrating on the child at her knee.

Later Mike pressed Ann into service at the steam tables, right beside him, scooping out warm German potato salad. He looked amazing in the leather shorts, and Ann had to steel herself *not* to look at the reverend's muscular legs.

Gloria made her way among the paper-covered tables serving iced tea and greeting people. But above her charming smile, her eyes kept darting to Mike and Ann. Her scrutiny made Ann uncomfortable, so she decided to leave as soon as the meal was over.

Before she got to her car, she felt a gentle touch on her shoulder. It was Susie Hobbs. "Ann, are you leaving already? I really wanted to talk to you about helping us with the Children's Arts Festival. That's where we sell the children's crafts and artwork right before Christmas. But we can discuss it another time. How's the house going?"

Ann rolled her eyes. "Painfully slow."

"That's not what I hear. The whole town is excited about the changed look of that place. Just getting those bushes trimmed was a massive improvement. Listen, before you go, I was wondering, why don't you join us for services in the morning? That is, if you like to attend."

"I do." She was a member of a large Protestant congregation in Washington, D.C., which she occasionally found impersonal. She'd never even spoken to her pastor. Might be fun to attend the small-town church headed by Mike Kirkpatrick.

"What time?"

"Sunday school at nine. Service at ten."

CHAPTER TWELVE

ANN COULDN'T BELIEVE how nervous she was. She, a woman who had argued before the United States Supreme Court, a woman who had waltzed at the White House, a woman who had spoken before a crowd of several thousand at a D.C. rally for women's shelters. *She* felt her heart in her throat as she walked down the graveled sidewalk toward the plain cinder-block building.

She had never in her life fretted so obsessively about what to wear. Her wardrobe wasn't extensive— simple and elegant was her style—but this morning she wished she'd packed a trunkful to choose from. Instead, she had no alternative but to wear the simple black sheath she'd brought for Edith's service.

Why was she so keyed up? she wondered as she walked through a set of open double doors into the worship area. The answer was obvious. This was *Mike's* church. The center of *his* world. *His* dream.

She was early, but already eighty to a hundred people had gathered and many more were rapidly filling the rows of folding chairs, waving and smiling at one another as they took their places. Everybody seemed to know everybody else.

Ann chose a place toward the middle on the side

aisle. As soon as she was seated, she felt a gentle pat on her shoulder. "Glad you could make it." Susie Hobbs. Ann relaxed a little.

"I still want to rope you in on this arts-festival thing," Susie whispered as she slipped in beside Ann.

"Oh, I want to help! In fact, I was thinking, if they haven't found a location, how about the pecan grove, weather permitting?"

"Wonderful! I'll mention it to Gloria."

Ann wasn't sure Gloria would welcome her help, but getting involved in the Children's Arts Festival sounded like fun.

Up front, a raised carpeted platform held a simple podium at the center and a large video screen behind, flanked by colorful banners. Plants and flowers were dotted around the front. A baby was crying somewhere in the back, and as Ann watched an old gentleman being helped to a seat down front, she felt a moment of chagrin. She should have offered to bring Ada Belle.

But her guilt was eased when she saw Ada Belle being assisted, walker and all, to a place of honor at the front by two strapping teenaged boys.

Gloria, all dressed up, came in with a flurry and seated herself at the end of the front row, where the redheaded Kirkpatrick children were lined up like stairs steps.

Before long an expectant silence fell and the choir entered from a side door, followed by Mike.

Ann's pulse raced at the sight of him. She ducked her head and hoped her cheeks weren't turning red.

He looked so handsome! Every hair in place. Tailored dark suit. Crisp white shirt. Tasteful tie. All eyes were on him as he stepped up to the podium, arranged his papers and raised his arms. The congregation stood.

The songs were familiar to Ann, and she joined in the singing with relish. Singing hymns always raised her spirits, and this bunch certainly did them justice.

After the third hymn, the crowd rustled into their seats.

Mike smiled, then leaned into the microphone. "How about those Titans?" His voice was rousing.

Murmurs of approval for the local football team, which had crushed the opposition on Friday night.

"Coach," Mike said casually to a bulky man several rows back, "I see you showed up to give your thanks."

Ann recognized Mike's father, Dan, who cupped his meaty hands to his mouth. "Prayin' over that next game, Pastor."

Laughter.

"Dad always asks me for a blessing for the boys. Funny though, he never asks me for any advice about the plays." Pause. "Maybe that's why we keep on winning."

More laughter.

"Today I want to talk to you about love. Let's take a look at First Corinthians Thirteen, because it tells us without a doubt what true love looks like."

There followed the whisper and shuffling of pages as people turned to the verse and lowered their heads to read along. When she noticed that Ann was empty-handed, Susie shared her Bible. Mike read the familiar verse slowly, confidently. As his resonant voice rang out, each descriptive word about love—patient, kind, trusting, hoping, enduring—registered in Ann's heart.

In later years she would often wonder if she hadn't made up her mind about her life that very day, the first time she heard Mike Kirkpatrick preach.

"Love is a powerful force. Nothing can destroy it." Mike was obviously building to his conclusion now. "In the Song of Solomon it says, 'Many waters cannot quench love...'"

A few ladies were dabbing at their eyes by now.

"'Nor can the floods...'" His words faltered as he looked up. Ann felt the intensity of his gaze all the way to her core. He looked down at his papers, then back at Ann for an instant. "'Nor can the floods drown it.' Now let's sing a song in celebration of God's love," he finished.

Ann looked down as he raised his arms, suddenly aware that her presence had thrown him. She should have told him she was coming.

The congregation stood and the singing started with gusto again.

Or maybe she shouldn't have come at all. She was behaving foolishly, coming to this place where she didn't belong just to hear Mike Kirkpatrick, to see him.

Yet part of her didn't regret coming. On the contrary, the minute she was out of the building, she knew she'd be back next Sunday to hear Mike Kirk-patrick preach again.

When the service was over, she left the auditorium quickly. But her heart fell when she overheard two women talking as they moved through the parking lot behind her.

"That was sure brave of the reverend to preach about love like that."

"Do you think he was thinking about Marsha there at the end?"

"When he got all flustered? Why, of course he was."

"It still hurts him, I'm sure."

"How could it not?"

"And did you see poor Gloria's face?"

"Yes, indeed. That girl is going to have to have the patience of a saint."

ON MONDAY MORNING the painters came before Ann had poured her first cup of coffee. The two men got right to work, and when she saw the first swath of color applied to the drab dining-room walls, she knew she had chosen the perfect shade of pumpkin. She loved it, and as she watched the warm vibrant color take over the drab room, she felt a small unbidden strand of attachment forming to the old house.

Mike showed up in work clothes after he had finished his real-estate business for the day. He emitted a soft whistle of approval as he stepped into the dining room.

"Isn't it beautiful!" Ann cried as the late-afternoon

sun poured into the bow window, which was now free of the crumbling plastic shades.

"Stay right there." Mike aimed a finger at where she stood in the center of the vacant floor, surrounded by the glow of the deep-peachy walls. I've got a surprise." He dashed out the door.

He came back carrying a very large framed picture wrapped in brown paper.

"What in the world is that?" Ann asked.

"Don't move," he said as he propped it against one wall and ripped at the paper. He grasped the antique barn-siding frame and hoisted the picture up to a spot above where the breakfront would stand.

Ann gasped.

It was an oil painting, a piece of exquisite Native American art, depicting a moonlit night over a waterfall in the mountains. A Plains Indian sat atop the falls on his pony in the moonglow. The ethereal blues and lavenders in the painting contrasted lusciously with the newly painted walls.

"Turner Falls," Mike explained as he leveled the piece. "You know, up in the Arbuckles, not too far from the Lazy J, matter of fact."

"I know," Ann breathed. "I've been there a few times."

"Of course." Everybody in Medicine Creek had been swimming below the falls.

"Oh, Mike. It's beautiful."

"Just consider it a gift from your Realtor. Believe it or not, I snapped it up at the rummage sale right before you arrived. I figured the way you like art and all." He smiled as he twisted to catch her expression, then frowned.

He lowered the painting down to the floor and crossed to her. "I didn't mean to make you cry. Here." And before either one of them had time to feel self-conscious about it, he had folded her in his arms.

She clung to him with her cheek pressed against his chest, not caring if this embrace was wise. For her it was the only comfort she'd felt in the past three weeks, and she needed it. She *needed* to feel his solid warmth, to hear the quiet murmurs coming from deep in his chest.

"Don't cry," he repeated. "It's okay."

"No. It's not okay," she said as the tears continued to run. "And you can't understand because you had a normal happy childhood. And now you have a family of your own. No one can understand what it's like to feel so alone."

"But I do understand. And you're not alone. I want to be your friend. That's why I bought you the painting."

"I know. And it's beautiful!" She sniffed. "It...it looks like it should have been hanging in this house all along. Why..." She choked, then started tearing up again. "Why did Edith always insist on keeping this place so damned bleak?"

"I don't know, but she's gone, bless her frozen old soul. And now the house is yours, and the painting, too. I hope you'll keep it."

"Oh, Mike. Always." She clung to his neck.

As they stood there in the soft afternoon light, Mike

held her tenderly. Her hair, he couldn't help thinking, smelled just as it had in high school. The realization rocked him as the fragrance that had to be essentially *Ann* snapped his mind back in time like a whip. Ever since she'd come back to town, he'd known he still had feelings for her. He'd known he wanted her. And he'd known he shouldn't be thinking these thoughts, but they'd formed again, whole and strong, as soon as he smelled her sweet perfume.

But his life was such a mess. He couldn't make it worse by getting involved with her. His divorce wasn't even final. And what about Ann? What about her feelings? She was vulnerable now, but she'd recover from all this eventually and go back to her senator in Washington. Mike felt a surge of protectiveness, followed by a swell of anger. Where was that guy when Ann needed him? *That's none of your business,* he warned himself, and tried to keep the hug comforting and platonic.

When he sensed that her emotions had calmed down, he patted her shoulder. "Listen." He pushed her away, gently, regretfully. "We don't want to mess up your pretty new walls trying to hang this thing. I've got a stud finder. Why don't you come over to my house with me and we'll get it," he urged. "I live right over by the church."

Ann dabbed her cheeks with fingertips and smiled. "Okay." She found herself unable to resist his constant invitations to do this and do that. In the three weeks she'd been in Medicine Creek they'd developed companionable habits. They only did simple things: grabbing a burger, trips to the hardware store, stopping to lock up the church. But those activities with Mike Kirkpatrick had become the focus of her world. She told herself it was because she felt so lonely in this oppressive old house, and because right now, she needed to be with someone. But the truth was, she didn't want to be with just anyone. She wanted to be with Mike Kirkpatrick.

HOW HAD ADA BELLE described this household? "Jumpin' like a box o' bugs"? As Ann stepped up to the two-story frame house, she wondered if Ada Belle had meant that literally.

Leaves cluttered the sidewalk, the newel posts beside the porch steps were grimy with fingerprints, and someone had picked a noticeable hole in the screen door. A Realtor lived here? A preacher?

When Mike put his key in the lock, opened the door and called out, "Dad's home!" it was obvious that disorder reigned supreme. Up the stairs a large-sounding dog barked and a door slammed. As they maneuvered through the living room, Ann noticed that sneakers and schoolbooks and soccer balls littered the floor.

Mike turned off a blaring TV that nobody was watching.

A gray-and-white-spotted mongrel dog padded down the stairs and trotted up to Mike, pushing against his leg. The animal had the wiry eyebrows and beard suggestive of wolfhound blood, but his semi-pricked ears and elongated face made him look sweet, like a collie.

When the animal tried to jump up on Ann, Mike grabbed his collar.

"Okay, Alfie! Outside!" he commanded, and the dog trotted off toward the back of the house. "I think my stud finder's under the kitchen sink," he said to Ann. "In here."

As Ann followed Mike back to the kitchen she thought, *What is that ghastly odor?* Ammonia? Acetone? Kerosene?

In the kitchen, Ann walked to the window over a sink loaded with unwashed dishes and looked out. "Where are all the kids?"

"Erin's supposed to be watching them," Mike explained as he dropped to one knee to dig around in the cabinet.

"Are they outside?"

Ann's question was immediately answered when a little cluster of children came whooping across the backyard, screeching to a halt beneath a giant old elm tree in the far corner.

The four children looked young, six or seven maybe, and Ann didn't see any twelve-year-old girl out there with them. Even though Oklahoma was experiencing an Indian summer and it was hot as blazes outside, all the children appeared to be dressed in their Halloween costumes: a gorilla, a cowboy, a ballerina, an angel. Alfie galloped up and stood expectantly beside the gorilla.

While the dog watched, the kids all fell to their knees, digging furiously in the loamy earth.

"Mike," Ann asked as she stared out, "what on earth are they doing?"

Mike, who'd pulled a rusty toolbox out, muttered, "Lord," as he straightened. "Please don't let it be anything illegal or life-threatening." He stared out the window, scratching his head. Then he raised the window and hollered, "Listen, kids! Y'all aren't supposed to be running around in those costumes till tomorrow night. Take 'em off!"

"Dad!" Ann recognized Brandon's piping voice coming from the gorilla head. "We got a dead bird here!"

Mike smiled and said thoughtfully, "Aha. The shoe box."

"Okay, then." Mike hollered back. "Just take 'em off when you're done."

"The shoe box?" Ann turned.

"The one that was missing from my closet when I changed clothes after work. Looks like a pretty fancy funeral is shaping up."

"Your children are playing *funeral?*"

At her appalled look, Mike shrugged defensively, "It's not as weird as it sounds. To a preacher's kids funerals are no big deal. I'm always doing them, so why shouldn't they? Sometimes they find dead animals out in the woods. Giving the poor creatures a proper burial is one of their favorite diversions. They get really creative about it." He gave her a sheepish grin and dropped back down to search for the stud finder.

Ann stood at the window, fascinated. Outside, the children were engaged in a loud debate about what to sing. Finally, at Brandon's command, they started marching around the yard in single file, howling ''Jingle Bells'' at the top of their lungs. After the second go-round Brandon, who was holding the shoebox aloft as ceremoniously as if it contained the remains of a pharaoh, came to a lurching halt.

''The stupid thing's not under there.'' Mike stood and headed toward the utility room. ''Lemme look back here.''

Ann nodded but kept her eyes on the spectacle outside.

''Dowwnnn he go-oes!'' Brandon intoned as he lowered the box into the hole.

''Poor birdie!'' Mary Beth, who Ann recognized in the pink ballerina costume, rushed forward, suddenly agitated. ''He's all alone!'' she wailed.

''No, he's not.'' Brandon stepped over to his sister and patted her shoulder. ''He's in bird heaven with all the other birdies.''

''That's stupid!'' the boy dressed as a cowboy said unkindly. ''There is no such thing as bird heaven.''

''Shut the heck up!'' Brandon flew at the unsympathetic boy, knocking him to the ground. They were soon locked in a wild tussle on the grass.

Their high-pitched yelling brought Mike running out of a side door shouting, ''Boys! Stop it!'' He jerked the flailing boys up by their costumes, holding them apart until they stopped their coltish kicking.

Ann watched while Mike listened, lectured, and then made the boys shake hands. She saw him gesture toward the box in the hole, and the children reassembled themselves around it.

Still scowling, Brandon grudgingly stretched his arm in front of him and shouted, "Oh, Lord! This bird is dead!" And after a long pause added, "Amen!"

The others muttered amen and fell to their knees, making a business of tamping the dirt over the box with grubby little hands. When they stood to leave, Mary Beth shouted, "Wait! We're not finished." The ballerina proceeded to do a sad, writhing dance over the fresh grave.

Finally the little gang ran toward the back gate, and Mike headed back into the house. He came up behind Ann, holding the stud finder out on his palm. "I found it."

When she turned her head, the smile he gave her looked careworn.

Ann smiled back. "That was quite a little drama out there."

Mike frowned. "It's not like Brandon to attack Kelly that way. They're best friends." He looked sadly at Ann. "My kids are having a rough time right now. They miss their mother. They don't understand why she left. Quite honestly sometimes I don't know, either."

Ann placed a gentle palm on his shoulder, but he didn't turn to face her.

"I get this close—" he made a pinch with his thumb and finger "—to forgiving Marsha, to letting go, and then my anger wells up all over again."

"That's natural," Ann said quietly. "It's been very hard on all of you."

"We're not always like this, you know." Mike examined the stud finder. "I like to think that we're basically a...happy family."

"And you will be again. You'll adjust eventually. In my work, I've seen families find all kinds of ways to heal after such a breakup." With a smile she added, "I thought the whole little scene out there—not the fight, of course—was pretty cute."

"They are cute, aren't they?" He looked out the window to the corner of the yard where the children had been.

"Very."

"Do you really think they'll be okay?"

"With time. They have each other. And they have you. I'd say that's a lot."

He turned and looked at her. His eyes were soft with gratitude. His gaze fell to her lips. He reached up and ran a fingertip just under her bottom lip. "You've got a little paint there," he said. His voice was suddenly husky. A current ran through Ann at his touch, and for a second, time was suspended. When he'd embraced her at her house earlier, Ann had felt so desolate she hadn't been aware of anything beyond comfort and solace, but suddenly with only the touch of his fingertip, she felt like a teenager again, magnetized by sudden desire.

"Dad!"

They whirled. Erin stood in the doorway with her freshly painted fingernails held aloft and her eyes burning with indignation. The air in the kitchen seemed suddenly charged with the girl's hostility.

"Erin!" Mike stepped away from Ann. "There you are."

Ann smiled at Erin, but got a defensive flinch in return.

"I was upstairs painting my nails."

"This is Ann Fischer." Mike put a palm to Ann's back. "Did you meet Ms. Fischer at Oktoberfest?"

"*Gloria* introduced us." Erin put a lot of emphasis on the name and looked pointedly at her father's arm, now braced against the counter behind Ann's back. Mike dropped it, straightened and jammed his hands into his jeans pockets.

"Yes, she did." Ann stepped forward. "How are you, Erin?"

The girl ignored Ann and glared at her father. "Dad, we're supposed to meet Gloria and go check out places for the Children's Arts Festival and the tree lighting."

"Oh, man!" Mike slapped his forehead. "I forgot." He looked down at his threadbare jeans. "Look how I'm dressed. Can you guys go on without me?"

"No, Dad, we can't! We promised Gloria." The child's voice was at once demanding and whiny. "Now hurry up and get ready."

Ann thought this daughter might need a little guidance in how to speak more respectfully to her father. But it was none of her business. "I'd better go," she said, taking the stud finder from him. "Thanks for the loan. I can just walk back to the house, Mike. You go and get ready."

Mike shrugged apologetically and went upstairs. Ann faced Erin, who studied her nails intently.

"You know," Ann started, "I was telling Susie Hobbs that I'd be happy to have the arts festival in the pecan grove this year, or even in my house if the weather's bad."

"That place is spooky." Erin frowned and licked a nail. "I've gotta get ready."

"Well, Erin, it was nice to see you again." Ann tried to end the encounter on a cheery note. "Good luck in finding a place for your event."

Without answering, Erin turned on her heel and disappeared in the direction of the stairs.

ANN FORGOT ABOUT the girl's rude behavior until two days later when she took her morning coffee out onto the porch.

"What the…" she gasped as she stepped out the door.

The freshly stripped floor of the porch was covered with a gooey mess of broken eggs, bits of shell sticking out here and there.

Her gaze was caught by a pink piece of paper, fluttering in the morning breeze. It was attached to the sanded newel post with a thumbtack. She crossed the porch, being careful not to slip on the egg.

Fingers trembling with fury or fear, she couldn't tell which, Ann snatched up the paper and read the typeset message: ''This house is hawnted.'' Erin's words. Suddenly the girl's hostile face came to mind. Ann forced the image away. Surely Mike's daughter hadn't done this. No, it was probably just a random Halloween prank. In fact, Ann decided, she wouldn't even mention it to Mike.

CHAPTER THIRTEEN

ANN MET THE LAST of the Kirkpatrick kids, the infamous Zack, at her open house the following Sunday.

The weather hadn't cooperated. Indian summer had come to an abrupt halt with thunderstorms and chilling rains that very morning. Ann hadn't packed many clothes—none for colder weather—and she debated about hosting an open house in sweats. In the end she was forced to launder one of Edith's old red turtlenecks and layered it under the navy blazer she'd worn on the plane. Jeans, loafers and white socks completed the outfit.

"You look nice," Mike said when he arrived. He was wearing a suit.

"Not too casual?" Ann looked down at her attire.

"No. Not that you didn't look great in that black dress this morning, but it would only remind people that the house and all the junk in it belonged to a dead woman. And that's the very idea we're trying to overcome."

He walked over to swipe a cookie off the breakfront.

He'd seen her in the black dress? She'd sat way in the back, hoping not to be noticed this time—by him or anybody else.

He crammed the cookie into his mouth, chewing and humming as he spread the promotional materials about the house on the table.

He didn't seem to think anything of her second appearance at his church. His sermon had been uplifting and flawless today. She supposed, eventually, he'd have to get used to having her there. *Eventually?* Eventually meant ultimately, finally. Eventually sounded like the future. Why was she thinking like this? She shook her head to clear it.

Despite the weather, plenty of folks showed up in their raincoats and church clothes for the afternoon event.

Zack Kirkpatrick arrived around three o'clock. He was a big boy with well-defined muscles. He smiled a lot, and the other people milling around in the living room all seemed to recognize him. He had another boy with him. Probably Laurie's son, Trent. Ann smiled, Laurie hadn't mentioned Trent's spiky hair— dyed bright blue across the top.

The two of them waved to the other people in the room and made their way right up to Ann.

"Ms. Fischer?" the big, broad-shouldered redhead said. "I'm Zack Kirkpatrick." A lady-killer smile, complete with dimples. Like his buddy, his hair was gelled up in twisted spikes. "And this is Trent Harris."

"Hi, boys." Ann gave them each a quick handshake. "Your mom and I were best friends in high school," she informed Trent with a smile.

"Yeah." Trent gave her his own very charming

grin, shyer than Zack's, but equally lethal. "Mom told me."

"We came to see your house. Dad said it was okay."

"Feel free to look around."

They made a beeline for the cookies on the dining-room sideboard first. Ann turned her attention to an older couple from Dallas who were considering putting a bed-and-breakfast in the area if the outlet mall became a reality. They wanted to see the back of the property, so Ann fetched one of Edith's many umbrellas and took them outside.

Later she saw the boys talking to Mike by the fireplace. The three of them were looking at the picture of June Starr. Ann couldn't hear what Mike was saying, but Zack had a solemn expression on his young face that touched her heart. The boy was the spitting image of his father as a teenager. Suddenly she wondered how she would feel if Zack were hers. Proud. Of course, any son of hers would have her dark coloring, wouldn't he? Her Chickasaw blood? Why was she thinking along these lines?

Mike and the boys ambled outside, and Ann crossed the room to stand in front of the picture of June. She wondered again, as she studied her mother's exotic features, what her own children might look like. Then she noticed a tiny triangle of pink sticking out from under the frame. Her heart drummed a warning as she slid the paper out and read the message. This one was no random prank—this one was personal.

MIKE UNFOLDED the piece of pink paper Ann handed him. "Get the heck out of town if you know whats good for you."

"Interesting," he said, giving it back.

"Is this kind of thing typical for this town?"

"Nah. Usually if they don't like you, they just egg your porch." He smiled.

"My porch did get hit with the eggs, actually. On Halloween. The night after the painters stripped the porch? And there was a note then, too. On the same pink paper."

"Really?" Mike's casual attitude abruptly evaporated. "What did that one say?"

"'Your house is haunted.' But I didn't keep it."

"Why didn't you tell me about it?"

"I thought it was just a prank, being Halloween and all."

"Hmm." Mike frowned, thinking. "You don't suppose Cagle could be behind this?"

"On pink paper?"

"Good point." Mike took the note again. "Do you want me to call the sheriff and report it?"

"I don't think that's necessary. It's probably another prank. Unless…"

"Unless what?"

"Do you think it might have something to do with the pecan-grove controversy?"

Mike was still frowning at the note. "People are awfully churned up about that. But this looks pretty juvenile."

Ann's mind flashed back to the angry expression

on Erin's face the day Mike had touched Ann's lip in his kitchen. Erin and her friend Josie had popped in briefly to ask Mike for some movie money. Ann looked at the note one more time before putting it back up on the mantel. "It's so *odd*. All these people were in here. It gives me the creeps."

"I know. Still, it does look like just another prank. I'd ignore it."

But Ann couldn't ignore the notes that followed. By Wednesday of the next week there had been three more:

Someone is waching you.
Your making a majer mestake.
You will regrett it if you stay here.

"Notice a pattern here?" Ann asked when she handed Mike the most recent one. She'd found it under the windshield wiper of her rental car. They were alone in Edith's living room, having just shown the last prospective buyer of the day out the door.

"Pink paper, terrible spelling." Mike sighed. "I believe I've got our culprit." He folded the note. "I suspect Erin wrote these."

Ann remained silent.

"Her English teacher is always saying that Erin is very creative, but that she's weak in spelling and grammar. And this paper's from Gloria's shop. I checked. Gloria has a computer down there and lets Erin use it sometimes."

"You're sure about this?"

"I'm afraid so. May I keep the note?" Mike held it between two fingers.

Ann nodded. "What are you going to do?"

"For starters, I'm going to question her. If I'm right, she's going to apologize. Then she'll be grounded for a month." He turned to leave.

"Mike, wait." Ann grabbed his arm. "Don't you see?" she implored. "She's only a child. In her eyes, I'm an intruder—one more person taking a piece of you. Your children already feel abandoned by one parent. And lately I've been occupying a lot of your time. Isn't there some other way to handle this?"

Mike planted his hands on his belt and sighed again. "Other people occupy my time, and Erin doesn't send nasty little notes to *them*. She doesn't resent Gloria like this."

"Gloria's different."

"From you? That's an understatement."

Ann gave Mike a surprised look, and he felt his neck turning red. He hadn't meant to say that—not with so much feeling. To cover his embarrassment, he shook his head ruefully, looking down at his shoes. "Like I said, if it were just a matter of resenting an intrusion, why isn't Erin hostile to Gloria? Or the people in my congregation? Or my other high-priority clients?"

"Erin is used to those people. Gloria, for example, is like part of your family. She's a friend. I'm the new woman in town, the outsider."

"No. That's not it."

"It isn't?"

"No. I'll tell you what I think. Erin is pretty sharp, and she can see that..." He hesitated, wondering if this was fair to Gloria. But maybe it was time to take a stand. "I think Erin can see that I'm not falling in love with Gloria, according to The Grand Plan." He made quote marks with his fingers. "Instead, I'm falling in love with—" He cut himself off and a loaded silence filled the air, while their resisting minds grappled with the truth.

Their eyes finally met and he took a step toward her. She shook her head slowly as if she could forestall what was about to come. But it was too late. It was as if a shaft of revealing light had shot into the air around them. And neither could deny its presence.

"It's true," he said, and his voice became so strangled with passion he couldn't say more.

She turned her head and closed her eyes. *No.* This was all wrong. She couldn't get involved with—fall in love with—Mike Kirkpatrick. They lived in different worlds—different universes. And he and Gloria... "But you and Gloria are—"

"Gloria and I are...truthfully, I don't know what we are." He studied Ann's face. "All I know is that I never wanted to do *this* to Gloria." He grabbed Ann's shoulders and pulled her roughly to him as his mouth—hot and demanding—claimed hers.

First kisses were bound to make an impression. That was how she'd rationalized her first kiss with Mike Kirkpatrick back in high school. She'd only remembered it because it had been her first. But the truth was no one had ever made her feel the way he did.

She groaned and he responded by thrusting his tongue more deeply into her mouth, and her whole body came alive. He wrapped her more tightly in his arms, and she marveled that she seemed to be able to feel his passion as clearly as she could feel her own. But they shouldn't, *couldn't* be together—for so many reasons.

"Mike—" she broke free "—wait. Stop a minute."

"No," he murmured against her lips. "I don't want to wait and you don't want me to." He angled his mouth over hers again. And again she succumbed like a woman dying of thirst, quenched at last.

He pulled her down on the couch against his muscular body as they kissed again. And again. Their bodies twisted in the effort to be even closer. He clasped her face in his hands, holding it still, so that he could kiss her the way he wanted to. They kissed wildly. Endlessly. For now, there was no spying Edith to stop them. There was no possessive high-school girlfriend. There was only—*a hostile town, a divided congregation and five hurting children.*

Ann broke away and pushed on his chest, feeling his heart thudding under her palm. "Mike, no."

"What's wrong?" He looked dazed, dreamy, as if he didn't want to focus on anything but the next kiss, the next touch.

She eased herself out of his arms. "Go home to your children. Think about this. Think about what you really want." She stood up and turned her back to him.

"All right." His voice was low, calm, as if he'd regained his senses. "If that's what you want. I'll think about it." She heard him get up from the couch. "But I already know what I want." He waited, and when she didn't turn around, he said, "I want *you*."

"Yes, but for how long?" She still wouldn't let herself look at him. "How long can you and I sustain a relationship? Think about that. Think about how I don't fit into this town, into your life."

She held her breath, listening, but behind her there was only silence.

Say something! Ann thought. *Tell me how wrong I am!* But he didn't. She heard his footsteps then, and the creak of the old door as he carefully closed it.

CHAPTER FOURTEEN

MIKE DID GO HOME to his children. And to Gloria.

Her minivan was in the driveway. As he walked past it and read the stenciling on the door—Gloria's Secret Garden—he wondered if parking her business vehicle in his driveway—she also owned a nondescript Saturn—was just one more of Gloria's signals to the people of this town that he was involved with her. But no more.

When he walked in the front door, Mary Beth—keeping her eyes on the cartoons on TV—informed him that Gloria was upstairs fixing Erin's hair for the school dance, an event Mike had totally forgotten about. He'd been too busy dealing with the church board, too busy hustling real-estate deals, too busy falling in love with Ann Fischer to think about what was going on in his own daughter's life. Discouraged, he went to the kitchen to wait.

Gloria finally came into the kitchen to check on a roast that was baking in the oven. It smelled delicious.

"Hi, Mike. I told your mom to go on home and that I would be happy to fix Erin's hair tonight." Gloria bustled cheerfully about the small space, grabbing oven mitts and a ladle, then crossed around behind him as he braced his palms on the counter and stared out into the darkening backyard.

"And I hope you don't mind that I went ahead and put this roast on. It just seemed easier that way tonight—to have something come-and-go in the oven. I swear, this is the busiest family! But as soon as we take Erin over to the Johnsons' for group picture taking—Herbie Morgan is her date for this do—then you and I can run back here and have a nice quiet dinner together. I already fed the little kids. Joseph's at work. God knows where Zack is. Have you seen him?"

Mike took a deep breath. "Gloria, why don't you go on and eat if you want to. I have go upstairs and talk to Erin for a minute, and when I come back down here, you and I need to discuss something... important."

Gloria pressed her mitt-covered hands against her chest and leaned around to examine his face. "Is something wrong? You actually look pale, Mike. Is everything okay?"

He pulled the pink note from his pocket. "Erin has been writing poison-pen notes to Ann Fischer."

Gloria jerked off a mitt, took the note and read it. She pursed her lips and handed it back.

"Have you any idea why she did this?" he asked. "What did Ann Fischer ever do to Erin?"

Gloria ignored the reference to Ann. "Erin shouldn't have done it, but must you go and jump down her throat about it right now? It's her first dance. She's all dressed up. We're taking her over to her friends. Can't you wait and we'll talk—"

"Not *we*. I want to talk to Erin privately," he said, and turned to face Gloria. "And later, after I've talked to her, *I* will take my daughter over to the Johnsons'—" He stopped himself, realizing how unreasonable he must sound. For one moment the familiar feeling of guilt about Gloria rose in him, arguing that she was only trying to be helpful. But why did she insist on inserting herself like this? Gloria didn't discourage easily, but Mike knew he had to be honest with her.

"I'm sorry, Gloria." He put his palms up. "I'm sorry. I can't...I can't do this anymore."

Gloria looked perplexed and genuinely hurt. "Can't do...? I don't understand."

"I'm sorry, Gloria, but it might be better if you leave now." He crossed the few feet to her and gently tried to take the oven mitts from her, but she backed away from him, clutching the mitts to her chest.

"I'm sorry," he repeated, really meaning it. "I'm sorry you cooked this roast. And I'm sorry Erin has become so dependent on you." He couldn't stop the words as they poured out in a torrent of painful truth. "I'm sorry I let you do things for my kids that I couldn't do. I'm sorry I've been so lonely and weak that I didn't face the truth about us sooner. I'm sorry about a lot of things, Gloria, but I can't go on like this, pretending."

At that, Gloria gasped and gave her head a tiny shake.

"Gloria, listen. I don't want to hurt you—"

"*Pretending?*"

"Yes, for want of a better word. We've been pretending that this cozy little setup is headed somewhere when it isn't. I've been unfair to you. You cook roasts, and I eat them. We drive Erin over to the Johnsons' together. Gloria! We never should have started doing these things—acting like a family—until we knew how we felt about each other."

"No!" Gloria backed up some more.

Mike let out a whoosh of pent-up breath. "I should never have let things get this far. Not when I...not when I don't have those kinds of feelings for you."

"No!" Gloria repeated. "We were fine. We were getting along just fine, you and me and the kids, until that woman came to town. That's what this is about, isn't it? It's about *her!*"

"No. This is about us. I want to be your friend, but I don't want to be your husband. I should have told you this—should have admitted it to myself—a long time ago. But I kept waiting for my feelings to...to deepen or something. You're a fine person, Gloria. A good woman. But I don't love you. You deserve better than that. I'm so sorry."

"No!" Gloria shouted, this time with real vehemence. "I won't listen to this! Not when you are finally about to get your divorce! I've been waiting for so long. Can't you see that? And then this...this strange woman comes to town. Out of the blue. What is she to you, anyway?" She flapped her hands, cutting off his answer. "You can't do this to me!"

"Gloria, please—"

"And of all the nights to bring this up! When Erin is going to her first dance!"

"There's really never a good time for these things, Gloria."

She threw the oven mitts at his chest. "You really are as selfish and egotistical as...as..." She sputtered to a stop, struggling to compose herself. When she started in again, it was with renewed venom. "Julius Harn tried to warn us all. He wanted to bring in a new preacher months ago, to force you to take a leave of absence. But no! I defended you! I said you loved the church! But the truth is, you don't love anyone but yourself, Mike Kirkpatrick, and you never have. No wonder Marsha left you!"

Gloria whirled and fled to the front of the house. Mike followed her.

In the living room, she snatched up her purse and jacket and jerked open the door. When she hesitated for an instant with her back to him, Mike had the urge to ask her to come back inside and talk this out, but, he realized, he had no right to ask anything of her. And there was nothing more to say, anyway. A clean break might be the best for everyone concerned.

"Where are you going, Gloria?" Mary Beth looked up innocently from her position in front of the television.

Gloria turned and stared down at the child as if only now realizing she was in the room. Her eyes raised to Mike. "You are going to regret this." Her tone was low, quieter now, and sounded more threatening than if she'd been screaming at the top of her lungs. "That woman is all wrong for you and she will make you miserable."

The door slammed and Gloria Miller was gone.

"What woman, Daddy?" Mary Beth asked innocently.

"Um. A lady. A lady at church." It wasn't a total lie. Ann had been at church a few times. "Gloria doesn't think she can help me."

"Oh." Mary Beth turned back to the TV. Mike stared at her thin hunched back, feeling bad for misleading his little girl, but also angry with Gloria for not controlling herself in front of the child.

Mike dialed up his mom, got no answer and spent fifteen tense minutes scrounging up a sitter for the little ones, the whole time mentally railing at Zack for never being around when he needed him. Then he went up and knocked on Erin's door.

He could hardly swallow past the lump that formed in his throat when he laid eyes on his daughter. His little Erin looked all grown up. She wore a mint-green princess-style dress with tiny iridescent flowers embossed on the fabric. Gloria had swept the front half of her hair up and anchored it in odd places here and there with delicate, sparkling butterfly clips.

When she smiled, the peachy lip gloss on her mouth shimmered softly. "Hi, Daddy," she said shyly. "Do you like it?" She fanned her short skirt out in a curtsy motion.

Mike decided Gloria had been right about one thing. This was not the time to confront Erin about the notes. This child had had enough shocks and disappointments in the past year. Even Ann had urged him to table the matter and show some understanding for the underlying pain that had caused Erin to act so inappropriately.

When he stepped forward and hugged his daughter, he wished she were a little girl again, instead of this half-woman, half-child who came up to his chin. He wished he could take away all her hurt and insecurity and keep her safe forever.

"Dad, don't muss my hair!" Erin stepped back.

He smiled and told her she looked pretty. He made some lame excuse about Gloria not feeling well. He answered the door when the sitter came, then took Erin to the Johnsons', where he shook hands with the other parents. He snapped pictures of Erin's gang of friends and thanked Herbie's parents for offering to pick the kids up from the dance.

On the way home, it started to rain, only a light fall drizzle, but the moody weather was enough to make Mike turn his pickup off at the Council Street entrance to the pecan grove. It was as if somebody else was doing the driving. And that somebody else was a cocky but tormented sixteen-year-old kid named Mickey Kirkpatrick.

He got out and slammed the door of the truck with extra gusto as if to prove to himself that he had nothing to hide. He was, after all, the agent selling this lot.

The moon shone full behind thin clouds, and there was enough of a chill in the air that he wished he'd worn his trench coat over his suit jacket. But then, he

hadn't known he'd be stopping in the pecan grove to
brood. What was he doing out here, anyway? But on
some level he already knew the answer.

A nighttime mist, perennial in this grove after the
autumn rains had started, hovered between the large
tree trunks and swirled away from his feet as he
walked over the damp grass to the spot. He remembered it—the exact spot.

When he reached the tree where they'd kissed so
long ago, he put his palm on the bark, closed his eyes
and let himself remember how she'd felt. How she'd
smelled. How she'd fit against his body as if she had
been sculpted just for him. He remembered how holding her had been such an amazing thrill. The chest-
to-chest, hip-to-hip glory of full human contact. Face-
to-face.

Heart-to-heart.

He lowered his head, doubled forward with the
most intense longing he had ever felt and drew in
great gulps of the misty air. All those years—lost.

What would have happened if he'd been more honest with Ann Fischer—and with himself—back then?
Maybe that was why he'd been so abrupt with poor
Gloria this evening. Fear. Fear that once again he'd
nearly allowed himself to be manipulated into a relationship that was wrong for him.

With Marsha he'd had the mistaken notion that
great sex could be a balm for their serious differences,
and with Gloria, he'd tried to tell himself the opposite—that sex wasn't all that important as long as they
were so compatible.

But neither was true.

Either way, a man ended up with a sad kind of half-happiness that didn't satisfy his soul. Neither relationship—the lusty one with Marsha or the sanguine one with Gloria—held everything he needed.

Because what he needed, in a word, was *Ann.* But why? He couldn't even articulate it. On the surface they seemed so different. She was sophisticated, urbane. He was small-town and folksy. He liked to plop on the couch with a hot dog and watch a good ball game on TV. She probably liked to nibble pasta salad in an art gallery café. She had a cat. And he had— he smiled to himself—good old Alfie. She didn't have any kids. And he had a houseful. None of it made sense, but despite the surface differences, all he knew was, she fit.

They fit.

And they always had.

The cold wind picked up, setting the tops of the pecan trees to bending and whispering. The mist on the ground swirled, running ahead of the coming storm. Mike shuddered and raised his head. He buttoned his jacket and turned the collar up against the shifting wind. He'd always tried to do the right thing. But had it been right to keep Marsha trapped in a life she clearly hated? Had it been right to keep company with Gloria out of simple convenience?

And was it right to feel as strongly as he did about Ann Fischer and deny it? If only he'd had the guts to be more honest with himself back when he'd first realized how he felt about Ann—right under this old pecan tree—they might not be struggling to make their lives mesh together now.

And no matter how he felt about Ann, she might still reject him. She could say—sensibly—that it was too late. That their lives could never blend now. She might not even—he felt his chest tighten at this thought—she might not even want to be a preacher's wife. She might want to be a senator's wife, after all.

It was crazy to go and confess his love for a woman when he had no idea how she felt about him. But he loved her too much not to try. And this was true love, he was certain of it. And another thing he was certain of: he wasn't going to let the opportunity for true love slip through his fingers again.

CHAPTER FIFTEEN

THE FIRST DROPS of rain spattered through the tall trees as he walked toward the old house. He hoped she was home.

The chandelier in the dining room shone pale yellow through the bare windows, casting an inviting glow into the rainy darkness. As Mike stepped onto the curb, he spotted Ann through the bushes. She was sitting at the table, with her back to the bow window. Was she eating? Doing paperwork? Was he coming to her at a bad time? Was there ever a good time for bursting in on someone and laying your heart on the line?

Lightning flashed, thunder boomed and the dark sky opened up. The rain beat down in thick sheets as he trotted up the sidewalk and took the porch steps in two giant strides. He stood before her door, while the rain pounded on the porch roof and his heart pounded in his chest. He felt young and vulnerable. Finally he shook off the water, raked his wet hair back and banged the knocker three times.

When she opened the door, she breathed, "Mike," as if she suspected that his unannounced reappearance at her door held some kind of import.

She had obviously bathed and changed clothes. Her

face was scrubbed pink and shiny, and she was wearing an oversize T-shirt and black leggings. Her damp hair was freed from its usual clip and contrasted, lustrous and black, against the clean white shirt. He glanced down—he couldn't help it—and saw her dark nipples pressing against the thin fabric. She was braless. She was also barefoot and was, he thought, the most erotic vision of a woman he had ever seen.

For one brief heartbeat he looked into her eyes thinking, *This is crazy.* Then he took that fateful step over the threshold and pulled her into his arms. He didn't give her a chance to utter a single syllable of protest before he kissed her.

This time he wasn't going to let anything stop him. He wasn't going to let her talk them out of their love as she had before.

He felt her trying to step back, but he held her more tightly to his chest, his belly, his already aching erection. Her hands found their way up inside his rain-dampened jacket, around to his back, and while he focused all his passion on her mouth again, her fingers curled and gripped his muscles. She managed another breathy ''Mike'' when he angled his head the other way for better access. He said ''no'' and kissed her even harder.

When he could feel that she was no longer resisting, he framed her face with his hands and said, ''I love you.''

She closed her eyes and swallowed.

He kept his hands where they were and pressed his arms into her breasts and danced her one step back, kicking the door shut against the wet darkness while he kept his eyes on her beautiful, beautiful face. The living room was lit only by distant flashes of lightning—and the light from the dining room—but he could read her expression clearly.

"Open your eyes," he said. "Are you going to marry him?"

"What?" A tiny crease formed between her brows, and she seemed confused.

He reached down and grabbed her left hand, then raised it into the air beside their heads, making the giant diamond flash. "The senator."

"Why are you asking me that?" Ann tried to squirm away from him, but he grasped her by the shoulders and brought their faces close again.

"Are you going to marry him or not? And if you are, why do you keep kissing me like that? Answer me!" He gave her shoulders a small shake.

"I don't...I don't know," was her answer.

"That's what I thought." He dropped his hands from her shoulders and backed up a step. He ran his hands through his hair, pulling his scalp tight, then turned away. His voice was dry, tortured. "We're running around this town pretending to be friends when we're both so attracted to each other that we ache." He whirled and pointed at her. "And don't you deny it."

"All right, I won't. I won't deny the attraction." Ann held her hands forth in placation. "I admit I've always been attracted to you. Okay? Is that what you need to hear? Okay then. But just because we felt that way back in high school, that doesn't say anything about now. Now, even if the attraction is still there, we have separate lives. I mean, good Lord, we barely know each other.''

''That's ridiculous! We know enough. We know we want to be together again. As for the rest, how are we supposed to get to know each other if I don't…if I can't…court you?''

''*Court* me?''

''Yes! Court you! Openly. Honestly. Like normal people. Here you are back in this town, and I can hardly think of anything else, and I have to keep making up stupid excuses to be with you. I want to just go to the movies with you, take long drives, wade in the creeks in Chickasaw Park, have an ice-cream cone on the bench in front of the firehouse, hold your hand during one of Zack's basketball games. I want to be *normal*.'' He paused, calming himself, and swallowed. ''No, I want more than all of that. Ann, the truth is, I love you desperately, and because I love you, I want to make love to you.''

Tears stung at Ann's eyes. Love? As soon as he'd said the word, the future flashed before her eyes. Living in this town with its bad memories. Giving up her career. Trying to be a stepmother to his kids. ''If it were only that simple,'' she said.

''For me it is. Because I've never felt this way before, except when we were together that time in the pecan grove. Do you remember that?''

Remember it? For years she hadn't been able to get

that night out of her mind. "Of course I remember," she whispered.

"Then what's holding you back. *Him?*" He grabbed her left hand again.

"No!" She jerked her hand away, stripped off the ring and held it up in front of his nose. "But this doesn't concern you, and I don't want to discuss it with you until I discuss it with him. Face-to-face."

Mike blanched. "Then what's stopping you?" he said quietly.

Ann waited, trying to form an answer. He deserved an answer. "Fear, I guess."

"Fear of what?"

"Fear of what will happen if we do this, fear of holding you and never wanting to let you go, fear of having you in my blood until the day I die!"

Mike studied her with narrowed eyes, and in the oblique golden light she noticed every detail of his face. The sandpapery russet stubble on his cleft chin. The crease between his brows. The deep lines that bracketed his solemn mouth. That mouth. She looked down.

"I had a life before I came here!"

"Was it a life filled with love?" he said. "Because I do love you."

"Oh, God!" She covered her face. It was a prayer. A plea that God would stop them, help them, make them sane and sensible. But then Mike touched her again.

He squeezed her arms and said, "I love you, and now I'm old enough, wise enough, to know how rare and precious these feelings are. And after sixteen years of living without that kind of love, I don't want to live without it any longer. And I'm betting you've been thinking the same thing since you've come back here. Haven't you?"

She dropped her hands, looked in his eyes and nodded.

He kissed her again, sucking the very breath out of her with his pent-up frustration and need.

When they stopped, she whispered, "Oh, God," again and collapsed against him. "We can't let ourselves fall in love."

"Why not?" He held her tenderly, pressing her head into his shoulder and stroking her hair. She could feel his barely restrained desire in his fingertips as strongly as she could feel her own. "Why not?" he repeated.

"Because…because you're a preacher now with five kids, that's why."

He frowned down at her. "So?"

"That is your calling—you told me so yourself— and those children have to come first, certainly before acting on some…some high-school crush."

He pressed his lips to her forehead. "Is that all you think this is?"

"I don't know what it is, and you don't, either," she said miserably. "It's too soon, Mike. Too soon to know anything."

He pushed her away from him and looked into her face. "Okay, then let's find out what it is. But that can't happen if we don't spend time together. And you can't get to know my kids any other way, either. That's all I'm asking. Give us some time. And don't throw the fact that I'm a preacher up to me again. Surely you aren't saying that a man of God isn't entitled to feel passion, to fall in love?''

''Mike. Be reasonable.''

''Listen.'' He stroked her beautiful mahogany hair back over her temple and pressed his hand firmly at the base of her skull. ''I am being reasonable. Because I know how I feel. This isn't about sex. I've had great sex, and maybe you have, too. But this is about *so much more* than sex.'' He pressed his fingers into her neck and touched their foreheads together.

''I know,'' she whispered.

''Then let's stop kidding ourselves. Okay?''

She nodded—that was all, just a small hesitant nod—but it was enough.

He kissed her again and this one was instantly demanding. She met that demand with demands of her own. The kiss deepened, hungry tongues stroking, pulling for more. Searching for everything they had missed.

When breath became a necessity, he stopped and gazed down into her eyes. She was breathing hard, as he was, and in the glow from the dining room he could see that her skin was flushed. He raised his chin and released an enormous breath over her brow. ''I'm going to go in there and turn off that light.''

''I understand. You don't want the whole town seeing us like this.''

''No. I don't care if the whole town knows about

us.'' He paused, fighting to control his harsh breathing. ''It's just that, now, I'm going to do things with you that I would never want to share with another living soul.''

CHAPTER SIXTEEN

ON SATURDAY MORNING, Mike found Steve Harris out in his north pasture digging a posthole. As Mike picked his way across the field in his business suit and loafers, Steve stood still, one arm braced on the digger.

"Can you take a coffee break?" Mike called, holding up two foam cups.

"Sure!" Steve called back. "What're you all duded up for?" he said when Mike reached him.

"The board had an 8 a.m. meeting."

"How'd it go? Did Gloria finally convince 'em to go for the land?"

"I'm starting to wonder if Gloria really wants me to build that church. Anyway, no, she didn't even show up at the meeting. Gloria and I...I think I hurt her very badly last night."

"Let's take a load off."

They sat on the tailgate of Steve's pickup.

"I'm in love," Mike announced after his first sip of coffee. "With Ann."

"Ah," Steve said. "Now that's complicated."

"That's what *she* said, but I don't care. I think I've finally found... I can't explain it. Did I ever tell you I had a big crush on her in high school?"

"Skinny little Annie?"

Mike smiled, remembering. "You saw skinny. I saw delicate and feminine. Even in high school, I felt like I'd been hit by a truck every time she was within ten feet of me. Now it's a thousand times worse. I'm telling you, Steve, being near her again this last month has been amazing. I think I've finally found the woman I truly love."

Steve studied his friend with a deepening frown. "Come to think of it, I sensed something when you two were sitting in that booth with me in the Pie a couple of days after she hit town. A body'd have to be deaf, dumb and blind not to see the sparks between you two. And if you are falling in love with that woman, then, buddy, you'd better watch out. You'd better slow down. She's no ordinary woman. And a man in your state of mind might do something stupid."

"Thanks for the helpful lecture."

"I charge by the hour." Steve sipped his coffee. "What about Gloria?"

"That's what Ann said, too. Fortunately I had the sense to call it quits with Gloria before I went back to Ann's last night."

"You called it quits?"

"Yep."

"Man. What'd Gloria do?"

"Left my house with her feelings all hurt. I haven't talked to her since, but I'm sure she'll stay angry for quite a while."

Steve nodded. "The woman scorned and all."

"Yeah." Mike sighed. "Well, I think I know what I'm gonna do. I'm gonna tell the kids first. Then on Sunday…"

Mike paused and Steve guessed maybe this was the real reason Mike had walked all the way out to the north pasture.

"I'm thinking about telling the congregation that I need some time off. I'm sure they're not gonna appreciate it that their preacher is dating a woman from Washington, D.C., who's not committed to their church."

"You're not thinking of resigning, are you?"

"From the ministry? Never. Not permanently, anyway. But I am seriously considering taking some time off. I could focus on selling real estate, on my kids and on Ann." He gave his friend a sharp look, as if reading his thoughts. "This is what I want, Steve. I've always loved Ann. I see that now. And I'm not gonna let the love of my life get away again."

"And what about Ann? How does she feel? What about this senator Laurie told me about?"

"I didn't press her about that."

Steve jutted his head forward, eyes wide. "Well, maybe you oughtta."

"I can't tell her what to do about that. She has to decide. And I can't ask her to give up her secure successful life in Washington after only one night of…passion."

Steve cocked an eyebrow.

"Don't look at me like that."

"Don't have enough kids, do you?"

"You think I'd make that mistake again? Fortunately Ann put the brakes on until I came to my senses. I wanted to stay with her, but she finally made me go home."

Steve nodded. "She's a smart woman."

"You bet she is."

"Awful smart."

"Now what're you getting at?"

"Well, like I said, Ann's special. I'm just wondering, what's a woman like Ann gonna do with herself in a backwater town like Medicine Creek?"

"Are you telling me a smart woman can't be happy living in a small town? What's that say about Laurie?"

"Laurie's different. She never left this place and her whole family lives here. She loves this town. Same way I do. Same way you do. But Ann doesn't. Ann doesn't have any family or anything else to keep her here."

"She's got me. I love her, and if she decided to live here, she'd also have my folks, my brothers and sisters, you and Laurie."

"Well, sure she would. But what about a job? I'm sure her life in D.C. is a sight more exciting than...Oktoberfest." Steve snorted.

"She told me she had fun!" Mike argued. But then his shoulders slumped and he sighed. "You're right."

"You gotta accept her the way she is, buddy."

"I know. I'm not going to make that mistake again, either. You know my history with Marsha better than anybody. I swore I'd never attempt to mold another person to my way of life again.''

"Hey, man." Steve clamped a consoling hand on Mike's shoulder. "That thing with Marsha wasn't all your fault, not by a long shot. Marsha was spoiled rotten by her mama and daddy, if you ask me. And she could have told you, a lot sooner than fifteen years and five kids down the road, that she wanted a different kind of life than what Medicine Creek offered. You would've tried to make her happy, I imagine, if she'd told you the truth.''

"Maybe. But I love Medicine Creek and I wouldn't want to live anywhere else. The trouble is, Medicine Creek holds a lot of bad memories for Ann. In the end she's going to have to be the one to decide, of her own free will, if she wants a life here with me. I can't force her about that.''

"A *life?* Is this thing that serious?''

"It is for me.''

"Man. I hope you know what you're doing.''

"If I knew what I was doing—" Mike grinned "—I wouldn't be wading through cow patties in the middle of the day to talk to my best buddy about it.''

They laughed and downed the last of their coffee.

As Mike headed back to the road, he thought how nice it would be if everyone in town could be as non-judgmental and easygoing as Steve Harris. Steve would support him no matter what he decided. No matter how this thing with Ann turned out. Unfortunately the rest of the town might not view his involvement with Ann Fischer as benevolently. But what he did with Ann Fischer was his own business, and, by George, he was going to keep it that way.

WHICH WAS NEXT to impossible in a town like Medicine Creek. Within the week Mike and Ann had been sighted picnicking in the Arbuckle Mountains State Park, at the movies down in Ardmore and holding hands on a Main Street sidewalk.

Gloria abruptly withdrew from the Children's Arts Festival committee, and Susie Hobbs brought Ann on. The pecan grove was confirmed as the location. As she made the arrangements, Ann got more excited about the event every day. She hurried her downstairs renovations along in case the weather grew too cold or damp. She started to get to know people in town as she lined up sponsors.

One day Erin and two of her friends showed up at Ann's on their bikes.

Ann showed them in. "This dining room is so pretty!" one of the girls gushed.

"Feel free to look around," Ann said. When the other two girls went into the dining room to look at the painting, Erin hung back. "This place is pretty," she said. Her tone was flat.

"I just hope I can get it ready in time for the arts festival."

"It's a big job," Erin allowed.

"Yes." Ann waited. The girl obviously had something on her mind.

"I can't believe Gloria bailed out on us like that." Erin avoided Ann's eyes.

"Mm." Ann didn't know what to say to that, and felt herself freezing up. She hated her inadequacy with children. "Would you girls like some cookies?"

"Not me." Erin shifted from foot to foot.

The other two girls came back. "Ready?" one said.

"You guys go on," Erin said. "I have to talk to Ms. Fischer."

"Erin, won't you call me Ann?" Ann said, after the other girls closed the front door.

"Okay." But Erin wouldn't look at her.

"Would you like to sit down?"

"No." The child stiffened and closed her eyes. "My dad says I have to apologize for sending you those notes and egging your house," she said in a breathless rush.

Ann splayed a palm on her breastbone. "Oh, I see," she said quietly. She took a step toward the tense girl. "Erin—"

"I have to go." Erin started for the door.

"Erin, please wait!"

The child turned around. Her blue eyes, so like Mike's, were wary, mistrustful, as she regarded Ann.

"Did you see this picture of my mother—" Ann crossed to the mantel and picked it up "—when you were at the open house?" Ann held it out. "Here."

Erin took it, reluctantly, Ann thought, and studied June's young face. "She's pretty," she said dully.

"I barely knew her. She died when I was five."

Erin's blue eyes flashed up, full of questions.

"Would you like to sit down?"

They sat with knees toward each other on Edith's

saggy couch while Ann told the whole story, and the child, silent, clutched the picture in her hands, studying Ann with increasingly sympathetic eyes.

When Ann was done, Erin Kirkpatrick, her tears brimming, had only one question. "Does it ever stop hurting?"

The next day, Ann found another pink note in her screen door. "Don't worry about the arts festifall. I have confidents in you." Ann decided to save this one forever.

MEANWHILE THE TOWNSFOLK talked. And talked and talked.

But Mike discovered he didn't care. One evening he dusted off his old tux, bought flowers—from a shop in Sulphur, not at Gloria's—and stopped at the Pie for two "specials" and two slices of coconut-cream pie to go.

"Dinner!" he said as he held the sack of food and the flowers aloft when Ann answered the door. She eyed the tux and shook her head in smiling disbelief.

Inside, he got dinner on the table while she dashed upstairs to change.

Ann switched on a lamp and felt a rush of giddiness. She bit her lip and slid the modest long-sleeved black dress off the hanger. She wished she had something really beautiful to wear for this occasion. Not the same old black dress he'd seen her in twice already.

She faced the mirror and unclipped her hair. She would wear it down. He told her he liked it that way.

Then she held the dress up to her front, hugging it to herself, smiling at her reflection. It didn't matter what she wore as long as she got dressed up and into the spirit of things. A tux! That crazy man. She threw her head back with joy and spun around, more excited than she had ever been over any elegant dinner in Washington, D.C.

They ate their meal in front of the bare dining-room windows by the light of two red votive candles Mike had found. After he fed her a few bites of pie, Mike produced a cassette tape from the pocket of his jacket.

"What's that?" Ann leaned close to see the label.

He snatched it away. "A surprise. We're going to dance to it."

"But I don't have anything to play it on. Edith didn't care for music much."

"Ah. Well, then. I am forced to be creative. Come on." He took her hand and led her out onto the wrap-around porch. "Wait here." He hopped down the steps and opened his pickup door, then leaned inside. Soon music drifted out from the cab.

Ann clapped a hand over her mouth as soon as she recognized the melody.

Mike came back up the porch steps slowly. His eyes, like Ann's, were shiny with tears.

"You are so very beautiful," he said as he came to a stop facing her, very near, but not touching. "Even when you're trying not to cry."

She looked into his eyes. "Where did you get that?"

"I've never been without a copy. I always thought

it was just because I like it, but the truth is, it's our song. Isn't it?''

He took her in his arms then, and their bodies settled together lightly, reverently. Then they started to waltz slowly, gracefully, around the old porch while the music floated out, sad and sweet, on the November evening air. Across the street, the unaccustomed noise caused someone to peek around a shade, the way Edith had done all those years ago. But this time Mike and Ann didn't care. They kept looking steadily into each other's eyes and slowly dancing. Dancing. Dancing. To the plaintive strains of "The First Time Ever I Saw Your Face."

THAT IMAGE—Preacher Mike in a tuxedo dancing on the darkened front porch of the old Starr place with that big-city lawyer in her funeral dress—spread around the small town faster than a cold virus.

Gloria, of course, was one of the first to hear of it. In the days following the breakup with Mike, Gloria had clutched her resentment to her breast like a withered bridal bouquet. She adopted the role of injured victim as readily as she had worn the mantle of the good Christian woman.

She made no secret of what had happened. No silent suffering for Gloria Miller. She told everyone who would listen that Mike had literally "thrown her out of his kitchen" while she was cooking him a roast, no less, and now he'd turned his eye to the exotic beauty occupying the old house on Pecan Street.

"I would have thought she'd have left town weeks ago," Josette Smith commented one sunny morning when she dropped by the flower shop to pick up some aging potted azaleas that Gloria had offered to donate to Sunset Manor. "What about her high-powered job and all?"

"She took a leave of absence," Gloria said over her shoulder as she bent toward the bottom tier of mums and azaleas. "Six weeks."

"Six weeks! What on earth for?"

Gloria stood with a browning azalea in each hand. "I expect now we know what for. And it isn't because she loves that old house so much. Grab those two." She pointed a toe at two other pots sitting on the floor.

"Ain't that the truth. She let it fall down around Edith's ears for years. And now she's fixing it up like it was the Taj Mahal. Doesn't figure."

Josette bent and picked up the other pots while Gloria shoved the door open with her bottom. Outside in the brilliant fall sunshine, they loaded the flowers into the back of Josette's SUV.

When Josette slammed the back door she said, "Thanks. This'll cheer the old ladies up. You're a good woman."

"Everybody keeps saying that." Gloria found herself with genuine tears springing to her eyes, right there on Main Street. "If I'm so good, why doesn't he want me?"

"It's okay, honey." Josette scooped her friend into a quick hug. "Just keep reminding yourself that you don't want that man. Not if he's going to act so shallow.''

With the pads of her middle fingers Gloria dabbed at the corners of her eyes. ''Well, I certainly never thought of Mike Kirkpatrick as shallow, did you?''

''No, I guess I didn't. Maybe I didn't mean shallow. I meant...you know how some men are, Gloria. Preacher or not, some of them just can't resist temptation. You're lucky you found out before you married him.''

Gloria sniffed and nodded. But after Josette had pulled away from the curb, Gloria went back into her shop with completely dry eyes. A realization had caused cold determination to vanquish self-pity.

She *did* want Mike Kirkpatrick, no matter what his weaknesses were. Besides, wouldn't any red-blooded man be tempted by a woman that glamorous—and that successful? Gloria had a sudden flash of insight. Ann Fischer was about to make some serious money from the sale of that house and that land. In her heart Gloria knew Mike wasn't pursuing Ann because of money, but what if Ann could be convinced that he was?

Mike's bills were piling up, and the whole town knew it. It wouldn't be hard to get some speculation going and make sure it circled back to Ann. Or Gloria could take care of it herself in one carefully worded conversation. The seeds of doubt might take time to sprout, to bloom, but sooner or later that notion would come between Mike and Ann.

A needle of guilt pricked Gloria's conscience. This was wrong.

No! It wasn't. It *wasn't* wrong to make sure everybody was happy in the long run. Mike would never be truly happy with that woman. She wasn't his type. She could no more fit into his life and make him a good wife than Marsha had. He needed to return to his pulpit, to his senses. And as for Ann Fischer, she needed to return to Washington, D.C.

THE NEXT FEW TIMES they saw each other, Josette continued to try to convince Gloria that she was better off without Mike Kirkpatrick. That there was a *reason* Marsha had up and left him. Preacher or not, the man was simply too dadgum handsome for his own good, and apparently he was fickle, to boot. Why, Josette repeatedly insisted, somebody ought to give him what for, shamelessly chasing that woman all over town only a week after he'd treated Gloria so shabbily. Those two were acting like lovesick teenagers. He was embarrassing himself, that's what he was doing. And his kids.

And the more Josette talked, the more Gloria was convinced that what she was about to do was the right thing.

She sighed. "I guess I just couldn't give him what he wanted."

"Now Gloria, you're very attractive."

"Oh! I don't mean that. I mean it seems to me he's after the money, the security. I'm sure Mike would rather hook up with a rich attorney than a struggling little shop owner.''

''Gloria! That's a terrible thing to say!''

''Well, don't tell me he doesn't worry about money. And the woman has that land, too. You know how bad he wants that land for his church and all. If he married her, he might even be able to stop being a part-time Realtor.''

Josette frowned. ''I don't think there's any call to talk rubbish like that.''

But despite Josette's sanctimonious attitude, Gloria knew she would haul this ''rubbish'' back to Tender Loving Care—and to Ann's friend Laurie Harris— faster than a speeding delivery truck.

IN SPITE OF HIS FEVERED HAPPINESS with Ann, Mike couldn't ignore the gossip and grumblings about their relationship forever. And he felt his own nagging obligations to his children, to his congregation. Obligations to set a good example.

Caught in a state of conflict between love and duty, he finally called his friend Sharon Norton in Dallas. Sharon, an older woman and a nondenominational minister like himself, headed a small flock. She and Mike had become friends in divinity school, and more than once during his trying times with Marsha, Mike had used Sharon as a spiritual sounding board. After an hour of long-distance soul-searching with this wise woman, Mike knew what he had to do.

But before he did it, he wanted to talk to one other wise woman.

He could see Ada Belle through the lace curtains as he stepped onto her porch. She had nodded off in her recliner in front of the flickering TV. He hesitated before he knocked, but it was only eight o'clock and he knew Ada Belle wouldn't mind company.

It took her a minute to rise and answer the door.

"Why, Preacher! What are you doing here of a Saturday night? Come in." Ada Belle stepped back to admit him.

The living room was stuffy and too warm, the volume of the TV could have shattered crystal, and the smell of strong liquid vitamins wafted from the kitchen, but Mike felt immediately at ease here. He sat down on the middle cushion of her couch without being invited, propped his elbows on wide-spread knees and pressed steepled fingers to his lips. He waited while she tottered over and flicked off the TV.

"Can I get you some tea?" she asked.

How sweet she was, Mike thought, still offering hospitality at age ninety-three. "No, thanks, Ada Belle. I came here for some advice."

"I see." Her lined old face grew serious. "I'll do my best, Reverend, but you're the one who should be advising the likes of me." With the help of her cane she made her way across the room and lowered her creaky frame into her recliner.

"I guess that's the problem." He dropped his folded hands between his knees. "I don't feel like much of a spiritual leader when my own life's such a mess."

"Why do you say that your life's a mess?"

Was she serious? Or just plain addled? "Well, uh," he stammered, "for starters, my marriage fell apart and my home's a wreck and my kids are out of control...and now I'm in love with the wrong woman."

"What's wrong with her?" Ada Belle seemed to know exactly who he was talking about. Ah, well. The whole town knew.

"Nothing! I mean, she's beautiful and intelligent, and kind and hardworking and fun to be with."

Ada Belle focused those sharp eyes on Mike again. "So you think you love her?"

"Absolutely," he breathed. "More than anything in this world."

"Then if you love her, why do you say she's the wrong woman?"

"It's not that she's wrong for me, it's that she's wrong for Medicine Creek. It's that it's wrong to ask her to take on all my...baggage."

"You mean them kids?"

He was silent, studying his linked fingers, flicking his thumbnails.

"Maybe you should let her be the judge of whether those kids are baggage."

Mike smiled. Ada Belle was so cute. But underneath the cuteness was her wisdom, plain and simple.

"It's more than that. It's that in my job as a preacher—"

"Your *job* is to live the truth."

Mike looked at her. She'd cut to the heart of it. This is what he had come here for. It was the kind of

thing people of Ada Belle's years could tell you with
absolute authority.

Outside, headlights fanned the front of the house.

"I imagine that's one of my nurses." Ada Belle
craned her neck.

"Then I'll be going. I don't want to tire you out.
You've helped me more than you know."

"I didn't do anything but flap my lips." Ada Belle
grinned.

He dropped a kiss on her soft wrinkled cheek.
"Good night, Ada. I guess I'll see you at church tomorrow morning."

THE CROWD WAS SIZABLE. The congregation often
started increasing again when the weather got cooler,
and by the second Sunday in November, new faces
always appeared. The skeptical, the undecided, the
hesitant, were always welcome at Windrock Nondenominational Church. Mike had been one of their
number once himself.

But what he had to say today was meant to speak
to the hearts of the faithful, those who took their
places in the folding chairs every single Sunday, rain
or shine. These people had come a long way with
him, and he wasn't going to let them down now. They
deserved to have this out in the open.

The choir's singing, as always, was soul-stirring,
and as Mike tried to sing along, he felt a lump in his
throat and prayed that what he was about to do was
for the good of all. Funny, he never felt nervous in

front of his congregation, but today his heart was pounding and his palms were sweating.

As he stood in his customary spot up front, he scanned the crowd for Ann's face. And she was there, sitting next to Laurie and Steve, in the sixth row back, on the side aisle. She looked radiant in a soft peach-colored sweater set that created a striking contrast to her sable hair. She kept her head lowered as she sang along from the hymnal. There ought to be a law, Mike thought, against a man watching a beautiful woman with her head bowed in worship. He felt the impact of it from his heart to his toes.

He made himself look for Gloria, and when he saw her, he silently apologized for the anguish he had caused. *Forgive me, Gloria. I never meant to hurt you.* But love is love—a gift from God—and only a fool would turn from it.

During the second song, an usher escorted Ada Belle up the aisle with her walker. She gave Mike a jaunty wink.

Next to Ada Belle, his children were lined up in the front row as always. He made eye contact with each one with paternal love swelling in his heart and hoped they would all understand what he was about to do. He hadn't discussed this decision with them or with Ann. As he told his friend Sharon, this was a decision between a man and his God.

After the last hymn, the people sat, settling in their places with the rustling contentment of a flock antic-ipating an inspiring Mike Kirkpatrick sermon.

He walked to the pulpit with his head down. For a

long time he looked at the notes he didn't really need and then swallowed down a spurt of fear-borne saliva before he spoke.

"Brothers and sisters," he began, "I won't be preaching a sermon today. Today I stand before you not as your spiritual leader, but as an ordinary man with an ordinary heart. And that heart, as many of you know, has been desolate this past year. There comes a time when a man must go on with his life as he sees fit."

The church grew uncomfortably still. People tried not to make eye contact, but Mike could see that a few did. Their sideward glances seemed to ask: *What in the world?* Maybe some of them were wondering if he was getting ready to announce some kind of reconciliation with Marsha.

"I hope you will understand what I am about to say."

He drew a deep breath and braced his arms on the side of the pulpit. "For the past few weeks I have started my life in a new direction."

The congregation showed faint signs of agitation. A few of them mistakenly glanced at Gloria, who got up and fled down a side aisle.

"Because of the energy I have devoted to starting my life over and because of other distractions, I am aware that my attention has been divided lately. I have even, at times, found myself guilty of short-changing my own children." He looked down at his kids. They were listening for once, fixated on him with wide-eyed concentration.

"So for the sake of my family and in the interest of peace in this congregation, I am stepping down from the pulpit. I will therefore ask the board to bring in a new minister to assume my duties."

The assembly broke into confused murmurs that picked up volume like a flock of noisy birds panicked into taking wing.

Mike raised his palm to quell the disturbance. "I know some of you don't want this change. And...I expect maybe some of you do. In any case, I am truly sorry, my friends, but this will be the last time I will stand in this pulpit for a while. I know you will keep me and my family in your prayers. It is my hope that we can all be reunited someday."

Quickly Mike stepped down from the pulpit and into the waiting arms of his five children, who had jumped up to gather around him with hugs. He raised eager eyes to where Ann was seated. But she was not there.

CHAPTER SEVENTEEN

OUTSIDE IN THE PARKING LOT Gloria and Ann stopped in their rush to their cars and faced each other like startled cats.

"Why are *you* leaving?" Gloria demanded. "You're the chosen one. You've won."

"I can't face the turmoil in there." Ann gestured at the cinder-block building behind them. "I didn't expect him to step down!" Her tone became regretful. "Gloria, you've got to believe me. Never in a million years."

"Didn't you? You didn't think there would be changes—consequences—if you swooped into town and made Mike Kirkpatrick fall in love with you?"

"I didn't make him—"

"Of course you did! He was lonely and confused, and you weren't getting enough attention from your big senator in Washington…"

At Ann's shocked expression, Gloria sneered.

"Oh, I *hear* things. And I *see* things. And one thing I can see is that you won't be satisfied until you've ruined Mike's entire life. It wasn't enough that you came between him and me and destroyed my efforts to mend that family. You have now alienated him from the one thing that matters most to him besides his family—his congregation.''

''Please...'' Ann held out a hand in placation, but Gloria ignored her.

''You're engaged to one man, but that's not good enough. You won't be satisfied until Mike is your victim, too.''

''No,'' Ann protested. She had taken off Kenneth's ring for good the night Mike returned to her house. ''I am going back to D.C. over Thanksgiving—'' She'd meant to say, *to break it off,* but Gloria interrupted before she had the chance.

''And what about those children? Don't you think they've been hurt enough by their selfish mother? I can understand Mike's attraction to you. You're well-off and he's broke.''

''Broke?''

''Almost. The whole town knows it. I don't imagine he's told you about that. I'm not implying that he's only attracted to you for your money, of course. You're glamorous and sexy and he's lonely and bereft. But those things don't qualify you to be a good mother. I don't imagine you've given that aspect of this situation much thought.''

''You're wrong!'' Ann tried to explain. What it meant to be a good mother and her growing love for Mike had been *all* she had thought about for the past few weeks. ''That's why I volunteered to host the Children's Arts Festival at the Starr house. I thought I could do something positive with the kids that way.

You're so wrong, Gloria. I love those kids, and I do want to make their lives better."

"You're just kidding yourself. A little arts festival is the fun part. These children need a real mother, someone who can fit into their everyday lives right here in Medicine Creek. That means sitting through soccer practice and mending favorite jeans and trips to the orthodontist in Ardmore and endless laundry and cooking and cleaning."

Gloria honed in on Ann's pensive expression. "Yes. I can see you really haven't given much thought to how *romantic* your life will be once you're mopping that cheap vinyl flooring in the Kirkpatrick kitchen." Gloria let a moment of silence pass so that image would sink in before she added her next dig. "I know he thinks you'll rescue him financially, but do you think he's going to be satisfied with someone who isn't completely devoted to that church?" Gloria pointed at the buildings, then lowered her arm and softened her voice. "I am not saying this because Mike and I were getting serious before you came along." Her tone indicated she was completely sincere. "That's over. But you really should stop this foolish affair before somebody gets hurt. Mike could live in peace and he'd probably forget about you like he did before, if you'd just go back to your life in Washington. If you really loved that family, you'd go back there," she finished with soft vehemence, "and just leave them alone." Then she whirled away and marched to her car.

Ann watched forlornly while Gloria drove off. It

wasn't images of laundry and cooking and cleaning that played before her eyes as she stood there with her deepest fears assailing her. Nor was it Gloria's hints about Mike needing Ann's money. She knew him better than that. It was the thought of being a poor match for the Kirkpatrick family. It was her knowledge that people like herself, people who had not been lovingly mothered, frequently made poor mothers themselves. In her case she feared that might be so. After all, hadn't she kept her life very tidy, very controlled and very...*sterile* until now? There had to be a reason for that.

She closed her eyes and thought about her own inadequacies and how those shortcomings might affect the Kirkpatrick children. By the time she learned how to be a good mother, Mike's children might be grown—and damaged. And then she thought about Mike never getting back up in that pulpit to do the very thing he did best and that was all she needed to make up her mind.

THAT AFTERNOON Ann moved quickly, efficiently. She was skilled at this sort of thing. Fortunately she had her plane ticket already, and since she'd arrived with few clothes, packing was a simple matter.

She called Jerrod Cagle and gritted her teeth while she told him she had decided to sell him the pecan grove and the house, but only if he agreed to keep the trees standing and let the arts festival proceed as planned.

The price she named was punishingly high, and she

thought he would choke on the figure, but Cagle seemed enormously relieved, even when she told him Mike Kirkpatrick was to get the commission on the deal. "I'll have my lawyer in OKC draw up the necessary papers, so you won't have to," he offered, then added casually, "I suppose you'll want me to get rid of all the junk in that old house, too."

Ann couldn't go that far. Though the past was past and though it seemed there was no way to either confirm or disprove Ada Belle's suspicions, some part of her still wanted to preserve whatever memories she could of her mother.

"No. I'll deal with the contents. But as soon as the house is empty—and once the arts festival is over—you can take possession."

There was a tense silence at the other end. "Well, you'd better take care of it pretty dang quick. You're getting top dollar here. I'd just as soon empty that place out myself." Cagle sounded scared, but this old man was the least of her problems.

"Abide by my terms, Mr. Cagle, or the deal is off."

Next, she called a highly reputable company in Norman that conducted estate sales for a reasonable fee. She was disappointed to learn that they didn't have an open weekend until January.

"And that's not really our best season, hon," the helpful woman named Janie told her. "You'd get better results if you waited until spring."

"No, I want it done as soon as possible. January is fine."

"Okay then, we'll come down tomorrow and look the place over. After that, you can just lock up and give us a key. Don't disconnect the utilities. We'll need them during preparation and, of course, on the weekend of the actual sale. With only a couple of months until January, getting them turned on again wouldn't be cost-effective. We'll do the rest. Of course, you should remove any items you want before we start our work."

"What if there is an item I want, but I simply can't find it?"

"No problem. Just tell me what it is and if we run across it, we'll set it aside for you."

"It's a necklace, a blue star-sapphire necklace on an antique gold rope chain."

"Oh, my. I'll make a special note of that."

"Oh!" Ann suddenly remembered something else. "If you run across a safe-deposit-box key, that would be helpful, too."

"Cash, keys, letters, legal documents and photographs—anything like that will not be sold."

MIKE COULD READ Ann's goodbye letter a hundred times, a thousand, and he'd never understand it.

He'd known something bad was coming when she had run from the church like that and then refused to see him all Sunday afternoon and evening. In the letter she'd explained that it would be healthier—*healthier?*—if they didn't see each other to say goodbye, given that their strong attraction only clouded their judgment.

How could she do this? It felt like another abandonment, just like Marsha's, and as the days after her abrupt departure dragged by, what Ann had done first hurt, then started to anger him.

On Monday Gloria wasted no time telling him about her talk with Ann in the parking lot. "She said she had no idea you were going to resign."

"She didn't."

"Well, the poor woman seemed genuinely shocked and upset, and then she told me she had been planning to go back to Washington before Thanksgiving all along." Gloria turned back to her flower arranging. "I wonder when they're getting married."

That was the last straw. Could he really have been so wrong about Ann? Had he been so blindly in love with her?

Without his pastor's salary, he couldn't be choosy, or he would have punted the pecan-grove deal to an Ardmore agent. The house, too. And he wouldn't have handled Cagle's cursed land deal with Powers, either. But now he needed those commissions more than ever.

The only thing that made him feel halfway normal was going to Zack's basketball game on Wednesday night. Every time he wasn't happy with a ref's call or if Zack did something impressive, he'd roar like a lion from high up in the bleachers. The game was packed because it was the Wednesday before Thanksgiving, and from down in the crowd people started to glance back at him. Once, Joseph even gave him a warning nudge.

He didn't care. He didn't care if Miss Ida plastered a picture of him screaming his head off right across the front page of *Medicine Creek Style*. He'd even suggest a headline: "Dumped preacher flips out."

The whole town probably knew the story by now, anyway. Even the shut-ins out at Sunset Manor had probably figured out that he'd made a fool of himself over a woman, even going so far as to resign from the pulpit for her, and then that woman had promptly ditched him—just like his dear wife.

Marsha, it turned out, was at the house when he and the boys got home from the game.

Mike froze right inside the door with the boys bunching up behind him. He stared in mute fascination as his estranged wife rose off the couch where she had been seated with Brandon and Mary Beth flanking her. As she moved toward him, he realized— happily—that though she was as gorgeous as ever, he didn't feel a thing. Except a certain ire.

"Marsha," he said calmly, "this is a surprise."

Zack, in black basketball warm-ups, muscled his way around his father, taking two giant steps into the living room and looming over his mother. "Let's see. You're our mom, right?"

"Zack…" Joseph warned.

"Zack, if you're going to be disrespectful, you'd better go to your room." Mike marveled at his own ability to remain so calm. He had almost wanted to say something like that to Marsha himself. Divine grace, he decided, really did come when one needed it most.

"Where's the sitter?"

"I sent her home. Children don't need a sitter when their mother is with them."

"Yeah. This is really a surprise," he repeated with careful civility.

"Mike, it's Thanksgiving." Marsha's tone was coaxing. She got to her feet. "Naturally a mother wants to see her babies on Thanksgiving."

Naturally? He wanted to say that there was nothing natural about a mother who stays out in San Francisco sending a check only when she's threatened with legal action, talking to her kids long-distance only enough to keep their feelings for her stirred up. But Brandon and Mary Beth were standing on either side of Marsha, smiling their best-behavior little smiles.

"We'd like to see you more often than on the holidays," he said mildly.

"You know I couldn't afford the plane ticket until now. It takes a long time to get going in the real-estate business, especially in San Francisco. I'll be staying over at Mother and Daddy's, of course."

"Of course."

"But you're gonna eat Thanksgiving dinner with us, right?" Brandon's anxious little face panned from his mother to his father.

"Of course," Mike repeated, and tousled the boy's wiry hair.

So they made nice. They played family. Marsha even cooked the turkey Mike had already bought, with all the trimmings.

When his in-laws had had enough of the strain and

left in the late afternoon, Mike started for his jacket, too. "I'll give you some time alone with the kids. I always have plenty to do at the office."

"On Thanksgiving? Come on, Mike." She stepped between him and the coat closet within the line of vision of his teenage sons, who were watching a football game on TV. She ran her fingers over his biceps lightly, then placed those long white fingers lightly above his heart. "I came to see *you,* too." She reached up and twisted the stray lock of hair on his forehead that she used to play with possessively.

Her wrist smelled seductive, familiar. And she had lost weight. Again. This time more than usual. After five pregnancies, she was an expert at peeling off the pounds. She looked positively svelte in a classy neutral getup of fluid fabric that emphasized her sloping oval breasts.

"I think we should talk about this decision you've made," Marsha purred.

"Decision?" He placed her hand back into her own space.

Marsha's mouth became pinched, as if she wanted to do nothing so much as stomp her foot, the way she used to in this house practically every day. "Yes, your *decision.* Mother and Daddy told me you resigned from your pulpit. You could have told me yourself, you know. You could have discussed this with me. After all, your obsession with that church had a lot to do with our problems, and now that you're not there anymore..."

Mike cut a glance at the boys, then stared at Marsha. *Not here,* his eyes said. He wanted to say that his being a preacher had absolutely nothing to do with their problems, but even now, after a year of separation, he wasn't so sure about that. When he joined the army after high school, Marsha had been excited, foreseeing a life of travel and adventure. It was when he decided to attend divinity school that her discontent had started.

Marsha lowered her voice below the din of the TV. "I just meant, if you *are* changing, then maybe we owe it to ourselves to give it another try."

Right then Mike realized that Marsha had heard about his relationship with Ann. Who spilled the beans? Erin, most likely. That might explain Marsha's sudden unannounced visit. He'd filed for divorce in mid-October, the week Ann arrived in town, but it wouldn't be final for ninety days. Since filing, he hadn't heard a word from Marsha except through lawyers. But now there was the threat of another woman. Marsha would probably shrug if Mike took up with a woman like Gloria. But Ann was another story.

He wondered about the poor guy she had taken up residence with in San Francisco. Had she dumped him now or what? He figured that as the father of these children he had every right to know—conceivably the kids might visit out there. He was about to ask when, upstairs, Alfie started barking wildly and Brandon sent up a bloodcurdling wail.

"Al-feeee!" the boy screamed. "You bad, bad dog!"

Mike adopted an ironic little smile. "They're all yours, sweetheart." And he was out the door.

HE ZIPPED HIS WINDBREAKER and took an enormous breath of the crisp fall air. He headed west, walking fast. He knew without a doubt where he was going, and there, he knew he could think. There, maybe he could even forgive.

What was Ann doing today? he wondered when he'd settled himself at the base of their tree in the pecan grove. Did the senator have a family that they would spend Thanksgiving with? Steve had told him the guy was from Kansas. Did they go to his home for the holiday? Was she in Kansas? Surrounded by her family-to-be? Being toasted and eating a lovely meal?

Part of him hoped not. Part of him hoped she was holed up in her sterile condo, with only a finicky cat for company, getting a good dose of time alone to think about all that she had run away from. That small part of him hoped she was missing him as much as he was missing her.

ANN HAD NEVER KNOWN such pain. How did one give up one's true love? Breaking up with Kenneth had been uncomfortable, merely uncomfortable. He had seemed mildly annoyed, not overly emotional, certainly not *passionate*. In the end she'd handed him back his ring and the thing was done.

She gently pushed her cat off her lap and walked to the massive sliding doors that opened onto her nineteenth-floor balcony. She had been very lucky, she reminded herself as she stepped up to the waist-high parapet, to snag this condo in the heart of Rosslyn. The air was crisp, and the view that spread below her looked like a postcard. The sun was inching down in the west, spotlighting the buildings in the mall beyond the ribbon of the Potomac.

From out of lush fall foliage, the Washington Monument rose like an enormous golden spike, and beyond that, the capitol dome glowed like a huge peach. She had underused this condo, hadn't shared this view enough. Maybe she would have a dinner party soon. She might enjoy that. Entertaining a few close friends. Maybe after a play or concert. She loved her life in Washington, she truly did. Then why had she turned down the smattering of invitations to Thanksgiving dinner? And why had she spent the day brooding and thinking about a passel of red-haired kids with blue, blue eyes like their father. And a sweet old lady who had a quirky way with words.

And a man who had kissed her like no other.

She wrapped her arms around her middle and fought off the terrible dark feelings that had threatened to envelop her since she'd left Medicine Creek. Tomorrow she would go back to work, and that would help. For now, she had to hold the black clouds of loss at bay.

Mike must have come to his senses the minute she'd left town, just as Gloria had predicted. If he hadn't, he would have called her by now. So apparently she had done the right thing. And that was what mattered.

With tears forming, she looked out over the treetops, kissed by the late-autumn sun on this day of thanks, when she felt no gratitude. This day of family, when she had none. Small sailboats glided under the bridges crisscrossing the Potomac. No place could be more beautiful than Washington at twilight—unless it was Main Street, Medicine Creek.

She swiped a knuckle under each eye. Maybe she should go for a jog before the sun went down.

THE E-MAILS STARTED a week later. This time Erin signed her name to her misspelled missives.

"The Xmas arts festifall wont be the same without you," the first one said.

Ann replied immediately. "Did you finish your short story? Did Mary Beth finish her drawings?"

Ann worried that by staying in touch, she was merely prolonging their inevitable separation. She countered those worries by telling herself that the last thing the Kirkpatrick kids needed was another adult suddenly disappearing from their lives.

"When are you coming back to town?" Erin asked, and it tore at Ann's heart. She gave a vague answer about maybe coming for the estate sale in January, then distracted the child with the latest antics of her cat.

"When my mom came home for Thanksgiveing, they had a big fight because my dad disaperred for two hours. My Grandma said she saw him setting under a tree over in the pecan grove when he should have been home with us. But I told my mom to not take it too personil. He does that a lot, and plays this tape of some old song, too, about whenever I saw your face. I can hear it coming from his room at night.''

Strangely Ann's spirits soared after she read that one. Mike had gone to the grove. And he'd been playing "The First Time Ever I Saw Your Face"? So maybe Gloria's prediction had been wrong. Maybe Mike hadn't forgotten about her the minute she'd left town.

But no sooner had her hopes risen than she got a coolish business letter from Mike with the papers for the sale of the house and the pecan grove attached, ready for her signature. "No need to be present for the closing," he wrote. "I can act as your representative." But her hand shook when she tried to sign the land away, and something made her put the papers aside for a few days. When she finally did sign them, she didn't have the will to give them a thorough perusal. What did it matter, anyway? She was never going back to Medicine Creek.

She reread his letter, and there was no indication that what Erin had written was true. His tone was polite, upbeat, but arm's-length and businesslike.

Then Erin started mentioning Gloria in her e-mails.

"Gloria said...

"Gloria came by today...

"Gloria didn't like the way the lights looked on the tree trunks...''

Ann tried to read between the lines, wondering if
Gloria was hoping to coerce Mike into picking up
where they'd left off, wondering about Gloria's mo-
tives during that last conversation in the parking lot.
But still, did she have the right to go charging back
to that town and interfere in a family's happiness?
Not when she herself didn't even know what she
wanted.

"Gloria said you are merrying a senator. When are
you getting married?"

"I'm not."

And then the call from Laurie came and Ann knew
she had to return to Medicine Creek—even if it was
to be for the last time.

"It's Ada Belle," Laurie's tone had been professional over the phone. "She's taken a very bad turn—
blood pressure's sky-high—and she wants to see you
before she goes."

EVER SINCE THINGS had cooled between Gloria and
him, Mike had encouraged Erin to use his office computer after school, instead of the one in the flower
shop. That arrangement proved inconvenient at times,
but he didn't want his daughter reestablishing a relationship with Gloria. One afternoon Erin didn't sign
off on her e-mail, and when Mike was backing out
of the program, he noticed the child's folder labeled
"Ann."

He shouldn't, he told himself as he opened the
folder. He should observe their privacy rule. But this
was about Ann. Had Erin been corresponding with

her? Apparently so. As he scanned the saved messages, it didn't take him long to put two and two together.

GLORIA TOOK THE PAPERS and examined them. She paled and looked up at Mike with both anger and fear in her eyes. "Erin's been e-mailing Ann Fischer?"

"As you can see, at first they were merely chatting about the arts festival. But later it gets more interesting."

Gloria didn't even have to look down at the pages to know what he meant.

"Mike, I can't be responsible for what Erin says! The child is...you know how that child is—"

"Did you lie in order to get Ann to leave town? Did you lie to me about why she left?" Mike shook the evidence—the stack of e-mails he'd printed out.

"Lie? I would never lie and you know it!"

"Maybe not technically, but you were certainly misleading. It looks to me like you misled Ann to get her to think she didn't belong here."

"Don't be ridiculous. She left to go back to her senator."

"Not true. Keep reading. She broke it off with him as soon as she got back to Washington."

Gloria read through the e-mails until she apparently saw the one saying that Ann was not marrying Kenneth, at which point she turned pink and bit her lip.

Mike sighed. "Look Gloria, I told you once. You and I can never make it as a couple. All I want to do now is give my children the attention they deserve and regain the confidence of my congregation after all my mistakes.''

"Well, you've made plenty, mister." Still in high color, Gloria went on the attack. "And taking up with Ann Fischer was your biggest one! I wonder what certain members of your congregation would say if they knew you'd had an affair with that woman!"

"There was no affair!" Mike replied hotly.

"Well, it wasn't for lack of effort on your part! And all this double-dealing about the pecan grove," Gloria rushed on. "Cagle's going to turn right around and sell that woman's land to the Powers people, isn't he? And you, Preacher, make a commission both times! And now my aunt Ida informs me that Cagle's going to let that Powers Corporation bulldoze those trees to the ground."

"He's *what?*"

"Don't pretend you don't know. That way you don't have to be the bad guy with Miss Perfect. Cagle gets blamed for the trees."

"Gloria, are you sure Ida has her facts straight?"

"The article will be in tomorrow's *Style*. The trees come down Monday morning. I have a half a mind to call some teachers, merchants, even members of your congregation—anybody I can drum up—and rally them to stop that destruction. Destroying those trees will ruin the looks of Main Street."

Mike's mind boggled at the complexity of human relationships. Gloria suddenly wanted the pecan grove preserved—Ann's goal—just to spite him and deprive him of a real-estate commission. But he couldn't worry about what this silly woman was going to do next. He had to find out if Cagle had double-crossed him—and Ann. Ann had wanted those trees preserved. Cagle must have found some loophole in that morass of papers the Oklahoma City lawyer had drawn up.

"I don't care who you call about the pecan grove, Gloria, but you stay out of my personal business from now on."

He was out the shop door before she could answer, the slam of the door and the clang of the bell chiming a note of finality.

CHAPTER EIGHTEEN

ANN TOOK THE LAST Sunday night flight to Dallas and accepted the quickest rental available—a Jeep. Driving up through the Arbuckles with the full moon low on the eastern horizon, she felt…as if she was coming home.

At Ada Belle's house Laurie filled her in. "Her blood pressure spiked earlier and now it's low. She's awfully weak."

When Ann bit her lip at this news, Laurie quickly added, "Don't worry. She's tough as a little old beetle."

From the front bedroom Ada Belle called out in a voice that didn't sound the least bit weak, "Don't talk about me as if I was some kind of bug! Is that you, Ann? Come in here."

Ann rushed to the bedside, and Ada Belle clutched her hand. "Sit down, hon." Laurie pushed a chair up behind Ann's knees, and Ann sank onto it.

Ada Belle was decked out in a lacy, cream-colored bed jacket and white silk nightie. Dainty rings sparkled on her fingers and her nails were painted frosty pink. Her bluish hair looked freshly done. Something was off here.

"I cain't believe you came all the way here from

Washington to see me," she whispered, and let her head flop back against the pillow.

"Ada Belle." Ann squeezed the old woman's hand. "Don't talk. You'll wear yourself out."

"You let me talk, hon, 'cause I've got something to say." She pushed herself up on one elbow with surprising strength and agility. "So?" she croaked. "You ain't gonna marry your senator, after all?"

"How did you know that?"

"Erin told Zack who told Trent who told Laurie who told me."

For a dying woman, Ada Belle certainly had her wits about her. Ann looked over her shoulder at Laurie, who was bent over the dresser, busily writing on Ada Belle's chart.

"What's going on here?" Ann asked.

"She made me do it." Laurie pointed her pen at Ada Belle.

"I had to come up with a reason good enough to make you come home," Ada Belle said in her own defense. "If you ain't gonna marry that senator, then we need you back here in Medicine Creek. Laurie, show her the paper."

Laurie whipped out the Friday issue of *Medicine Creek Style* and handed it to Ann.

"See what that horrible man is about to do?"

Ann read the piece. "He can't do this!" She slapped the paper on the bed. "We had an agreement!"

"Well, it sure looks like he is fixin' to do it, agreement or not. But I think I know a way to stop him."

"You do?"

"Yes, I do." Ada Belle hoisted herself up higher against the stack of pillows, as full of energy and excitement as any teenager. "Listen. In the olden days the Chickasaws had eleven whole counties and part of two others in this state." She held up two fingers. "The Choctaw was a bigger tribe, and we ended up making some kind of land deal with them, but I cain't say about all that." She waved her hand, rings flashing.

"Here's the point, all of those counties had some of the original allotted lands, including most of this area around the Arbuckles. That allotted land can never belong to anyone but a Chickasaw descendant. As long as the lands stay in a Chickasaw family, no problem. Your pecan grove and that ranch, too, were allotted lands."

"Ada Belle, are you sure?"

"I'm pretty dern sure. And that means Mr. Cagle, being white, cain't own 'em."

"Then how did he get the ranch?" It was Laurie who asked this.

"Nolan, or maybe Edith, must have finagled a way to sell it to him. But Cagle's got a real problem. He can never sell it, and he can't buy that pecan grove from you. The land has to go right back to the Chickasaws if you don't want it."

"There's got to be a way to check into the legality of all this." Ann was suddenly agitated. "First, I've got to ask Mike what the title search turned up. What time is it?" She looked at her watch. After ten.

"You don't have time for a bunch of legal stuff. Read that article." Ada Belle tapped the paper with a twinkling pink nail. "They are taking those trees out first thing tomorrow morning."

"Gloria's called the media down from the city."

"Gloria? What's she got to do with this?"

"Who knows?" Laurie said. "Maybe she thinks the mall is going in there. The downtown merchants were against it from the start."

"If anybody's capable of attracting TV cameras to a speck like Medicine Creek," Ada Belle allowed, "it'd be Gloria."

"It's Christmas break, so she's using the kids," Laurie added. "She's got them making protest signs for the cameras over at the church tonight."

"I will find a way to stop this," Ann vowed. "Those trees aren't going to be touched."

"That's my girl!" Ada Belle thumped Ann's knee with a skinny fist. "I knew we needed you back in this town."

"Now." Ada Belle rested her palm on Ann's knee. "There's something else."

Ann waited.

"I want you to go see Mike—about the two of you."

"Ada Belle," Ann said softly, "I can't do that."

"Why not? It's a dying woman's wish, dadgum-mit."

"Ada Belle—" Ann gave the elderly imp an unsparing look "—if you're a dying woman, then I'm Pocahontas."

Behind them Laurie suppressed a giggle.

Ann twisted toward her friend. "And you! Shame on you for lying and making me come all the way back here."

"I didn't lie!" Laurie was indignant. "Her blood pressure was sky-high this morning. And now it's low. Look." She held out the chart.

"Your exact words were 'She wants to see you before she goes.'"

"Oh, for pity's sake," Ada Belle huffed. "She didn't say *where* I was goin'."

"And I bet your blood pressure zigzags around like this every day, doesn't it?"

Ada Belle and Laurie exchanged abashed glances.

"Listen here, Miss Priss—" Ada Belle flipped the quilt back and swung her bony legs off the bed, going on the attack "—this is for your own good. I don't know what happened to make you hightail it out of town the way you did, but that man stepped down from his pulpit for you."

Ann frowned. "He did step down for me, and that's the trouble. I feel I'm the reason he's estranged from his congregation. If I had just stayed out of his life—"

"Nonsense. Mike Kirkpatrick's not estranged from anything. In fact, he's finding things he thought he'd lost. And you're one of 'em."

Ann looked at Ada Belle in surprise.

"Oh, he talked to me. And way back, when you was a pretty young thing, I saw you two out in that pecan grove once under a full moon like we're havin' tonight. I know what true love looks like, girl, and I seen it that night."

Ann's cheeks blazed as she imagined Ada Belle watching them from behind one of her lace curtains.

But the old woman didn't seem to notice Ann's embarrassment. "You cain't turn your back on feelings like that. That'd be a terrible sin. Whatever is wrong, you cain't just run away, girl. You've got to be strong." Ada Belle slapped Ann's knee. "Don't forget—you're a Chickasaw!"

Ann lowered her head and laced her fingers with Ada Belle's fragile ones. "Thank you," she said softly, simply.

Laurie stepped around and sat on the bed beside Ada Belle. "We care about you, Ann, and we care about Mike. And we want you both to be happy."

"Are you sure he wants to talk to me?"

"He once told me that he loved you more than anything in the world, and it didn't sound to me like he was ever gonna change his mind."

Ann smiled. No, Mike Kirkpatrick wouldn't change his mind. He hadn't in sixteen years. "Okay, then. I'll call him in the morning."

ANN PUT THE SKELETON KEY in the lock and opened the door to Starr House. She stepped inside the dark foyer and felt a chill that went deeper than the cold air. When she flipped the light switch, there was no power.

A blown fuse?

She shivered. It was freezing in here, but she didn't

dare fumble in the dark with the pilot light on the ancient wall furnace. She felt her way into the kitchen, where she had last seen Edith's flashlight. When her hand came into contact with the surface of the stove, she turned on the burners. The oblique light of the blue gas flames cast eerie shadows in ways Ann had never noticed before.

And then she saw it. A bump, a *lump* under the corner of the framed sampler hanging over the stove. She reached up and lifted the embroidered piece off its nail. The metal frame and the glass were sticky from years of Edith's greasy cooking. "God Bless This House," the stained muslin read. It was, she recalled, the only creative thing Edith had ever attempted.

She tilted the frame toward the light and under the glass, under the cloth, there was definitely a wrinkle. With shaking fingers she loosened the cardboard backing and immediately a key—a safe-deposit-box key—clattered onto the enamel stovetop.

Ann gasped, picked it up and quashed the sudden urge to call Mike. They had searched for this key for so long. But it was after eleven o'clock at night, and though crafty Ada Belle had done her best to clear the way for their relationship to begin again, this time Ann wanted it to be on the right foot. She would call him at a decent hour, after she found out what was in the box.

The bank opened its doors at eight o'clock in the morning, and Ann would be there, key in hand.

"A LOT OF GOOD it's doin' us to be on Christmas break if all we're gonna do is work all week." Zack slumped in the seat and donned his shades against the morning sun, which had barely peaked over the mountains.

"And you can bet your ass that old man'll work us into the ground." Trent took the curves in the winding Arbuckle roads at breakneck speed. His dad would kill him for driving so recklessly when he'd only gotten his Jeep back yesterday. But they were already late. "I wish to heck we'd never raced that stallion."

"Yeah. That was two whole months ago. You'd think the old geezer would've forgotten about it by now. Who the heck starts dragging brush at seven o'clock on a Monday morning?" Zack grumbled.

"Old farts with nothin' better to do."

Jerrod Cagle met them outside his double-wide trailer with the keys to his pickup, a list and a crude map of Lazy J roads.

"Hope you two troublemakers brought your own lunch," he snarled. "Don't expect me to feed you nothin', 'cause my Mexican woman don't come on Mondays. Ain't no help here to feed on Mondays."

"Trent's mom made us sandwiches." Zack snatched the list.

After a couple of hours of dragging brush, loading hay and fixing fence in the cold December wind, the boys were hungry, exhausted—and very bored.

"How about some sandwiches and chocolate milk?" Trent said.

"But it's—" Zack checked his watch "—only nine-thirty."

"Who cares? I'm *starving*."

They sat in the pickup in silence, running the heater, eating their sandwiches and swilling the cartons of milk.

Suddenly Zack said, "Hey! Look there." He pointed up the slope in the distance at a crumbled old limestone chimney peeking out from among a cluster of fat red cedars.

"I'll be. That must be the old burned-out homestead my dad told me about. Indians used to live up there."

"Let's go look." Zack killed the engine and hopped out of the truck.

"Are you sure we should be going up there?" Trent said worriedly.

"Cagle can't see us way out here," Zack said as they climbed the hill. "We're stuck on this place all week whether we bust our asses gettin' that list done or not. Might as well explore a bit."

There was little left of the old place. Weeds had overtaken the charred foundation. But an ancient warped hewn-wood cellar door immediately attracted the boys. It was heavy and took some prying with a big stick to get it open, but when they finally poked their heads down into the musty air, the boys were amazed.

The inside looked solid and hand-built. Where the aged white paint and concrete had chipped off the walls, chunky red clay blocks were revealed, stacked tight without mortar, like the walls of a pioneer soddy. Shafts of winter-white December sunshine came through two small air vents at the back.

"Cool!" Zack said. He propped the stick in the door and started down the steps. "Come on."

"Forget it, man. It's spooky. There's probably bugs and spiders and snakes and things down there."

"Don't be a chicken."

Trent followed reluctantly.

No sooner were they inside, exploring the dark recesses and avoiding the puddled water on the hard-packed dirt floor than a gust of mountain wind snapped the stick and banged the door shut.

The boys were big and strong, but the skewed door was wedged tight by the force with which it had slammed. After some minutes of putting their backs to it, they retreated down the steps.

"Now what?"

"Somebody's gonna have to use a lever on it from the outside, like we did."

"Helllp!" Trent hollered toward the ground above them.

Zack punched him and pointed at the two little air vents high on the back wall. "Let's yell out those."

The boys grappled at the bricks to boost themselves up, screaming "Help!" at the tops of their lungs. On Zack's third try a brick came loose and he went tumbling onto his backside into a puddle.

"Look!" Trent cried. Behind the brick a small metallic box glittered.

"Wow. Gimme a hand," Zack ordered, and fitted

his muddy boot into Trent's locked palms. He pulled the box out. It was a small strongbox, like they used at his dad's church to hold the offerings until the bank opened on Monday. But this one had no padlock. They unlatched the lid. Inside was a zippered plastic bag. Inside that was a bundle of newsprint. And inside that some rolled-up cotton batting. And inside *that*— Zack let it slide down into his palm like a trickle of baptismal water—a giant star sapphire on a gold chain.

"Holy crimoli!" Trent breathed.

"I'll say."

Zack angled the nickel-size stone into the oblique shaft of sunlight from the small window above and the perfect six-ray star danced and rolled.

"Man." Trent's eyes bulged. "Wonder what something like that is worth?"

"What's old man Cagle doing with it?" Zack frowned.

"Maybe Cagle didn't even know it was here. Maybe an old Indian hid it."

"Grow up," Zack said. "It looks like the one Ann's mom had on in the picture. Dad said she died when Ann was five." He was already examining the dates on the newspapers in the dim light. "And see? These are all dated in 1973. Hey! If Ann's mom died when she was about five, wouldn't that be about 1973?"

"Come on, man, you know I'm crappy at math."

Outside they heard a car engine roaring up the slope and crunching to a halt.

"In heeere!" Trent yelled upward.

"Push on the damned door!" an obviously irate Cagle ordered from outside.

With their combined efforts, in seconds the door scraped open and a very red-faced Cagle looked down at the spooked boys.

"Goddammit!" he spat. "When I heard you yellin', I figured you ornery cusses was messin' around in this old cellar. Get your sorry little asses up outta there!"

As they climbed the steps, Zack had the presence of mind to zip the necklace into his pocket.

"What were you all doing down there?" Cagle yelled as the boys emerged.

"Come on!" Zack commanded Trent as soon as they backed away from Cagle, and they hightailed it for the truck.

"Hold it!" Cagle yelled. "You stop right there!"

But the boys had already jumped in the pickup and fired it up. They fishtailed down the rutted road, hellbent on getting back to the Jeep.

CHAPTER NINETEEN

THE WOMAN AT THE BANK, Mrs. Lucas, remembered Ann. "I heard you'd left town and that you'd arranged an estate sale of Edith's things in January. I figured you'd given up on this box." She led Ann into a vault where brass boxes were imbedded into three walls. A plain library table with two chairs provided workspace.

Mrs. Lucas inserted a key into one of the larger boxes. Why would Edith need such a big safe-deposit box? Ann wondered as she handed over her key.

The woman turned the lock and said, "You just slide it out." She lifted the handle to demonstrate. "I'll give you your privacy. Just call out when you are finished."

Ann drew the box out of the wall, raised the lid with held breath and peeked in. Documents. On top of the stack Ann recognized a yellowed mimeographed copy of a title abstract—for the Starr of the Arbuckles ranch.

She took the heavy box to the table and removed the pile of papers. She plopped them on the table and riffled the stack, then checked the empty corners of the box with her heart drumming. But there was no star-sapphire necklace. She sank into a chair and stared.

But surely Edith had a reason for locking all these papers away. Palms sweating, Ann lifted the thick ranch abstract, dating back to Indian Territory days just as Ada Belle had said, and then the abstracts for the pecan-grove property and the house. She set them all aside. She'd go through every line of these things later.

Then she sucked in a breath. Under the abstract was a card the size of a driver's license—with *her* name on it.

It bore the seal of the United States Department of the Interior, Bureau of Indian Affairs. "Certificate of Degree of Indian Blood," it read. "This is to certify that Ann Louise Starr Fischer born 2-8-68 is 19/32 degree Indian blood of the Chickasaw Tribe." It was dated March 11, 1968, and signed illegibly by the issuing officer. Her mother apparently put her on the rolls shortly after she was born.

Seeing it, Ann felt a dizzying disorientation. Somewhere she was on the rolls of a Native American tribe she knew nothing about.

Under the card was her birth certificate, then her mother's, then her mother's CDIB card and finally, June's death certificate. Ann lifted it lovingly and read the cause of death: cerebral concussion secondary to accidental fall. She spread the documents on the table—her paper path back to the Chickasaw people.

She analyzed the other papers with a swift legal eye.

June must have died without a will—as any twenty-five-year-old might—because an attorney with an Ardmore address had named Nolan guardian ad litem for Ann. She shuffled the papers. Why hadn't she had a separate attorney and guardian? Ann always made sure her child clients' interests were protected individually. Maybe things in the small-town world of 1973 were different.

She quickly scanned the other documents. One giving Nolan, as guardian, the right to sell all property, an order allowing sale of real property, another showing the guardianship court approving the final sale of the property, Starr of the Arbuckles, to Jerrod Cagle. Everything was dated three to six months after her mother's death.

There was Nolan's later will, leaving everything to Edith for her lifetime, and then reverting the estate to Ann.

And finally, bound with a rotting red rubber band, were several *uncashed* checks from Jerrod Cagle's account at the Murray County National Bank, dated immediately after her mother's death. They were in increments of one thousand dollars—made out to Edith Sloan.

Ann sank back into the chair, trying to make sense of what she was seeing.

Apparently, as soon as Edith got her hooks into Nolan, she had found a corrupt lawyer in Ardmore who made sure they could get their hands on Ann's property. All that lawyer had to do was find a lazy judge and not mention the Indian-land issue in court. Slip. Slap. Documents done.

Was Cagle behind it all somehow? Or had he and Edith been working together? Either way, Jerrod must have been paying Edith for some reason. To keep quiet about something? Maybe Edith had been holding these documents and uncashed checks over his head.

Ann wondered if Cagle knew that without a good title he could never sell the ranch. She wondered if he cared. Maybe he *had* discovered this when he first tried to sell that strip of land by the interstate.

It must have freaked him out when she came back to town.

Thus, the removal of the trees. If he could rush the sale of the grove to Powers, this legal tangle would become their problem. If they'd already made expensive improvements to the property with his permission, they were more likely to go to court to fight for the property.

Of course, Ann's selling the pecan grove to Cagle wasn't legal, either. As original allotted lands, the property had to remain with the Chickasaws.

She scooped up all the paperwork. "Mrs. Lucas! I'm finished. You can have your keys now."

She had to find Mike right away.

JERROD CAGLE whirled around as soon as the boys took off. Had those brats found the necklace he'd hidden there? He propped the door open with a sizable rock and descended the dirt steps. The sight of the loose brick nearly stopped his heart. It only took seconds to locate the empty strongbox in the dark corner. He threw it against the wall and roared a curse, looking for the necklace on the murky floor and wishing to hell he'd never taken the thing to that jeweler in Texas and found out its value—its 1973 value—forty-five thousand dollars. He should have thrown it in Arbuckle Lake, but he couldn't make himself dump something so valuable in the bottom of a lake. Of course, he couldn't sell a necklace that distinctive, either. So he'd buried it way out here, telling himself, *Some day, some day.*

Maybe those boys wouldn't find out what that necklace meant, but he sure as hell couldn't take that chance. There was, after all, no statute of limitations on murder.

No, it wasn't murder. It had been an accident. He shouldn't have followed her horse, shouldn't have tried to talk her into giving up the land again, shouldn't have grabbed at her when she slapped at him with the reins. When her horse shied and stumbled off the cliff, somehow the necklace had gotten caught in his fingers as he grasped to save her. But would a jury ever believe that, especially with June's nosy lawyer daughter poking around that house? Those checks had always worried him. Edith had come to him after June died, ready to help him get the ranch. Nolan would sell, she said. A corrupt lawyer would take care of the Indian-land documents. The child was only five. Edith swore she would never tell. Then, to keep silent, she'd started demanding money. But she hadn't cashed all the checks, so they must be in that house somewhere. As long as Edith was alive and the house sat empty, he felt safe. But then Edith had died and that daughter came back to town.

And now the necklace.

He had to stop those boys before they showed it to anyone.

ANN LEFT THE BANK, headed for Mike's office, but out on the Main Street sidewalk there was a commotion. An agitated contingent of teenagers, Erin and Joseph Kirkpatrick included, were hoisting themselves and their homemade signs into the bed of a pickup parked in front of Gloria's flower shop. Mike was there, in suit and tie, following Gloria, who was rushing toward her store van. His outstretched arms indicated he was trying to stop her or appease her.

One look at him filled Ann with longing.

"Mike!" She ran across the street, clutching the papers to her chest.

"Ann?" He froze. "What are you doing here?"

"Hey, Ann!" Erin called. The other teens squealed and screamed as the truck lurched away from the curb. "Hurry up! We're gonna save the trees!"

Gloria glared at Mike and Ann, facing each other. "Perfect," she spat, and slammed the van door. The three other women in the van gave them quizzical looks as Gloria backed out.

"Mike, I have to talk to you!"

"Ann—" he spread a palm over his chest "—I

can't believe you're here.'' Ann hated this. She had imagined a quiet gentle reunion where they would confess their love and bare their souls. Not this chaos.

"I don't have time to explain," she said. "Is *Gloria* going to try to stop them from bulldozing those trees?"

"Yes. It's a long story. But I tried to tell her I've got a lawyer coming from Oklahoma City with an emergency restraining order. Cagle can't destroy your trees. I stayed up all night searching the contract and the abstract and that land—''

"I know.'' Tears stung Ann's eyes. This man had fought for her, for her trees, even though she had hurt him. "I've just discovered the same thing—I have the proof right here."

Mike stared at the pile of papers in Ann's arms. "Maybe we can use that stuff until my guy gets here. Come on."

He grabbed her hand and dragged her to his pickup. He roared down the two blocks to Pecan Street and parked in front of Ann's house.

As they jogged across the street to the grove, Ann saw the Channel 9 satellite truck. Other heavy equipment, cherry pickers, bulldozers, limb shredders, had furrowed deep ruts in the earth. Some large tree limbs were already on the ground. The teenagers were busy chaining themselves to the massive trunks of the two largest trees.

Fists on her hips, Gloria stood facing an angry-looking man in a hard hat, while a cameraman circled them. The church ladies had gotten some of the kids singing a hymn about the tree of the cross. They raised their voices higher when the whine of chain saws threatened to drown them out.

"Gloria!" Ann called as she ran ahead of Mike toward the woman. "I don't know why you're doing this, but thank you."

Gloria looked bewildered for an instant before she turned back to the guy in the hard hat. "Go ahead and call your boss," she shouted, "but you're not sawing off one more limb!" She yelled louder as, behind them, the chain saw ripped into wood. "These trees belong to this town! They are part of our heritage!"

"That's right." Ann stepped directly into the line of the camera, holding up her papers. "I have documents here that prove this land was part of the original lands allotted to the Chickasaw people. The sale of this property to Mr. Cagle was illegal, and the Powers Corporation cannot buy it, either. And they certainly have no right to touch these trees."

"Who are you, ma'am?" The reporter asked as he stuck a microphone into Ann's face.

"I am Ann Louise Starr Fischer," Ann said as she gazed steadily into the camera. "The Chickasaw heir to this land." And as she spoke the words, for the first time in her life, Ann felt her Native American blood.

The guy in the hard hat turned and gave a sharp whistle with his fingers. "Hold it, boys! We got a problem." The crew in the background stopped working and gave one another disgusted looks.

The cameraman swung to the cheering teenagers, and Gloria bustled off in their direction. "Children! Keep on singing!" she called.

With the crisis temporarily averted, Ann's mind turned to Cagle. "Mike, we've got to talk."

"At your house," he said, and took her elbow.

The reporter tried to stick a microphone into Ann's face again while he fired more questions at her. "Not now!" Mike waved the man away.

Once inside her door, he said, "What's wrong?"

"Look at these checks from Jerrod Cagle." She went directly to the dining room and spread them on the table. "Why do you think they were never cashed?"

Mike picked up one of them. "Considering what Ada Belle told you—"

"Do you think it means—" her voice shrank to a whisper as the horror of it collapsed in on her "—that maybe my mother's death wasn't an accident? Maybe Cagle killed her. And Edith knew it. Edith *used* it."

Mike nodded sadly. "If these were for a legitimate purpose, why wouldn't she have cashed them?"

Ann covered her eyes. "They were just a way for her to prove that Cagle was paying her to keep quiet. I wonder exactly what Edith knew." She started to tremble.

"Whatever it was, she went to her grave with it." Mike came around the table. He gripped Ann's arms with warm palms, calming her. "We'll get to the bottom of it, but first..." He pulled his phone out of his jacket and punched in a number. After an interval during which he and Ann studied each other's worried eyes, he said, "He's not answering," and hung up.

"Who?"

"Cagle. The boys are working out on his ranch this morning."

"Oh, Mike." Ann covered her mouth. "I do *not* want them out there with that man."

"Me, neither. Come on." He grabbed his jacket. "Once we've got the boys safely back here, we'll contact the authorities about what you found."

ZACK KEPT CHECKING behind them.

"Is he chasin' us?" Trent asked.

"Don't see him."

"What do you think he'll do? Call our dads?"

"Hope so. Is your dad home?"

"Nobody's at my house. My dad went into town to get feed today. You hope Cagle calls your dad? Man, if he does, we are in big trouble."

"No, man. Not us. *Him*. My dad told me Ann had been looking all over that house for this necklace. My guess is Cagle isn't supposed to have it. That's why it was hidden, man. Don't you get it? That's why he was havin' a stroke about findin' us down in that cellar." Zack craned his neck to check behind them again and jumped when he saw Cagle's old pickup coming around the last bend. "Hell. Here he comes."

"My man Zack—right again." Trent mashed the Jeep's gas pedal to the floor.

"This isn't funny! Come on!" Zack yelled as he

buckled his seat belt, then reached across and fastened Trent's. "We gotta leave this old guy in the dust!"

As Jerrod Cagle closed the gap between his truck and Trent's Jeep, he paced himself. He hoped they'd assume he simply wanted the necklace back, that this was just a high-speed joyride to outrun an old man. But he knew these twisting roads far better than the boys, and there was a spot, a quarter mile or so up the road, where a sheer wall of rock fell away sixty feet to a waterfall below. That was where he'd pull up on the mountain side of the boys and run them off the road. Served 'em right for digging around on a man's private property.

The right wheels of the Jeep left the ground as the boys rounded the next hairpin curve. He'd have to be damned careful or he'd get killed with them. But not far beyond the cliff was a large scenic turnout where he could spin off and correct his course if he got out of control. The main thing was to make sure they hit the cliffside rail at a high speed. No one could survive that drop.

Trent had started to sweat like a horse, and both boys were cussing like sailors. "He's gonna kill us!" Trent cried.

"There's that big scenic turnout around the next bend." Zack fought to keep his wits about him. "Try to whip in there and go back the other way."

"What good will that do?"

"It'll put some distance between us. He'll miss the turnout."

"But he'll just keep chasing us—" Trent righted

the wheel ''—and then we'll be headed away from town.''

''You've got a four-wheel drive and he doesn't. We'll take a bumpy side road and outrun him. Then we double back to town.''

''My dad's gonna kill me!''

''Only if this crazy old man doesn't do it first. Here comes the turnout.'' But just then, the front bumper of Cagle's truck whacked the rear end of the Jeep.

The air bags popped as soon as Trent hit the guard rail, and Zack felt the weightlessness of being airborne. Then came that funny slow-motion thing you always hear about.

He thought, *God, don't let me die,* and saw each one of his brothers' and sisters' faces. And in that drawn-out instant he could see how beautiful they were. He saw his mother and felt the strangest mixture of love and compassion and forgiveness. His last clear thought was that he'd never told his father how much he loved him, how glad he was to be so like him.

''WE SHOULD TAKE my rental,'' Ann said as they dashed out the door. ''That Jeep Cherokee beside the house. The tank's full.''

Silently Mike blessed this woman for always being so organized, for being prepared, for being so generous.

''I love you,'' he said when they slammed the doors of the Jeep.

"I know." Ann fired up the engine. "And I love you, too. Got your cell phone?"

He nodded and smiled as she backed onto the street. "And I'm never letting you go."

"Fine by me." Ann put the Jeep in gear and roared off toward the mountains.

ZACK WOKE UP to the sensation of frigid water rising around his ankles. He batted down the collapsing air bag and looked out the shattered passenger window up a sheer wall of rock. The only sound was the rushing water and under that, the hiss of the Jeep's destroyed engine. His face felt wet, and he reached up, touching, wincing, then saw the blood on his fingers. He felt his head and tried not to panic. He seemed okay except for the pain in his legs.

"Trent! Trent!" He tried to shake his friend. Trent was slumped forward with his face smashed into his air bag, and when he didn't come to, Zack pushed his head back out of the airbag's way.

They were deep in a ravine, sitting upright smack in the middle of the creek with the falls just ahead of them. The top of the Jeep had caved in just above their heads. Zack was amazed that he was alive.

"Thank you, Heavenly Father," he whispered with closed eyes, then panicked and shook his friend again. "Trent! Wake up!" Zack started to tremble. What if Trent was dead?

He heard a vehicle pull up on the road above and started to climb out and scream for help, then had the cold realization that it could be Cagle. On instinct, he angled his bloody head toward the window and played dead. Before long he heard the vehicle move on.

He had to get Trent out of here. He had to get help. He turned Trent's battered head sideways and was relieved to see him draw a big breath. "You hang on, buddy," he said to the unconscious boy. "I'll get help." His seat belt had already come unhooked, but he couldn't budge the door. He'd have to crawl out the broken window. When he moved his legs, the pain in his ankles was excruciating.

He covered his knuckles with the leather sleeve of his jacket and punched the remaining chips of glass away. As he levered himself out of the narrow opening with all of his considerable upper-body strength, he cried out in torment. It was a relief to plunge his feet and ankles back into the icy water, but when he tried to bear weight on them, he realized both ankles must be broken. Dismayed, he raised his eyes to the sloping wall of rock again.

"Help!" he screamed. But his only answer was the gurgle of the creek and the rush of falls beyond. Tears stung, but he steeled himself and got mad, instead, because it looked as if he was going to have to crawl up that cliff. How often had his Grandpa said at football practice, "No pain, no gain"? Zack knew he was in for some hellacious pain, but the gain was his best friend's life.

FOR AS LONG AS HE LIVED Mike would never forget the heart-stopping moment he saw his son at the side of the road. One minute he was holding Ann's hand, squeezing it, never wanting to let go. And the next he was coming around the bend in the winding mountain road and seeing Zack.

Zack.

There was no mistaking the combination of letter jacket and wild red hair. The boy was sprawled spread-eagled on the shoulder with his shoes off. His face was covered with blood.

Ann brought the Jeep to a screeching halt. Mike threw the door open and ran to the boy with Ann right behind him.

Mike fell to his knees and Zack groaned, "Dad?" His eyes were slits of pain.

Mike said, "Hold on, son," and started to check for any bleeding that needed immediate pressure. "Ann, go get my cell phone." She ran back to the truck.

"Trent," Zack gasped, trying to sit up. "He's down there. Hurt bad."

Mike craned his neck to see over the cliff and spotted the wrecked Jeep at the bottom in the creek.

"We'll get help. Rest now." Fear for his son and his friend coursing through him, Mike stripped off his suit coat and used it to cover Zack's upper body.

"Where are we?" Ann cried as she ran toward them with the cell phone pressed to her ear.

"West on 53, first county road north to Little Falls. Tell them we're just south of Medicine Creek."

Ann repeated the directions to the dispatcher in Ardmore.

Zack roused himself to say, "Dad, get Trent."

As Ann dropped to her knees on the other side of Zack, Mike stood. "I've got to go down."

She nodded distractedly, her whole attention on Zack. She folded her jacket and gently pushed it under the boy's head.

Mike stood at the side of the precipice with his heart thundering, wondering how he could get down to Trent quickly. He could see the boy's blue hair sticking out of the broken window. He was completely still. He might be unconscious or...*no. God, no.* But how had the boys survived that fall? And how had Zack gotten up onto the road? The sloping limestone bluff stretched for a hundred yards each way, curving to match the mountainside. It was dotted with brush and a few cedars, but there was very little else to give purchase. Maybe, he thought, Zack had been thrown from the vehicle before it sailed over the cliff.

He cupped his hands and hollered down, "Trent!"

But the boy didn't move. About twelve to fifteen feet below where he stood was a shelf, and ten feet below that, another. From there the ravine angled more gently into the creek, so maybe once he got that far, he could scoot down the incline, grabbing brush for support along the way.

He ran back to the Jeep, grateful when he found jumper cables in the back.

"Ann," he yelled, "how is he?"

"I'm okay!" Zack replied. "Please! Help Trent!"

"Come and help me, Ann." Mike waved her over.

"Once I'm down to that first ledge," he said, "you unhook this cable and toss it to me."

"Okay." She held out the cell phone. "Take this. You may need to talk to the paramedics while you're down there."

"Good idea." His eyes locked with hers for one telling instant. "Ann, I love you."

"I love you, too. Be careful."

Mike lowered himself, knocking loose rocks into the ravine sixty feet below.

WATCHING HIM DANGLE from the end of the jumper cables and drop to the narrow ledge made Ann's heart lurch. Her hands shook as she unhooked the pinchers from the guardrail where Mike had tied them. She coiled the stiff cables as tightly as she could, then leaned over the rail, concentrating so that her toss wouldn't overshoot the ledge. Mike caught the cables and waved. She watched him tie them to the trunk of a small tree and lower himself again with a slight rappelling motion of his legs. Then she lost sight of him as he dropped to the second ledge.

Please don't let anything happen to him, she prayed, *now that we've found each other at last.* She held her breath.

As soon as she saw him emerge from the brush at the bottom, splashing through the knee-deep water toward the crumpled Jeep, she started to breathe again. Then she saw him ease the blanket he'd carried down through the window, covering the boy.

''Your dad's with Trent!'' she called to Zack as she ran back to him.

It seemed an eternity before they heard the wail of sirens echoing around the mountain.

Finally the boys were loaded into separate ambulances and the firemen got busy bringing Mike up. Ann turned away from Zack's ambulance as it pulled away and saw Mike swinging over the railing with the toes of his loafers grazing the gravel on the shoulder. At the sight of him hanging there, mud-smeared, his russet hair disheveled, her heart soared with relief and love.

She ran to him and threw her arms around his neck before the firemen had even started untangling him from the harness. They clasped and clung, their mouths instantly grappling in a wild, hungry reunion kiss. It was the first time they'd kissed in four long weeks, but the firemen and cops standing behind them, grinning, didn't know that.

''Your husband's okay, ma'am,'' the one climbing over the rail with mountaineer's equipment reassured her.

''I'm okay,'' Mike repeated as he unlocked her arms from around his neck. The guys lifted him out of the sling and slapped some dressings on his bleeding knuckles. Then Ann and Mike hurried to the Jeep to follow the ambulance to the hospital in Ardmore.

''Mike,'' Ann said as soon as she turned the Jeep onto the highway, ''you aren't going to believe this. Zack told me that Cagle ran them off the road.''

''What the hell?'' Mike looked gut-punched.

"I told the sheriff. He went directly to Cagle's place to arrest him. And as they were loading Zack into the ambulance, he handed me——" Her voice caught and she shook her head, but she kept her eyes on the road. She fumbled in the side pocket of her purse. "This." She handed Mike the star sapphire.

Mike accepted the thing onto his open palm and shook his head, gaping at it. "Your mother's sapphire? I don't believe it. How did Zack…"

"It's a pretty fantastic story, and we've got the whole drive to Ardmore to get you caught up. But let's start with this. Your son is very brave and very, very special."

Ann steered with one hand while they clasped their hands between the seats. "He's strong, too," Mike said, choking back his emotion. "I'm just glad they're alive." He strained against the seat belt and kissed Ann's jaw. "And I'm glad to have you with me."

After they'd gone over the details of what had happened, and after Ann had filled him in on what the paramedics had told her about the boys' respective conditions, Mike reached over with his bandaged hand and stroked her hair. "Did you hear that fireman call me your husband?"

Ann smiled. She wondered if he'd heard that. "I sure did."

"Did you like the sound of that? At all?"

Ann blinked back sudden tears. "Don't make me cry. I'm driving."

He stroked her luscious black hair back over one ear. "Okay. Then let me put it another way. Ms. Fischer, how'd you like to take up residence in a dull little town that you absolutely loathe, with a poor country preacher, his five wild kids and a mongrel dog that'll probably make your cat's life miserable?''

Ann smiled through her tears. ''Like I told you, Mike Kirkpatrick, please don't make me cry.''

ANN HAD NEVER SAT vigil in a surgery waiting room before. People in clusters of two and three occupied the turquoise vinyl chairs, waiting for news of patients. Ann, Mike, Laurie and Steve had seated themselves in a corner by the windows. A TV mounted near the ceiling mutely flashed scenes from an afternoon soap opera—doctors and nurses engaged in tense conversations. Ironic, Ann thought.

At the moment the place was quiet except for a young woman having a loud, chatty cell-phone conversation with a co-worker. She must not be in their situation, Ann thought, waiting to hear a damage report.

Mike reached over and squeezed Ann's hand, and she forced a smile. All afternoon she'd tried to take her cues from Mike and Laurie and Steve. But in order to match their calm courage, she had to set aside her own guilty doubts. She couldn't help feeling that if the boys had never seen that picture of June Starr wearing that sapphire, none of this would have happened.

Why had she insisted on digging up the past? Why couldn't she have left well enough alone? Now the boys were in critical condition, and a once-peaceful town was about to be thrown under the dark cloud of a shocking crime. She should have buried Edith, sold everything and headed straight back to Washington the way she'd planned. She could have lived out the rest of her life without the horrible knowledge of what had happened to her mother.

But then she looked at Mike.

He raised the hand he'd been squeezing and kissed her knuckles. He turned his head and stared out the window. "We'll just have to trust in God," he said softly, as if speaking to himself.

Ann studied his profile. His features were so strong, so beautiful. That face. She loved that face so much already. She could only imagine how she was going to feel about him after a lifetime together.

If she'd turned her back on Medicine Creek, she would not have this man sitting beside her now. Her life would be as it had been before. Marked by the incipient emptiness and loneliness that comes from denying who you truly are, from never seeking what you truly want.

Steve got to his feet and moved directly in front of one of the long banks of windows that looked out over the winter-brown hospital grounds. He stood there like a big hurt bear with his face angled near the glass, the way people do in airports while they are waiting, waiting.

The boys had been whisked into surgery more than two hours ago. Trent had been in the worst shape. The doctors hadn't seemed quite as optimistic about his chances. His spleen was ruptured, his right lung was punctured and his brain was possibly damaged.

Zack had fared better. He was having his crushed ankles and tibial bones set with pins and plates. He had a nasty concussion, as well—the physicians had debated about the anesthesia—but as Mike had repeatedly pointed out on the long drive down to Ardmore, Zack was strong as a bull. He had to be to have pulled himself up the side of that rocky ravine. Zack would make it.

Ann said another silent prayer for Trent. *Please God,* she repeated over and over like a mantra, *protect him, protect him, protect him.*

Laurie got up and joined Steve and pressed a palm to his back. A commotion at the waiting-room entrance caused everyone to turn their heads. There was Trent's sister, Julie, with a small gaggle of her cheerleader friends. The energy of teenage vitality rushed into the room with the girls like a crisp breeze. "Mom! Dad!" Julie cried as she ran to her parents. They stood for some seconds in a tight hug while the other girls looked on tearfully.

"Mona at the Sheriff's Department called me at school," Julie explained in a voice loud enough for the whole room to hear. Her daughter's tears had encouraged Laurie's own to flow, and Steve moved them off to a corner.

"Should we give them a moment alone?" Ann suggested.

"Sure." Mike and Ann walked over to the three

girls who had driven Julie down to Ardmore. "You girls want a hot chocolate?" Mike said.

The girls checked one another with glances, then nodded.

Mike crossed to where the Harrises had retaken their seats and said a few quiet words. Ann studied his back. Her husband to be. A thoughtful ER nurse had brought him a set of baggy surgery scrubs and some paper boots so he could change out of his wet, mud-caked clothes. His hair was raked back in wild furrows, and his shoulders were tense with worry, but to Ann, he had never looked more handsome.

On the first floor they found the coffee shop and got the girls settled at a table with their hot chocolate.

"The chapel's right across the hall," Mike said to Ann. "Would you go in there with me for a minute?"

"Of course." Ann took his hand and didn't let go, not even when they sat down on the short chapel bench.

For some moments they sat there holding hands and silently praying. "I guess," Mike finally said in a voice hoarse with emotion, "this is when a man needs his wife the most." Ann wasn't surprised—only thrilled—to hear him calling her his wife so easily. It was funny—and wondrous—she thought. She had been thinking of him as her husband all afternoon.

Ann looked into his eyes. "I've never felt this way before."

"Me, neither. I was thinking about it when I was writing my sermon."

"Your sermon?"

"You know, the one I wrote when I resigned."

"Are you telling me this relationship is…spiritual?" Ann teased.

But his expression was serious. "No. It's more like…sacred. I was thinking about that verse from the Song of Solomon, 'Many waters cannot quench love, nor can the floods drown it.'"

Ann's teasing gaze grew solemn. "Oh, Mike."

Mike reached up and traced her lips lightly with one fingertip. "When I saw you that day at my church, I knew that I could never stop loving you even if I wanted to. I honestly never imagined being this happy."

"Me, neither, but I think this is the way love is supposed to feel."

He put his arms around her right there in the chapel. "When I hold you like this, it's as if my soul is wrapped around your soul. It feels as if my soul fits around yours as perfectly as my body does."

"Mike—" He cut off her words with a searing kiss. A *soul*-searing kiss, truth be told. She knew what he was talking about. Way back when, this whole thing had started out physically—or had it ever been only physical?—and now it had become so much more. Even at this moment while his mouth claimed hers, it felt as if, at the same time, her soul was being tenderly cradled by his.

A nurse in surgery scrubs opened the door. "Reverend Kirkpatrick?"

"Yes?" Mike jumped up and faced her.

"The boys are out of surgery now. They're both doing fine."

Ann jumped up beside Mike and clasped him in a fierce grateful hug. Then together they went to check on the boys, just as they would do so many things for the rest of their lives...together.

EPILOGUE

Two years later

A BRUTAL FEBRUARY WIND whipped around the old cemetery high on a rocky hill in the Arbuckle Mountains. Ada Belle Green had come to rest among the ancient craggy bluffs where she'd been born almost a century before.

As Mike stepped up to the small portable podium, the cold wind gusted, flattening Ann's maternity dress against her rounded abdomen. He shot her a concerned glance that said, *Why don't you go to the car?*

Ann raised her chin and gave him a responding look that said, *No. Ada Belle had been one of her dearest friends, and she wanted to hear every word Mike had to say.* She folded her raincoat closed and hugged Erin against her left side while Brandon and Mary Beth huddled on her right. Joseph and Zack, arms crossed, towered behind them, in the wide-legged stance of sentinels.

Mike smiled at the little cluster—his family—and shoved his fingers through his hair, which the wind immediately blew askew as he braced his hands on the pulpit.

He looked at the other faces assembled under the flapping canopy. Some of them were too old and frail to be out in this biting wind, but Ada Belle had had loyal friends, who wanted to give her a proper send-off. Still, he'd have to keep it brief for their sake.

He was as chilled as anybody in the small group of mourners, but when he began to speak, he made sure his voice rang out clearly.

"Ada Belle Green, ninety-five years young, lived a long and fruitful life. She was born Ada Belle Roye in Indian Territory and married Willis Green in 1927. Though they were not blessed with their own children, the couple enriched the lives of many youngsters during their tenure as devoted schoolteachers. They shared a joyous example of the marriage covenant for over fifty-four years before Willis went to his Maker.

"My wife and I visited with Ada Belle not long before her passing. We gathered in her sweet little home, with her nurse Laurie Harris in attendance."

In the back row of mourners, Laurie and a couple of other nurses dabbed at their eyes.

"I asked Ada Belle how she was feeling, of course, but Ada Belle was always concerned with other people first. She flipped her hand and said, 'Tolerable,' and then demanded to know what I had gotten Ann for Valentine's day."

Even the tough old farmers in the small assembly chuckled at that one. Ada Belle Green—nosy to the end.

"I told her I'd managed a single rose that I swiped

from an altar arrangement, and she aimed an accusing finger at me and said, 'Buster, you'd better do a sight better than that. A pregnant woman needs extra courtin'.'"

The group chuckled appreciatively, and Mike hoped he'd captured Ada Belle's spirit.

"That was Ada Belle. Not afraid to call her minister buster. Not afraid to chastise him for his shortcomings."

"The last two years of Ada Belle's life in Medicine Creek have seen tremendous growth, and she told me she was glad she got to witness it.

"She was especially thrilled to be present at Christmas when Starr House opened its doors as a children's arts center. And she will long be remembered for leaving her estate to the cause of Starr Park so that tennis courts and a swimming pool can be built among the pecan trees. And her generous gift to the church will allow us to start construction on a new building at the south end of the grove within a year.

"Yes, Ada Belle made her life count. But mostly she will be remembered for her love of people. She liked nothing better than to sit and visit for a little while. And weren't we all blessed that she visited us here in Medicine Creek—for a little while."

Mike led a short closing prayer, and as the assembly shuffled to the vehicles parked on the shoulders of the winding gravel road that wound to the top of the hill, he took the time to greet each one of the townsfolk who had come out on this blustery day. When Ann came up beside him to help in the greeting and consoling, he broke from his duties and turned his attention to her.

"Aren't you cold?" His voice was low.

"Freezing," Ann said under her breath. Then, to one of the elderly mourners. "And how are you, Gladys dear? It was so good of you to come."

"Harriet." She touched the arm of another frail lady. "I've been keeping you in my prayers."

Mike, still smiling, took Ann's elbow and murmured, "Then go to the car."

"I have one more little thing to do."

"I'll go with you." It was Erin, who had come up beside Ann.

"Please go to the car soon," Mike said.

"What are we doing, Ann?" Erin asked as they walked back toward the canopy.

"Taking a flower to remember Ada Belle by." Ann slid one pink rose from the casket spray Gloria had created. Gloria was working harder than ever these days, getting her new shop established in Ardmore, yet she'd taken the time to make this beautiful arrangement for Ada Belle. A sign, Ann hoped, that Gloria was getting on with her life. Ann pulled out another rose and handed it to Erin.

"Mary Beth will want one, too." Erin took a third one out.

"One more," Ann smiled.

"For who?" The child looked puzzled.

"You'll see."

Ann and her stepdaughter walked slowly over the

rocky ground, arm and arm, to a marker under a twisted scrub oak tree.

"That was your real mother, wasn't it," Erin said as Ann traced her fingers over the engraved name.

"Yes, June Starr Fischer." Ann laid the extra rose at the base of the stone.

"I want to put mine here, too," Erin said. She twisted at the knees just as Ann had and put her rose down carefully. Erin, at fourteen, was becoming quite a lady now.

Ann gave the girl's shoulders a squeeze. "I'm freezing, aren't you?"

"Yeah." As they walked back to the car, Erin said, "Ada Belle sure was a nice lady, wasn't she?"

"Yes, she certainly was. I'll always be grateful to her."

"Because of the money she donated to the old pecan grove?"

Ann smiled. The kids would probably always call it the old pecan grove.

"Because she helped me see who I truly am, where I truly belong."

"You mean here in Medicine Creek?"

"Yes." Ann smiled. "Right here in Medicine Creek with you kids."

"And with our dad." Erin looked up sincerely. Ann's heart swelled with gratitude. Winning Erin's trust and affection had been a slow and cautious process.

Ann looked back at her handsome husband. "Yes, and with your dad. Right here…where I belong."

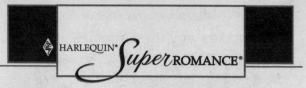

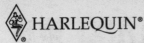

TRUEBLOOD, TEXAS

Coming in January 2002…

THE BEST MAN IN TEXAS
by
Kelsey Roberts

Lost:

One heiress. Sara Pierce wants to disappear permanently and so assumes another woman's identity. She hadn't counted on losing her memory….

Found:

One knight in shining armor. Dr. Justin Dale finds himself falling in love with his new patient…a woman who knows less about herself than he does.

Can the past be overcome, so that Sara and Justin may have a future together?

Finders Keepers: bringing families together

HARLEQUIN®
Makes any time special ®

If you enjoyed what you just read,
then we've got an offer you can't resist!

Take 2 bestselling
love stories FREE!
Plus get a FREE surprise gift!

Clip this page and mail it to Harlequin Reader Service®

IN U.S.A.	IN CANADA
3010 Walden Ave.	P.O. Box 609
P.O. Box 1867	Fort Erie, Ontario
Buffalo, N.Y. 14240-1867	L2A 5X3

YES! Please send me 2 free Harlequin Superromance® novels and my free surprise gift. After receiving them, if I don't wish to receive anymore, I can return the shipping statement marked cancel. If I don't cancel, I will receive 6 brand-new novels every month, before they're available in stores. In the U.S.A., bill me at the bargain price of $4.05 plus 25¢ shipping and handling per book and applicable sales tax, if any*. In Canada, bill me at the bargain price of $4.46 plus 25¢ shipping and handling per book and applicable taxes**. That's the complete price, and a saving of at least 10% off the cover prices—what a great deal! I understand that accepting the 2 free books and gift places me under no obligation ever to buy any books. I can always return a shipment and cancel at any time. Even if I never buy another book from Harlequin, the 2 free books and gift are mine to keep forever.

135 HEN DFNA
336 HEN DFNC

Name	(PLEASE PRINT)	
Address	Apt.#	
City	State/Prov.	Zip/Postal Code

* Terms and prices subject to change without notice. Sales tax applicable in N.Y.
** Canadian residents will be charged applicable provincial taxes and GST.
   All orders subject to approval. Offer limited to one per household and not valid to
   current Harlequin Superromance® subscribers.
   ® is a registered trademark of Harlequin Enterprises Limited.

SUP01   ©1998 Harlequin Enterprises Limited

CALL THE ONES YOU LOVE OVER THE HOLIDAYS!

Save $25 off future book purchases when you buy any four Harlequin® or Silhouette® books in October, November and December 2001,

PLUS

receive a phone card good for 15 minutes of long-distance calls to anyone you want in North America!

WHAT AN INCREDIBLE DEAL!

Just fill out this form and attach 4 proofs of purchase (cash register receipts) from October, November and December 2001 books, and Harlequin Books will send you a coupon booklet worth a total savings of $25 off future purchases of Harlequin® and Silhouette® books, AND a 15-minute phone card to call the ones you love, anywhere in North America.

Please send this form, along with your cash register receipts as proofs of purchase, to:

In the USA: Harlequin Books, P.O. Box 9057, Buffalo, NY 14269-9057
In Canada: Harlequin Books, P.O. Box 622, Fort Erie, Ontario L2A 5X3
Cash register receipts must be dated no later than December 31, 2001.
Limit of 1 coupon booklet and phone card per household.
Please allow 4-6 weeks for delivery.

**I accept your offer! Enclosed are 4 proofs of purchase.
Please send me my coupon booklet
and a 15-minute phone card:**

Name: _____

Address: _____ City: _____

State/Prov.: _____ Zip/Postal Code: _____

Account Number (if available): _____

---

097 KJB DAGL
PHQ4013